To Slay the
Lonesome
Night

FOR MY FATHER AND MOTHER

Acknowledgments

I want to express my sincere appreciation for the help provided by Stewart Applin, Patrick Jones, Francie Loveall, Susan Paden-Garling, and Barbara Anderson Beard.

A kind note from a friend,

"Great work! Good luck on the new novel."
—Ray Manzarek, The Doors

To Slay the Lonesome Night

Life is like a circle that should always lead back home.
A novel for all ages.

AUBREY RUSSELL

[1]
BREMERTON, WASHINGTON, 1969

I crouched in the high grass and watched the fool stealthily approach the car, pondering the ill-conceived plan and wondering if our combined idiocy had ever been disputed. The question took only another second to answer. Rick cupped his hands around his face and peered through the driver's window, prompting it to burst open with explosive force, discharging an immense giant who grabbed him in a vicious death lock, slamming him hard to the ground with the force of a bone-crushing hammer! My friend struggled futilely against the mammoth's withering assault, his pitiful moans choked and garbled by the brutality of the sudden surprise. Yet it got worse, as such things often do. Instantly, and with equal malice, another crazed creature sprang from the other door, attacking Rick head-on, violently ramming a rag into his mouth and pounding him ferociously with his fists. It was all unexpected and surreal and filled me with staggering disbelief.

Now look at him! A mere moment ago he was just a young man returning from a joyride to Canada, and now he's tightly wound inside the unmerciful clutches of the two meanest-looking cretins on earth. How quickly our fortunes had faded —and all for running out of gas.

I froze in fright but not panic. Mesmerized, I could do little else but gaze stricken upon the image of them as a thing of maddening pandemonium. Rick's hapless head was a crumpled marshmallow inside of the giant's massive bicep, and the creature's strong hands pinched the poor boy's face tight, demanding that he reveal his motives or die.

I was primed to turn and run. Any location except here would do just fine. Fear assaulted my unproven valor, and I fought hard to resist the urge to seek safety. I had not expected to be tested so bitterly tonight, and I was unaccustomed to tasting the shame of the coward's sweat. Astonishingly, after scrambling to my feet, I started running straight toward them. I tripped and fell twice, struggling to outpace the muddy sludge that crippled my every stride, the thick muck adhering to the soles of a fool's mad folly. "Damn! Damn!" I cried. Onward hero. Onward.

But it was adrenalin—the cheaper form of courage we are all born with—that chased my forebodings away, leaving me vulnerable to the obvious downside of such a rash decision. With each fall I arose to new heights of cursing the angry sod, denouncing the day I was born, and fate and Rick and bad men in the night. I was soon upon the grotesque figures battling in the dark, my heart pounding and my breath short. I had impudently arrived.

Rick's willingness to fight back was truly wondrous, a righteous attempt to stay alive. He had amazingly gotten the upper hand, if only briefly, managing to free his head from the giant's iron grip, gulping for air, discharging the ungodly rag, capping off his herculean efforts with desperate pleas for reason and restraint. The victory was short lived. With deaf ears and cold-blooded hearts the two thugs wasted no time regaining control, beating Rick unmercifully back to the ground. In a fit of unmatched brilliance they decided not to gag him again: a clever move that would actually allow him to speak. Even so, genius was generally unbecoming to them, as you will soon see.

The giant nodded at his churlish accomplice in a strangely causal manner, alerting him to my hasty appearance. It was the same relaxed demeanor that would eventually prove to be the baffling antithesis of his violent nature. I had stopped a few feet short of their exact position, blurting out an obscene objection to their overly harsh treatment of my friend. Their first reaction was one of childlike inquisitiveness, rather than the surprise and intimidation I hoped might strike them dead.

"No shit, Moe, there's another one! What the hell do you think about that?"

Moe was in no thinking mood, only calling out his friend's name, urging him to lower his voice. He then seized upon me with overwhelming speed and fury, swiftly pinning me to the ground, rendering me crippled, perplexed, and a failed hero. Still, his intention wasn't to mortally wound me. Just the same, he hoisted me up roughly by my feet, dragging me toward my fallen friend. My humiliation lasted some 20 feet, and Moe loudly listed his indictments against me. He finally dropped me next to Rick, in a heap of human rubble, where I could only think of one thing to say, "Way to go, John Wayne!"

But Charlie had plenty to say. He kept jabbing Rick with a question he couldn't possibly answer, and he wasn't pleased with the response he was getting. "Well, kiss my butt, kid, if I don't know that's a lie. Where's that shit-sucking colonel? Give him up, or I swear I'll kill you—right now!"

It was the same question and demand that Charlie would

use to torture us throughout the night. Regardless, we had nothing to reveal about the mysterious colonel.

Charlie had been gleefully entertained by my degrading arrival and now turned his attention toward me. At the very least, it provided Rick with an earned reprieve. "Well, look at what the cat dragged in," he chimed, still fuming.

"Charmed, I'm sure," I foolishly snapped.

He promptly grabbed me by my neck to assert his authority, my throat constricting severely from the pressure of his stranglehold. Pulling me full face to the ground, he punched me several times on the back of my head with the same wicked force he had used on Rick. I fought to remain conscious in the fast fading light of my great misfortune. He was truly a natural born killer, and had not Moe forcefully restrained him at that moment, he would have finished me off without further delay or moral qualm. Charlie adeptly wrestled out of Moe's grip, lunging at me again, grabbing at my right hand, snatching away my prized burglar's tool. I had forgotten I still held it.

"What the hell is this, kid? Hey, Moe, look at this, will ya? Sweet lilies if it ain't a butter knife." Charlie was beside himself. "I'm getting the willies just holding it, Moe," he said, laughing madly, making his hand tremble fearfully in prankish pretense, genuinely pleased by his new found powers of roguish depiction. Jumping quickly back to his feet, he performed several outlandish stabbing gestures in the manner of a crazed stage actor, striking out at the dark in all directions, in sneering attack to slay the lonesome night. It was a childish exercise. He finally swung the blade toward me, snarling, "What the hell were you planning to do with this, Buttercup, conquer the world? I bet you couldn't butter a loaf of bread with it. Well?"

I had nothing quite so noble to confess, and I cared only marginally for bread. Still dazed, I decided to say nothing. Charlie slapped me across the face, blood spewing from the inside of my cheek. I spit, instinctively. "The big cat hauled you over here," he cried. "He didn't get your tongue. And don't spit at me!"

The dire situation couldn't be made worse by revealing the truth, yet I found myself strangely embarrassed to admit it. "It's for stealing stereo tape players, sir, but we've never actually done it before. It's a long story."

"The hell you say? Did you hear that, Moe?" Charlie was excited and bemused by what I said. "They've never really done it before? It's a long story? Yeah, right, Buttercup. You know, Moe, I'll be a son of a bitch if we didn't just catch ourselves the legendary Butter Knife Stereo Thieves. Yeah, I've heard about these two bandits. I bet there's a reward for them. Woo! Woo! Woo!" Charlie shrieked, tapping a one-handed drum roll on his thigh, steadily growing more delighted in our buttery blunder. Not wanting to lose the moment, he decided to examine the butter knife in the car's bright dome light spraying on our feet, rotating the blade at precise, sharp angles, causing it to reflect brilliantly in the scattered glow. Sadly, it had become the flaming sword of our sorrows.

Suddenly bored, Charlie tossed the knife aside, turning to once again sneer murderously at me. Rick languished nearby, still gasping for air, carefully searching himself for serious injuries. Moe hovered over him, content now to ignore me and let Charlie have his way. Charlie's way was not to give me a good old-fashioned choking or another brutal thrashing. He used a doubly-terrifying method of torment this time, one molded out of steel. My first reaction was to roll my eyes away from the twin barrels. I could not bear to look directly at them. Then I heard the awful sound of the pump-action and the rounds load, Charlie smirking with deadly satisfaction. The bastard.

From 100 yards away the bright neon lights on the roof of the old motel quietly illuminated my despair. The fragile, wine-colored glass blinked erratically, flashing out of sync, as if purposely humming out of tune to the song of my unfolding demise. Nearby, the towering, thick shrubbery encircled our position on the abandoned road, standing guard: hushed, tombstone sentinels indifferent to this miscarriage of justice. Above the silence, I could hear Rick weep gently, the way I would expect. He was always brave, despite his untimely stupidity.

The events of my life did not flash before me as some have said happens. Rather, I could think of nothing more than my convulsion and dread for the initial blast, heartbroken that my parents would have to see me in such a condition. Moe, moving next to me, broke through my horror, whispering in my ear that it would not hurt. He said it would be as a child who braves a pinprick just before falling off to sleep. Hell, I wouldn't even hear it, he muttered softly, strangely trying to console me. How peculiar that my final comfort would be a killer's pity.

"I have to shoot you in the face, kid. I can't risk it another way," Charlie declared, almost by default. Then he snickered and sneered and gloated, "Then I'm going to cut off your hands and feet. No one will ever know who you are!"

Moe laughed, betraying me. It would be the first time I would experience his mood swings, and he proved to be a puzzling enigma.

"Screw you both," I shouted at them. "It's good news! I don't wish to be identified." My loved ones would grieve only the mystery.

Moe had inspired me by telling the truth—it would not hurt. I challenged Charlie, still indiscreet in my foolish chivalry. "I don't know who you think we are, mister. But if you were asleep in that car, I'd own your stereo by now. Let us go and I'll steal you a better one. I'll steal the colonel's stereo, if you want me to." This declaration had its desired effect.

"You got balls, kid. I'll give you that. And did you hear that,

Moe? First he says he's not a thief and then he says he is one. Sounds just like the colonel, doesn't it? I think this kid really knows the colonel, or maybe he's just a funny guy? I've heard that funny guys aren't afraid to die." He lowered the shotgun from my face, studying me intently, turning to study Moe. He twisted back again and confronted me suspiciously, "So, you'll steal the colonel's stereo for us, huh? That just proves you know him, and you know how to find him. Doesn't it, Buttercup?"

The gravity of our plight would have made lying easy, but I denied Charlie's insinuations, honestly, yet reproached myself for mouthing off about the colonel's stereo or even mentioning his name. Moe exerted his authority again, saving me for the moment. He wanted to huddle with Charlie. They stood some 20 feet away, whispering as if they were polite parish nuns at a hanging. How empathetic of them.

I looked at my forlorn friend, miserable, curled up on his side, his face hidden from me. Something had to be done. I kicked him in the ribs, but it was a huge mistake. Charlie's meanness had broken some of them. He lurched in agony, rolling over to confront me.

"Damn you, Rusty. Knock it off. I'm hurt!"

"How hurt? Can you get up and run?"

"No, man, I think my ribs are busted."

"Oh."

"You two shut up over there," Charlie barked. Moe scolded him for the clamor he made. They huddled again.

"Rick—hey, man, can you try to run?" I exhorted him, again, desperately.

"I don't think so, man. I feel real bad, kind of broken up—all over."

"Come on, let's give it a try. I got a plan to get us out of this," I whispered. My plan was to run.

"You don't think they really want to kill us?" Rick stammered, meekly, dissolving my plan in his shattered pain. He couldn't run anywhere, only befuddlement and anguish were left to him. He was hurting much more than I realized.

"I don't think they want to kill us *here*. The shotgun will make too much noise. Somebody is sure to hear it," I reasoned, finding new strength in such sound logic.

"Why don't we just say that we know the colonel?"

"Because we already said we don't. If we change our story now they won't believe anything we say. I think this could be bad. We stumbled into some real trouble here."

"I wonder who the hell the colonel is. I wonder if it's better to pretend to know him, Cosmo. It might keep us alive."

Such a gamble stank of our final undoing. I told him so. "I think not knowing him will keep us alive. I'm not going to listen to another one of your stupid ideas. First the steak and now this. You're the worst thief in the entire world. Now, keep a level head, and let's try not to fall apart!"

"God, I hope you're right about this, Cosmo. I think I need a doctor."

This time it was Moe who told us to shut up before turning his ire on Charlie. He chastised him for talking too much, quick to expose whom they were looking for—giving them away. Moe grabbed the shotgun from him, shaking it angrily in the air, opening the car's trunk and slamming it in hard, then slamming the trunk harder. He never stopped cursing the whole time. Apparently, this means of execution was ruled out for the reason I explained to Rick.

This infuriated Charlie, and his livid response sank the two confused ogres into an argument that thundered with mutual contempt. Moe launched biting accusations at Charlie, all denouncing his professional incompetence, leaving Charlie so furious that he countered with stupefying excuses for why this could not be, pleading with Moe to consider each one, carefully. And Moe did, condemning each one, hotly, energizing the quarrel beyond all good reason. Outwitted, Charlie fired back with the only thing left of his chastised inanity.

"Then if you're so smart just use your knife," he cried, in frustration and embarrassment. It was clear now that they despised each other, both unpredictable. I hadn't thought about a knife. Charlie's suggestion sunk me to a new low.

"Shut up! You don't tell me when and where to use my knife. Capo warned us not to get the car bloody. It is one of his. Do you remember that?"

"Then kill them outside, Moe. Nobody says you have to use the car."

"So someone can see me? What an ass you are. We're not killing these boys here, and we can't let them go now. Your big mouth settled that!" he boomed. "Besides, I'm sure to hell not paying for new upholstery." Moe, though blistered by rage, conveyed this as little more than good, common sense. "If I have to use my knife, it will be when and where I say—not you! Got it? There's time enough to find out the truth about these two." His decision had all the sound of a hung jury's frustration and would buy us a needed pardon for now.

On Moe's return, I could feel the ground rumble beneath his feet, the earth straining to maintain its orbit under the weight of his gigantic frame. Moe was easily the biggest and scariest monster I had ever seen. He remained intensely annoyed with us. "You two sure talk a lot for pissants with their butts in a tight sling," he grumbled, adjusting his privates and spitting precariously close to me. He leaned hard into my face, point blank, his breath as hot as flaming fire. I cringed but didn't cower away. "Tell me why I should let you live?" he scowled.

Was he kidding? No question was ever easier to answer. The hard part was deciding where to begin among a galactic host of good reasons. Yet amazingly, the question stumped me. Why should he let me live? Is that it? Is that all? It was surely a trick question, too simple. It made me crazy, and I set about to prove it.

"I'm not looking to die tonight, sir," I began, boldly. Then it happened—something I had never experienced before and couldn't manage or stop. A sudden whirlwind of certain doom overwhelmed me. Sweat began to pour from my face and hands, mixed with blood and dirt, and I labored hard to breathe, shortness of breath uncommon to me. I was trembling from head to toe, a shaking palm branch in a raging wind. A panic attack is what my friends call it. It's something they say their mothers get and impossible to rein in. Whatever it was, my powers of reason were momentarily shut down. I was unable to utter a single, sensible thing, except to ramble on shamelessly and not remember a word of it. Once again my disgrace was complete—Moe unimpressed by the long, confused dissertation about my good reasons to stay alive. Finally, I ended up right back at where I started, 'I'm not looking to die tonight, sir, *ESPECIALLY FOR SOMETHING I DON'T KNOW ANYTHING ABOUT!*' This final proclamation was delivered in hostile contempt for him, and he didn't miss it. The only thing I had to fight back with was anger. I didn't know it at the time, but it proved to be my best weapon.

Moe just spit—he liked to spit—shook his head, unconvinced, somewhat puzzled by me. Still, the dark part of him enjoyed my meltdown. From the start of my impassioned plea, I had instinctively stood up, unwittingly animated, waving my hands, trying to express by gesture what I couldn't think to say. It was late and I was beat up, bleeding, and exhausted, shocked by the sudden misfortune, afraid of dying and at a loss to know how to get out of it. A real bummer, to say the least.

Moe reacted with a sweeping hatchet blow from his muscular, powerful arm, connecting squarely on my shoulder blade, sending me crashing back to earth. "Damn it. Don't move around so much, kid. I don't read sign language. And what kind of fool notion makes you think we need your help to find the colonel? Two sorry pissants like you. Hell, I've got a legion of devils to call on whenever I want—whenever I choose. I can get a new stereo too, boy, and I don't need to steal it."

My animation had provoked his. After scolding me, he sought out the discarded butter knife to prove the point. He found it a few yards away and broke into a full war dance, a sort of hop and bop and crazy chock-a-block circle, over and about it, gangster style. Then he turned snidely to confront me again. I thought him deranged.

He stooped over me, dropping low, his blistering breath scorching my ear. "So, I believe I asked you a question, didn't I, pissant? Eh? You ain't given me nothing but nonsense, and I already brought that with me. So, tell me again, why should I let you live?"

"So I can be around to murder your children!" is what I wanted to say, but this time I stuck to the simple truth, too weary to mount another long appeal. "Because I want to."

"You want to? Isn't that tender." With this, his next move was into his pocket, letting his hand linger there. I feared he changed his mind about the knife. He pulled out something and put it into his mouth. It was chewing tobacco. He reached into his other pocket, adding, "Your carcass ain't worth spit to me, boy. I can skin it right now, you know! You made a lot of trouble for us tonight. Do you realize that, pissant? Capisce?"

I barked back, impertinent and aggressive, informing him that even if my carcass wasn't worth spit to him, it had a great deal of value to me. I further told him that we were willing to fix this trouble by any means possible. All they had to do was stop acting like diseased children and ill-nurtured maggot-pies! Only God might know why I was so dangerously combative, but as I said, it proved to be the smartest path. Moe was actually a little impressed by me, unsure of my forced bravery but amused by it. Few men had ever shouted at Moe and had it turn out well. Oh, to be young and bulletproof.

"What the hell is a maggot-pie, kid?"

"You two!"

"You're about the goddamnedest pissant I ever met. You know that? Why always me?"

I used this moment to try to reason with him, once again. "Please, listen, Mr. Moe, this is a big mistake. We are not who you think we are. We were just trying to get some gas money. We thought we could hock a good stereo for a few bucks to buy some. If you just give us a chance, we'll prove it to you." Then I got stupid again, suddenly despising the colonel for getting us into this mess, whoever in God's name he might be. "In fact, we can be of great value to you," I said, insisting that we could help. "Why take the risk yourselves? Why? When you can risk us? Hell, we'll even hold him down while you do him in. From the looks of this crap, he deserves it." A fine tactic, stupidity. I was certain to blurt out anything I thought might help. My words had again poured out in a flood of desperation.

"OK, kid. I got it. I'm not stupid," Moe scoffed, impatiently. "You realize that anyone in your predicament would say the same things, don't you? Besides that, I don't need a couple of candy-asses to help me do my killing. But I think you're about scared enough to do anything I say. We'll see about the colonel." He snatched me by the hair of my head, examining my face so intimately that I could smell the hot mixture of wrath and tobacco on his breath. "And don't ever lie to me, kid. I kill liars."

"You don't have to worry, sir. I don't have any reason to lie to you. I've told you only the truth. We're just two guys from California, coming back from a ride to Canada."

"OK, just as long as you understand, pissant." He released me and patted me on the head, as if I had been a good puppy.

"Draft dodgers, I bet," Charlie snarled. "We might as well shoot them now and save the Army the trouble."

Moe reacted as if it dishonored him to hear of such a possibility. "But that can't be right. Can it, kid? Hell, if that was right you two California shitbirds would still be in Canada. Right?" Moe's reasoning powers eclipsed Charlie's. We weren't draft dodgers, and he wasn't looking for just any vague reason to murder us. He was the more dominant personality among goons, obviously, but only to our slightly better advantage.

Still, grim Charlie was uncaring. Having missed his first chance, he fumed and pranced about wildly, growing steadily more irritated by finding no real fault in us, save our planned heist of their stereo tape player, which even Moe acknowledged he could afford to replace. Charlie had seen Moe pat me on the head and read it as a sign of warming to me. In his mind, this spelled betrayal. Charlie let him know it.

"Don't let your guard down, Moe. You remember Sammy the Sucker, don't you?" With this he regressed into an unfathomable tale of poor, unfortunate Sammy, dead now, murdered in his innocent sleep by the most unlikely of killers, two freckled-faced runaways, orphaned kids he had befriended on the highway, hitchhiking. They slit his throat and hijacked his car. Then for the sheer kicks of it, they cut off his ears and tied them to the rear-view mirror. Beyond ghastly, one might agree, and I guessed that Charlie was guilty of exaggeration. The Mob suffered a long delay in locating the lost car, he reminded Moe, and they were unable to bury the Sucker as a whole man. It took two weeks and the Sucker stank. Being surpassed on the scale of evil, the Family was nervous and put on high alert. This event had apparently just occurred, and the outrage of it was paramount in Charlie's mind. It was the most astonishingly weird story I had ever heard.

"They got a butter knife, Charlie, and we ain't asleep!" Moe obviously considered Charlie's comparison to our meager threat as asinine but still responded as if it equaled a challenge to his authority. He rebuked Charlie once again for revealing far too much in front of strangers, shaming him for his outburst of Mob business. Charlie looked at us, sheepishly, obviously embarrassed. It was enough to temporarily shut him up.

"So what do you think, kid?" Moe asked, his attention back on me.

"About what, sir?"

"About what Charlie just said. Were you going to hack off our ears with this butter knife and maybe feed them to the colonel? That seems like an easier job than stealing a stereo with it." However salty, his inflection was one of humor, and it provided me with my first relaxed breath. "How do you cut the wires?"

"You don't have to, sir. The knife is used just to snap the window loose, crack it open enough to get to the lock. A butter knife is sturdy and doesn't bend. Then the wires can easily be popped loose from the back of the player. Most people don't even secure it to the bracket. It's that easy."

"Just a snap, crackle, and pop, then you got the poor guy's tunes, huh?"

"That's another way to put it, I guess." Then I thought it the ruin of me to realize that Moe was so concerned about those who lost their source of music. Rick also perceived this and did his best to right the wrong, thus further confusing the issue.

"But it's not a personal thing, sir. Not at all," he groaned.

14

"It's not our nightly business, and we would never take any music, just the player." This made no allowance for the obvious —no player, no music—but it seemed to comfort Moe. That part about genius I mentioned.

Soothing as such a statement was to Moe, it provided Charlie with more ammunition, and the ridiculous accusations started again. "How much does the colonel pay you for the stereos, Buttercup? Damn it, Moe, can't you see these boys are double-dealing? I'm telling you, this is a ploy, some damn thing the colonel thought up. He's a shrewd bastard. You know that's true. I can smell a rat, and it smells like these boys."

Moe announced his verdict, "I don't think they know jack-squat about the colonel, Charlie. They're just a couple of pimple-brained kids who made a big mistake tonight. But just in case you're right, we're taking them with us. There is time enough."

"Good, that's real good. We'll take them with us." Charlie seemed to eagerly embrace the idea, and it would, indeed, give us more time. Still, I suspected that he had his own devious scheme in mind, and I wondered if he might turn on Moe should the big guy decide to go easy on us. Moe was wily enough to have considered the same without my input. After all, Charlie was the devil.

"You're not going to kill these boys unless I say so, Charlie. Understand?" It was more of a direct order than a question and delivered in a cadence demanding respect, adherence to the mobster's chain of command. "We'll do what we have to do, but I say when and where. Capisce?"

"Sure, Moe, whatever you say."

"Now let's get busy."

Charlie consented submissively, reduced to making muddled threats against us, binding our hands and feet together with strong, fine cords, intended to cut flesh. He enjoyed it. Then he finally secured us together with a coarse rope, one that burrowed deep inside our clothing, pinching our skin and sucking the air from our collapsing lungs. This produced a groan of sheer agony from Rick, two of his broken ribs in direct contact with it. Moe loosened it slightly and then pushed us into the car. "Don't worry about nothing, kid," he whispered to me. "If you're clean, I might not let him kill you."

It wasn't the Sermon on the Mount, but I embraced it.

~~~

PART 2

All manner of signs roared past my window dispensing useless information. It was of no consequence to me who cooked the biggest and best burger. I didn't care what fine establishment offered the cleanest sheets and softest beds. It didn't matter one bit which gas station was only two exits away or that Willie's Used Cars could finance anyone, dead or alive. The whole world now had the quality of a bad horror film, and in every flashing frame I was certain that the end would come soon. Rick disappeared into a cloud of fetal sleep, and his motionless bundle provided me an opportunity to gently loosen the rope that bound our destiny together. My hands were impaired, and I feared that tugging on it too aggressively might startle him, causing him to unwittingly betray me.

Moe eyed us every few minutes, keen to stay aware of any movement. The small, dark openings in his face still showed little that could be predicted, except maybe a harsh reaction to foolish behavior. I think God would have advised me to keep pecking away at his softer side, his inner child, but not expect too much. Every time he looked at me I decided to smile back at him, broadly. It was too much for him, and he finally gave in.

"Goddamn, kid! Now I'm sure you're about the bravest squirrel I ever saw. What in the world do you got to smile about? Do you really think all this is funny?" He then bellowed a Bunyan's bellow, a laugh so loud and sweetly rich and warm that it spread a soothing blanket over the night and my fear, energizing me. I was getting to him, and he dug me in a curious sort of Cosa Nostra way. Then he leaned across the seat and felt the area of rope I had loosened, winking at me, pulling it tight again. "Good try," he said, once more briskly rubbing my head, then adjusting the blanket he used to hide the lashing rope.

Meanwhile, Charlie never shut up. I hated him, and I drew exotic pleasure from imagining what hellish delights God had in store for his kind, and how I'd be first in line to book passage to the bottomless pit, a quenched, happy, satisfied witness to the glorious, final roasting of his pathetic carcass. Until then, I endured with much prayer his dreary compulsion to babble endless nonsense and spew out intimidating threats. It all went something like this.

"There is no way to convince me that you two just stumbled upon us," he would proclaim heatedly, condemning our blunder as a crafty trick on our part to somehow conspire with the colonel. "The colonel sent you out to the car, didn't he?" He would demand the truth by slamming his fist hard on the dashboard. "What lie did he use to get you to spy on us? Boy, nobody could have known where we were in that field, except the colonel. Nobody! That means he told you."

I would reply in the following manner, just as fervently. "I swear to you mister that we don't know anything about the colonel. We just happened onto your car, taking an evening walk, and made a bad decision. People do that, sometimes. I don't know what else to say to you. It's the truth and the only story you are going to get out of me. It's the only one I know!"

17

Moe secretly enjoyed how my anger would flare up and was satisfied just to take in the show, now on its umpteenth rerun. "You couldn't beat a bad lie out of me, Mr. Charlie. I swear to you, we just happened to come upon your hidden car, and my foolish friend here—well, he decided to go for it. All we wanted to do was hock your tape player for gas money. Just some lousy gas money, that's all. We're trying to get home."

Regrettably, Charlie wouldn't budge, his suspicion an impenetrable blockade to youthful reason and truth. At random moments he would change the tactics of his prosecution in order to twist and turn the essence of my honest answers, coming at me from directions that would make a bad lawyer cringe. It became obvious that Charlie simply wanted somebody to murder tonight. One recklessly forgets about the existence of evil: The unyielding reality of such madmen as him, those truly deranged souls living among us who take perverted pleasure from the mere act of killing. Lucky for us, Moe was Charlie's alter ego, and for the moment it was enough to keep us alive.

I'm moved to tell you that Rick and I were not even practiced thieves, stereos or otherwise. The worst of it for me amounted to a few candy bars when I was very young and I think Rick even less than that. Yet here we were, and as I repeatedly tried to explain to Charlie and Moe, we only wanted their car tape player in order to hock it for gas money. We hadn't managed our finances very well during our return from Canada, and now we were broke and desperate. We had decided against calling home for help. Rick had suggested it, but my idiotic pride ruled against him. One way or the other, it goes without saying that we should have mapped a more sensible and safer course. It was our butter knife blunder, one might say. Whoever the colonel might be, he must have been highly devious and tricky, perhaps having gotten the better of them in similar circumstances, and they simply were taking no foolish chances this time. I had heard that the Mob's credo was to trust no one for any reason, until they were dead certain of what the truth actually was.

So it went, with Moe seldom speaking. Yet I knew he believed me. He had practically said as much. Charlie knew he believed me. Still, when Charlie wasn't insisting that I tell him a lie just to appease his murderous logic, he told more horrific stories to Moe. He was seemingly fond of revealing secretive Mob business, vomitive ditties about how some of his now dead sucker buddies had been unluckily guilty of showing their gentler dispositions, paying an awful price for this error of compassion. They were exhortations that Moe was, in fact, very familiar with, having once witnessed—up close—the death of a brother mobster, himself a victim of his own good and careless transformation of consciousness. No good deed goes unpunished. In his strange, delusional dogma, it appeared that Charlie had a good point to make. So our predicament left Moe torn between his secret desire to let us go and his firsthand knowledge of how the innocent sometimes come back to slay the guilty. Just the same, I sensed that he had grown to appreciate my defiant attitude, and I hoped this progress would somehow pay off.

Yet we weren't making any sensible progress in the car. Good for us. It became clear that all we did was drive in a circle. I began to recognize specific landmarks and highway signs we had passed a number of times, especially the abundant and pompous billboards that assured our conquest of a better life, if only we dared. Specific sounds became very familiar. I could detect the whining machinery of overburdened factories straining on the night shift, working through the holiday, the roar of traffic's ebb and flow at distinct locations; and furthermore, the unmistakable sounds of an athletic contest nearby, where life and death played out in derisive make-believe. I took in the unmistakable din of fans cheering loudly for the home team, taunting the visitors with jeers and sneers—but never with death. I wished to be in such a contest, where I could win or lose or quit and still go home in any fashion I pleased.

Coincidentally, at that very time, Moe decided to quit. He was finished, tired of covering the same ground. "Give it up, Charlie, we're lost. Pull in at the next gas station and we'll get directions." In a few minutes, we had found one.

Moe rolled down his window and called out to the attendant, but first he issued a firm warning to me, inspecting the snaky rope. My injured friend was still unconscious, dead to the world but thankfully alive. Moe quickly covered Rick's head with his muddy jacket. It was hard to tell he was even there: beaten, bruised, and perhaps seriously hurt, and it was my fault. I had been blaming him, but it was my fault.

It was late and the station was empty, not another car in sight. A rather tall, stony-faced young man eyed us indifferently as he advanced toward the car, whistling a sad tune, a distressed sound that seemed to mirror my own unsung groanings. Wearily, and before answering Moe's question, he leaned with tattered elbows upon the car's roof to steady himself. Then for a split second we locked eyes, and when he dropped his arms I could see his injured hands and bandaged fingers, betraying a barely competent mechanic. His face was pale and worn, and it had the markings of broken dreams, perhaps the result of long hours devoted to the spirit-killing routines of gas station work. I tried to make my eyes express my silent misery, but he didn't recognize it. Obviously, he was too dismayed by his own troubles to take much notice of mine. Our eyes unlocked when he leaned his head back to get a better look at Moe and answer the buffoon's query.

"You need to get back on the freeway going north," he pointed, studying Moe closely for directional comprehension. Satisfied, he continued, "Then take the third Bremerton exit, turn left under the overpass and then turn right on Industrial Drive and continue due north." He paused to clear his throat, his voice crackling a bit. "A large sign will say Carter's Wrecking Yard. You'll see it near the entrance to the last cul-de-sac on Industrial. We do business with them. It's late though, they'll be closed. But you know that, right?" James, I could read his name tag, looked at me as if to poll me, to see if I realized as much. I projected only anguish, and once more, he didn't seem to comprehend it.

"Yeah, kid, I know that," curly Moe proclaimed to him, a little too confidently. "We're going there tomorrow."

This didn't satisfy stooge Charlie. He had to get in it, misreading James' tone of voice as insulting. "When we get there ain't your concern, buddy. You monkey-wrenching, asshole loser. We know what our business is and it ain't none of yours!" he sneered, shouting, catching James by complete surprise.

Startled by the retort, James lurched away from the car, instinctively. I cheered Charlie's mistake, but the frazzled kid was alarmed and irritated, his attention far from me. "Tomorrow is the Fourth of July, Independence Day," he barked. "If you two gentlemen didn't know already, this is America, and they will be closed.' He was showing real anger, the hair on his arms bristling like a frightened cat. "If you dumb shits had any monkey-wrenching, asshole business going there, you would know that. Now screw off, losers. I'm busy!"

Wow! How great it is that youth is defiant. I had heard that young men raised in Washington State possessed the spunk of the oak and the gumption to use it.

21

Moe only glared at James, his eyes torched by vehemence, strangling him in the tense silence that followed. The young oak held his ground, glaring back, afraid but sturdy. The tension burst when Moe let out a booming, baritone bawl, another Bunyan's bellow. Hearing it a second time, I imagined it to be common laughter heard in faraway parlors, where Mafia paramours and other silly, lonesome dames must delight in him.

"I'll be a son of a bitch if this place doesn't rain down some of the goddamnedest kids I've ever seen! We could use some balls like this in Chicago. Don't you think, Charlie?" He slugged his fellow deviant in the arm, with some force. Charlie just grunted and then slammed on the gas. As we sped away, Moe swung around quickly, sticking his head out the window and pumping his fist in approval of James, yelling something to him that I couldn't make out.

I'm positive that it was with incomparable relief that James watched us fade into the distance. He hadn't recognized our plight, but I prayed that he still might figure it out, and he was calling the police right now. They never came. It seems we all have our broken dreams.

We drove on for what felt like another hour. Neither of my Neanderthal friends said much now, the thing that happens to cave dwellers when they get lost, I imagined. Rick remained unaware, a void of rigid sleep, his breathing more labored than before. Mile after mile ticked by.

Finally, the silence was broken when Charlie erupted wildly, suddenly stupefied with renewed anger. "Damn it. Where the hell are we? For crying out loud. This is taking way too long. Do you remember those directions, big man? Speak up, Moe. Aren't you the navigator?"

"Yeah, yeah, I got it," Moe said, waking up from whatever private journey he had been on, insisting that we try yet another new heading, one that resulted in only further confusing and exasperating Charlie. Heckle and Jeckle they were, in all their prime-time glory. Of course, it was still to our advantage.

After five more unproductive miles, Charlie's growing impatience once again exploded into a raging wildfire. He began to lash out uncontrollably, aiming sharp criticism at Moe's navigational skills. This went on for some moments and might have been downright funny under different circumstances. The insulting attack brought only scathing wrath in return. Big surprise. The big cat was furious in defending his skill, doing so at every rebuke, even if he had no idea where we were. He kept insisting that Carter's was just around the next corner, demanding that Charlie just shut up and drive. I thought it certain they would turn on each other with grisly consequences, their petty bickering far eclipsing any former disagreements. The pot was beginning to boil over.

But Charlie was not yet finished turning up the heat, and he continued to denounce Moe's careless propensity for dishing out impromptu directions, chastising his insistence that Carter's was "just around the next corner." Incautious Charlie wasn't taking a cue from James or me; his verbal abuse of Moe had become a regular game, a dangerous one for him. Moe was keeping score and fired back, increasingly determined to prevail, unmercifully berating the antagonist for his outbursts of harsh judgment and doubt. His authority—right or wrong—was never to be questioned. The frenzied squabbling just got hotter by the second, threatening full-scale war.

The instructions James gave them had been concise, but these two bungling sociopaths proved to be as unfamiliar with this area as Rick and I were. They had miscounted the correct number of exits and continued to plow northward for much too far. We were approaching the community of Chico and had left Carter's

Wrecking Yard far behind, hopefully to be salvaged by better than these two. In another second my disheartenment returned.

Charlie suddenly veered onto an old dirt road, and we stumbled into what appeared to be an ancient forest, a menacing black hole encased in impregnable hostility. A place for wayward kids to disappear. It had the feel of being haunted.

"Hell, this looks like a good, secluded place. I'm tired of this crazy runaround, Moe." Charlie was making his final stand, emphatic, turning up the heat again. "Come on, big man, let's get this over with. It ain't nothin' to worry about. It's just business. There should be a good spot in a mile or two. Screw Carter. "

Sadly, Moe offered no resistance. I despised his outrageous disloyalty. You can't trust anyone. "Just find a spot, Charlie, and we'll see what happens." He looked back at me, mournfully, as if sorry for the inconvenience.

I had been remarkably quiet for an extended time, emotionally drained by this unlikely and shocking ordeal. It was surely a fate meant only for other people. Regardless, the timely realization that I was soon to draw my final breath in this dark and damp forest filled me with new inspiration for life. If Moe and Charlie were going to kill us, I would rather it be at Carter's Wrecking Yard, where I hoped we at least stood a chance of getting noticed by someone, anyone. We must return to civilization, at once.

I fired my best bullet: a wild shot in the dark. "Hey, you two, Lewis and Clark, you were supposed to turn right miles ago. You drove past the right exit at least three times," I said, forcibly, sarcastically, desperate to change course. I would shame them into turning around. Then I thought of something else and poured it on thick. "I know this area, and it's a place known to be haunted. Very haunted. There are certain places where bad men disappear and are never seen or heard from again. You can hear the ghouls screaming at night, flying around with human heads wobbling on a stick. They think it's funny. It will be your heads next!" I shot a third round, with a conviction that even impressed me. "And it's patrolled nightly by park rangers and the local police. One wrong move and you'll bring the entire world down on your heads. They are out here everywhere, like the ghosts, constantly looking for stupid men like you. And this is Independence Day weekend, idiots. There will be lots of campers out here, everywhere. If the ghouls and ghosts don't get you, the cops will. You two will be in handcuffs before you can make it back to the car. Better yet, some devilish forest fiend will eat both of you! Capisce?"

OK, then. Poets and prophets have yearned long to understand the mighty weapon called the tongue, a tiny fire that burns red hot and untamed, capable of shaping a man's fear. So what happened in the next few seconds, I can only attribute to my big mouth and dumb luck.

"What the hell? Did you hear all that, Moe?" Charlie fumed, insanely. "If I had the shotgun up here, Buttercup, I'd shoot your ass right now! You two are the only ones not coming out of this forest tonight. I don't scare easy 'cause a shit like you says so, and ghosts don't scare me either, punk."

"They'll get you," I said, firmly.

"You better shut the hell up, Buttercup. Right now!"

My outburst had been too much for him. I was working on pure adrenalin. No matter how foolish, I would say anything that came to mind if I thought it would keep us alive.

"Damned if I don't think he might be right, Charlie," Moe said unexpectedly, in a cowed, fearful demeanor that both surprised and excited me. Could it be true? The big bad man was afraid of ghosts?

"He's right about what?" Charlie shot back, astonished by the mere idea of Moe's suggestion.

"It's summer, Charlie, there are likely campers out here all over the place. I don't know about the cop business, but I bet there's got to be a few rangers around," Moe replied, his manly countenance suddenly returning. Then his voice tailed off, unintentionally, giving him away. "Doing a thing like this out here could be a real mistake. This place is really creepy. I don't like the whole setup."

Bingo! Shakespearean poetry. Moe was genuinely frightened and convinced by the first lies I had told tonight. Maybe if we stopped here, he really would have occasion to call on the devils he bragged about earlier.

"Go ahead, Charlie, turn around," he said, explicitly. "I really think the kid might be right about this." His voice tailed off again—flat, dull, and subdued. He was as a man-child. Ghosts! Of all things.

I firmly believe that Charlie was also alarmed by my preposterous story, although he denied it. Whatever got to him, he obediently—with no more fanfare or complaint—turned the car around in the middle of the road, having finished his say. Still, he didn't fail to offer, one last time, that it would have been a good place to kill us. That Charlie, always the debonair one.

I led them to exactly where they wanted to go, Carter's Wrecking Yard, everything I knew it would be.

[2]
MEMORABLE BEGINNINGS
TWELVE DAYS EARLIER

For sure it wasn't the tenets of youthful rebellion that drove me from the home that kept me safe and dry. It was a warm home swarming with bright siblings and sparkling parents, and the latter were the kind that spoke softly, meant what they said, and provided their children with daily examples of grounded living. They were genuinely honest and humble about their approach to life, and I couldn't have asked for better. My dad was a shipbuilder and a patriot, a veteran of the *big* war. Modest and temperate, often kind to a fault, he was a brilliant man who completed crossword puzzles in ink and read the Sunday comics with equal ease and joy. Mr. Mellow is what we called him.

On the flip side, my mom was also a child of the Great Depression, reared in the mountains of North Carolina. It was a time and a place that molded her steel backbone, sharpening her eyes and ears to detect folly and nonsense at a glance and a whisper. We kids referred fondly to her as the "Pink Wall" because of her love for this delicate color and the gentleness it expressed about her, combined with the firsthand knowledge of the brick wall of discipline built just behind it. The two of them made a persuasive pair, and they were serious about teaching their children the foundational principles of self-respect and personal courage, American style. Most of all, they were my friends, and sometimes I had to be reminded that they were my parents.

Rebellion set aside, some might think that my secret adventure was a vain, illusory quest to find my place in America's ephemeral Camelot, tragically lost to me in my youth among the ghosts of slain American heroes, most of them assassinated, and a dirty little war. Or, maybe, as my older brother had been pleased to tell me, it was nothing more than a futile pursuit of rainbow wisdom and uncertain enlightenment, and one didn't need to take a road trip to find them. Everyone should have a big brother.

Or, sadly, a still more plausible analysis might be that Rick and I were fleeing to Canada for the singular purpose of avoiding the Vietnam War. That was absurd, of course, but understandable in the context of the times. No, sometimes a body just needs to get out of the house and go somewhere, with little concern for the time and effort—even danger—it may involve in getting to somewhere and back. The two of us planned to take an innocent joyride, nothing more, and if our aesthetic senses were awakened and our social consciousness developed in the process, then so much the better. Honestly, I think most Americans long to be set free to see and discover the sharpened details of their homeland—and plenty more after that. Our collective, manifest destiny is the way one might put it. It's the American urge to keep moving that comes to us as our national birthright.

Naturally, it was the sensible and proper thing to inform my parents that I was planning such a nonchalant drive, *The*

Great White North being my chosen goal, after seeing the wonders of America. Yet, surprisingly, spontaneously, I decided against it. I suppose I dreaded hearing about how America's highways were dangerous, and there was serious concern brewing in Canada over young American men. It's not that they wanted to keep me on a short leash. I was never raised to be a momma's boy. Except from their perspective it was my summer to prepare for college, and there was much to be done. They just wanted me on a secure line for now, one attached to something meaningful and something that could be directed, like a ship's rudder. Hadn't my older siblings, all four of them, done it this way? As far as my folks were concerned, I could paddle to Hawaii if I so dared and hang out at the beach, growing a beard and going broke, as long as college and a degree came first. My first year would set the tone. I think parents, whether they admit it or not, live vicariously through their children. "Put it off for a year, son, there will be time for joyrides. What's the rush?" That kind of stuff.

Despite that kind of stuff, I was going, anyway, and no one was going to stop me. After all, I was 18 and practically a man. What was the harm in a simple summer drive? I'd be back in less than a week. Besides, the Pink Wall, the final authority in all things sensible, had just recently encouraged me to explore my independence. The way I reasoned it, morality still mattered, and I doubted there was less of it to threaten me two thousand miles away. I had a very personal reason, as well, something to live up to, but I think I'll say more about it later. I believe you might enjoy it.

When it came time for our brash departure, Rick arrived at my doorstep a full hour before sunrise, his gusto to get moving impossible to restrain. It reminded me of what the young hippies and rockers fondly called, "The Full-Tilt Boogie."

When I answered the door, he magically appeared and then vanished, only to rematerialize in a puff of smoke at the back of the Princess, loading her trunk madly, the essentials of life on the road safely in his hands. All this time he smiled jovially at me, fumbling about some more, urging me to pick up the pace and get a charge on! He was a lovable goofball, sweet and kind, with few rough edges, and a real wizard about some things in life. Sometimes his temper would flare up but only on occasion. He was also my best friend, and this fact helped us quickly disappear: two smoking firebrands heading for hell.

"You didn't tell your parents, did you, Rick?"

"No way, Cosmo. I told my sister, Carmen, but she won't rat us out."

"What?" I asked, mortified by his betrayal. "I thought we agreed not to tell anyone until we got on the road. Why did you do that? Are you trying to outdo Benedict Arnold and surrender before the first mile is won? Damn it. What the hell is wrong with you?"

"What if something goes wrong, man?"

"Like what? A flat tire, maybe? We run out of gas? Dang, Rick, I wish you hadn't done that. You sound like my parents."

He sulked a little while from this whipping. Then his magic returned. "Hey, man, it's all OK. I just remembered that I told her we were heading south, Disneyland, or someplace benign like that. Don't worry. She won't get a wild hair and bust us. Must have slipped my mind."

"Must have slipped your mind? Is that the truth, really?"

"Yeah. It's the truth. I just forgot. Anyway, I'm pretty sure that's what I told her. Dang it, Cosmo, stop worrying like an old woman, and stop hassling me. She's not going to burst our bubble." He was calling my bluff. "She hopes I won't come back."

"Just get the maps out of the glove box, Ruiz, in case we need them. And try not to hurt yourself." I suspected that he was telling the truth, at least the important part. Maybe I was making too big a deal out of it, and it unfortunately produced a brief occasion of stiff silence between us. Within 50 miles we were best friends again, as it was always meant to be. With the passage of 200 more, the excitement created by conquering new, majestic horizons was enough to bind us together forever, inseparable, suckling little sugar ants raiding the sweet honey jar of America.

This is my home, California, the American equivalent of the Biblical land of milk and honey, luscious and extravagant in her proud, sunbaked fleece of fine gold that garlands her silver peaks to the east; and to the west, her jagged coastal cliffs, where the continent falls off precipitously into the Pacific Ocean. It's a glorious land and the end of the line for many. In our case, it was just the beginning of our known world.

Thus, finding our way skirting along like this, heading northeast from the San Francisco Bay Area, it was with untainted enthusiasm that we landed upon a great number of magnificent vistas, each one displaying its expansive view of breathtaking forests, peaks and mountains, and silver ribbons of implausible, mystic rivers. Time after time we were overwhelmed by the vast beauty of a state like no other, where every stop is different but the same, and where there is no end of nature's beauty—the unspoken poetry of God. And when we looked on high, we could see the rush of billowing clouds, riding the winds of a summer blue sky, sometimes spotting majestic eagles, powerful raptors, more magnificent than angels and dominating the heavens. They are a proud symbol of a proud nation, soaring grandly on long, broad wings, keeping them aloft and flying faster than light.

31

It was with great longing that I wanted to share all of these places with strangers and friends or anyone who has never had the chance to take in such dazzling sceneries, contemplating them softly in the mind and exploring them with the eyes. Such marvels left us hungry for the awe of wonder, where no single location can satisfy one's sense of sight, hearing, smell and touch. We were never fully satisfied to taste any particular stop, only teased back into the car, anxious to be bewitched by the next display of the splendor of our state.

On random walks, bursts of personal discovery, we hurried along, our footsteps excited to explore these improbable, magical places, where we often found tantalizing little brooks and streams. These gushing runlets helped cloak us from the heat of the midday sun, and we soaked our heads and faces, taking prolonged drinks of fresh mountain water. In the summertime, as the snow is quick to melt, they are everywhere, yet isolated and uninhabited. The seclusion was idyllic.

On one stop we found a large beehive, mangled and scattered upon the ground, and we thought a cantankerous Brown Bear must be close by, its diet consisting of almost anything, perhaps including young men, so we quickly hustled to a different location. The scare brought back the reality that nature is both friend and foe.

At yet another stop we encountered hundreds of swarming dragonflies zigzagging at startling speed over a large, stagnant pond, on the prowl for flies and gnats and mosquitoes. They appeared to be searching for any insect they could pounce on and devour. I guessed it to be their favorite hunting ground, awash with an abundant variety of nourishment. We sat for some moments, near to them, watching this slaughter with curious fascination and dread, knowing that the sheer numbers of them prevented any escape for those marked out as lunch. It was an electric light show of red and blue and orange, a frenzy of changing colors in the streaming sunlight, and I was thankful not to play a part in this fierce drama that absolved few victims. No matter, for them it was a happy and healthy feeding site.

All in all, the grandeur of our new world was offering up a delectable table of goodies for our consumption, and we began to relish the romantic idea of coming back and homesteading any of these fine places, where no intruders could find us and no interlopers were welcome. We abandoned, only for now, the allure of returning one day soon and staking out our own unchallenged claims. It was a longing for a bygone America, but it was fun to think about.

By design, most of these aesthetic triumphs were conceived on short notice or by pleasurable cravings. Little of importance was missed. If so, another roadside attraction was surely just around the next curve. Then almost prophetically, it was the very next curve that revealed an attraction we weren't expecting. We spotted an elderly man struggling to change a flat tire and decided to offer to help. It was a good thing because the lug nuts on the wheel were so tight that he could not loosen them. In fact, they were so snug that it required putting on a pair of gloves, and then my trading off with Rick, just in order to bust them loose. To complicate things, the spare was so brittle and bald that we offered to follow him to the next town so that he could find two replacements. He thanked us repeatedly for our kindness and kept saying that providence had been good to him throughout his life, and he hoped it would also serve us well.

The adventure cost us almost two hours of daylight and fun time, and the providential outcome of God's care for the universe led us to drive much faster, with the consequences often resulting in sudden blast-braking, smoking peel outs, and needle-threading exits, to make up for lost opportunities. These impulsive forays did surprise and distress an unsuspecting fellow traveler or two, causing more than one admonishment to keep our exuberance in check. I doubted it was the kind of divine outcome the old fellow had in mind, but I can't say we were entirely surprised. Still, we were quick with repentance on these occasions, disarming such earnest remarks by smiling warmly and articulating our sincere apologies. Each time we represented ourselves as forthright, malleable gentlemen, swift about recognizing our errors and pledging to correct them.

Such embarrassing encounters have convinced me that Americans, when receiving genuine apologies, are easily the most forgiving people on earth. I've come to believe this because we are not really strangers—not at all. Are we not, in fact, brethren locked up together on the same continent, with no better place to go? I think Americans are so intertwined because of our vast and similar commonalities, that, well, we might just as well have been born from the same parents, conjoined in the corporeal and the spiritual. We are a gracious, free people who freely forgive—and we do it from sea to shining sea. I love this place, right or wrong.

Admittedly, things did go wrong one time. We finally met the episodic killjoy and malcontent, the kind of person who will not relent or take a softer line. We found him on a lonely outcrop, sleeping comfortably in his car, in the shade of a mighty ponderosa pine. We rudely awoke this Lone Star Texan, one who turned extremely annoyed by our rowdy arrival, and he served us up a portion of his considerable longhorn wrath, a ten-gallon hatful, I'd say. I will not be quick to forget him. Nonetheless, we managed to be safe and careful, as the overall order of things, and thus we retained a respectable level of social acceptance. Two American boys just having fun—and forgiven for it.

It's only fair to say that these abrupt and sometimes playful excesses were openly advanced by our intimate association with another friend. We happened to be armed to the teeth in a new Chevy Camaro, dream class of 1968. If you will forgive me, I'll brag that I earned her myself, every penny. I picked more than 7,000 big boxes of tomatoes, over three summers, on a large farm in Dixon, California. I saved every cent and bought her for cash when I was only 17. I'll tell you the full story later, and I'll only add now that if one wanted something at our house it had to be earned. Mr. Mellow and the Pink Wall were not pushovers.

Anyway, I named the car the Princess, aptly, because she was pretty and petite and as explosive for her size as any little darling that has ever hailed from the motor state, Michigan. She was a young man's divine dream machine, sexy in her cool black dress, and her heart pumped with a big, vivacious engine, 327 cubic inches of it—revved up much more than just a little. It was a love affair in full bloom and the generation of the true muscle car. The Princess was a decent version.

Honestly, we were never carelessly reckless, God forbid. Both Rick and I had a passionate love for the art of fine driving, and we respected others skilled in relationship to their machines. It can make all the difference in a tight shave. We certainly had a healthy respect for the rules of the road, and if we occasionally stretched them, it was always and only within the limits of our abilities.

My driving skills came by the good fortune of learning in a professional environment. My hard-charging brother-in-law was the direct cause of my early induction into such storied, masculine matters. His passion, beyond his daily vocation of stevedore and good family man, was to build fast cars and race them on weekends. Keith, his name, was a professional dirt track racer at a time when local race tracks could be found in many small American towns. One of my great boyhood memories is recalling the thunderous roars that came from the local race track on weekends, blasting away the night sky. In the calm air of a soft summer night the sounds could be heard for miles, and maybe as far as the next town, where the same thing was likely taking place. It was the growl of life in America at the time, and the town's heartbeat growled right along with it.

Keith always invited me to assist him in pit row on race nights, and I was proud to be a member of his team, learning much more than I ever contributed, but always striving to be useful. Long after the night's thrills and spills were over, and the fans were heading home on slower, saner roads, he would let me burn off as many slapdash laps as I wanted. The cleanup crew never seemed to mind and enjoyed seeing me improve. Keith most often rode with me, repeating, "Always drive within yourself and your machine, Rusty. And, at all times, avoid the outer limits. They will kill you!" I thought the bit a little corny and overdone, the way older people can get about such weighty matters, but, all in all, he was a man's man, thriving on self-control and practicing it daily. As his young student, I admired him immensely, and his word was golden.

Rick was also talented, in his own right. His older brother, Joe (Big Ugly is how Rick referred to him), owned a fine, diamond-blue 1966 Pontiac GTO, considered by many to be the decade's premier muscle car. Its brute force was simply unmatchable. Joe finally gave in to Rick's constant pleading for some personal training and agreed to school him thoroughly on what it took to tame the angry beast. Rick then left his initials in rubber on every unpatrolled county road, right next to Joe's. So it goes that every American generation has its own collection of unique trademarks and ours was no different. We were all cohorts raised on cheap gas and extremely fast, gut-busting muscle cars.

That was the long road around explaining that we were not terrorists or simpleminded hooligans on the loose, just young American men doing what young American men are apt to do in young America, from time to time, without much thought or reason for it.

~~~

PART 2

Meantime, the vistas and other extraordinary sights certainly didn't care to reason with us, not in the least. From my perspective—as one in awe—these piercing, unspoiled spots of nature's beauty went far beyond merely dominating their surroundings. Rather, they spoke their own spiritual language, a parlance of sweet exhortations that begged for the consideration of God. Who else could craft and mold such astonishment, cupping it softly in his strong, celestial hands, before serving it up to us on a silver platter, without money and without price? I marveled at the budding of such grand thoughts, when one is sure that God must have something to do with all things. What I had seen today called for a satisfactory explanation, and the idea of accidents left me cold and empty. In the clouds of such lofty reflections, I was summoned to earth.

"Cosmo, we better be moving along. There's a lot more to see. Are you going to do this every time we stop?"

"Do what?"

"Whatever it is you do when your eyes glaze over like that. It really spooks me out. You remind me of some lost mystic or hippie on a bad LSD trip."

"You're afraid of mystics and hippies?" I teased him, amused by his choice of oppressors. But when it was silent again, I thought I could hear a mighty, forceful wind rippling throughout the painted landscape, a thundering song of sweet invitation and acknowledgement rushing to embrace us with its mouthwatering cry of beckoning, ancient welcome. Each time we left such a pretty place behind, I was disheartened when saying goodbye. Is there nothing at all that won't finally break your heart?

We stopped again soon, this time at a flat expanse of earth, a bare-bones rest stop and quaint picnic area. The wide drive-thru, where we entered, was layered heavily in California red clay and speckled over in sharp gravel, the kind of thick, crunchy road grime that slimes your tires and bounces off the side of your car. In a minute more we realized it lacked restrooms and we were obligated to slip behind a large tree to take care of our more immediate business. That aside, and all hazards and inconveniences duly noted, it did come with a lovely emerald valley framed by massive forests and stuffed with verdant ponderosa pine and ageless Douglas fir. The sight of this much timber, surrounding us on all sides, reminded me of the western TV show, *Bonanza,* and the family, Cartwright, who, in the distance, I could see riding happily on gallant steeds—straight toward us.

A short distance away, a turbulent river flowed swiftly through the valley's carved belly, born of a rich Sierra snowmelt. Rick swore that he saw mischievous leprechauns on the opposite bank digging in the luscious topsoil for hidden treasure. I didn't see them. Nonetheless, knowing the magical aura that sometimes surrounded him, I naturally took his word for it. After all, hadn't I just seen the Cartwrights? At any rate, we were pleasantly refreshed by strolling close to the cool, swirling spray, a delectable mist that kissed lightly off our brows and energized us.

Just as we arrived back to the car our transcendence was abruptly shattered by a colossal truck, a big-rig beast of burden that came crashing through the calm air, spraying clouds of dust and assorted rocks, then finally grinding to a seismic halt very near to us. I surveyed the Princess, now covered in red filth and pelted by the fierce gravel from hell. Outraged, ready to defend her honor to the death, I arose from where I sat on her hood to express my fury. Then I remembered the recent easygoingness displayed by my fellow countrymen. I came to my senses and quickly let it go.

It was just as well because a monster was descending from the cab, looking impatient to relieve himself, seemingly oblivious to our close presence. Such urges were not lost on us, of course, so having witnessed his hurried, dramatic entrance, we could fully sympathize with the seriousness of his mission.

I considered his manifestation to be a great intrusion, to be sure, but grandly entertaining. The sudden appearance of the infamous Sasquatch arriving in a blinding rush of necessity was unmistakably Rockwellish, an American portrait painted right in front of our very eyes. His side of the world shook when he hit the ground, said Bigfoot unexpectedly breaking into a funny and fluid Bojangles' kind of jig-boogie, a stationary, rhythmic tap dance to heat up the blood in his road-sore joints. His presence was loud and alarming and a little brazen in its own peculiar way. It impressed upon me the subtle reality that the American trucker was still king of the road. And his kingly arrival, after all, had not been much different from a few of ours, so we already felt kinship to him. I wondered if he would dance that jig again if he knew that kin were watching.

Almost as dramatic, as his rowdy arrival, were his theatrical garments: a road-soiled, holey T-shirt with a delightful picture of the Mona Lisa etched on it, and blue work breeches, sorely blanched and fitting loosely around his waist. He wore no belt, so they seemed to defy the law of gravitation and would have taken Newton off guard. Just as comical was his baseball cap, loud and painted with wide zebra stripes, which struck me as the perfect camouflage to ward off highway horseflies and other odd road dangers. Hidden beneath this cartoonish assembly was a chest so thick and firm that the sheer girth of it could crumble a mountain if he fell against it. His arms and shoulders resembled massive, steel girders, a robust foundation to support his monolithic bridge of neck and head, and his brown, wavy hair protruded in all directions beneath the wily zebra. I imagined it a real burden to carry around such immensity. Then he moved and I saw a different man, vigorous and agile, darting forward like a dignified and dominant mountain lion, sure of himself and his surroundings. It spoke of his ability to move freely and unthreatened, and it was a metamorphosis that caught me by complete surprise. He greeted us with a quick wave, a tip of his cap, and a gregarious smile, disappearing in a trot down the gentle slope that led to the river. We nodded in understanding of his urgent need.

By the time he returned we were plowing through peanut butter sandwiches and gulping warm Kool-Aid. Our carved up and rustic picnic table faced the valley and the stream, and as the huge man passed by again, Rick surprised him by offering to share our lunch.

"Hey, mister, we've got plenty to go around. Are you hungry?"

"How's that?" he asked, evaluating the two of us more closely now.

"I said we got plenty to eat. Are you hungry?"

"Oh. Well, I don't know. Yeah, come to think of it, I might be. Got ice?"

"No, no ice. But the bread is nice and fresh. We just bought it today," Rick bragged, happy he could atone for the curse of warm Kool-Aid. He held the loaf of bread high over his head, accentuating the positive, as only he could.

"Well, I'm not one to turn down the saving bread," the giant said, won over by Rick's friendly insistence. "If you'll give me a minute, I'll fetch some ice."

Without further ado, he bound his way to the wide double doors at the back of his immense tractor-trailer (T-Rex, we later named it), bringing back a hefty cooler filled with ice-cold drinks. I wished we could have afforded the same. Such things were a luxury on this trip. "Got a little of everything in here. Take your pick, men," he said, cheerfully.

"Thank you, mister," we said in unison. Rick was a scoundrel, reaching in first and snatching the only bottle of chocolate milk in sight, using two pincer-like fast fingers, the same ones I've seen him use to snatch fish off a hook. It's dreadful. They are practically skinned before they know they've been caught. It's one of his special talents, if one should care to view it that way. In reality, the little demon was just being ornery for the sake of a cheap laugh, knowing my undying affection for chocolate milk. It was only one of four things I'd die for, besides God, family and country.

After getting his full measure of fun, he tossed the milk at me a little too quickly, causing me to bobble and then drop it, watching the bottle roll away in the loose dirt, stopping some 10 feet away. He tried his best to wrangle his way out of this embarrassment, hastily informing our new friend of the innocent humor intended by his little joke. He then made apologies for my lack of catching skills, as if it was my fault all along, and explained that I had long ago sold my soul to the Chocolate Milk Devil. He was only trying to save me from further damnation. In the end, he's always paid a high price for such practical jokes but never seemed to learn his lesson.

"They say it's a small world. My son also loves chocolate milk." The colossus finally replied to Rick's defensive banter,

41

not at all shocked to hear of another person having the same affliction. The tall story was already coming back to haunt Rick. The titan's loyalty to the cause erased any idea that he found the joke funny. I liked him very much already. I even thought we might together butcher Rick.

"He does?" I asked, appreciative of his effort but not entirely convinced.

"Yes, absolutely. It's not something I'd kid around about. I always bring him some on my run home."

"I'll be glad to put this one back, mister, if you'd like?" I had fetched the bottle and carefully wiped the dirt away, my devotion to my love overcome by the grief I knew his son would endure. Life is full of these kinds of sacrifices—and they will find you. I tried to place it back inside the cooler.

He would not abandon his kindness so easily. "No, no. Please don't put it away," he said, shoveling it back into my hands. "Drink it and enjoy. I'll get some more. No problem—at all—young man. Please, I insist."

Feeling reassured now, I offered one more weak appeal in behalf of his son's welfare and then drank it in deep, guiltless pleasure. It was only when the crime was done, and the bottle empty, that I thought I heard the desperate, withering moans of a faraway boy's tragic despair, coming from hundreds of miles away, fast overtaking me, suffocating me under the weight of sorrowful, searing laments of great mourning and misery. Wow! Chocolate milk is serious business in a serious world. Just so you understand.

On par with such seriousness is the universal mystery of why teenagers find it so hard to introduce themselves first. It's a widespread riddle, I've come to think. Naturally, we waited for him to do the honors. And, of course, it was a real honor to meet one Roscoe Van Hamilton, a regal name. The noble sound of it seemed to mold well with his physical stature and perfectly matched his natural goodwill. He now struck me only as a giant, lovable mountain of a man, and his genuine display of warmth disarmed my initial anxiety at being in the presence of such a formidable stranger.

Then, without warning, he suddenly howled, "The Rusty, Rick and Roscoe Show!" bobbing and weaving his head from side to side as a boxer might do in a dance of joy, when he realizes he can't be hit. All the while he threw punch after punch of inspired glances our way. It was the strangest thing. I thought he must be truly a daisy of a man, to go with the mountain. Comically, the daisy wasn't finished. "I got it!" he shouted, even louder, as if heaven had suddenly provided him with a stirring revelation. "By golly, I'll be darned if we don't sound just like a circus act. It has the ring of a real barn burner to me, men! Yes, sir, a real fire in the tent. It's time to break out the buckets, boys. The circus is in town!" He was very funny and so delighted by this silly gag that he repeated it again, even more animated the second time. His behavior was preposterous, of course, and I didn't know what to make of him. His display of childlike enthusiasm for all this silliness made me think he'd make a natural politician. With such an affable personality and unique delivery, people would agree with everything he said and believe it could happen. He was just a cool guy, and I was happy that we had stumbled upon him. What followed was a meaningful discussion about the professional merits of roustabouts—his excitement sparked our interest—then we settled down to finishing off the peanut butter sandwiches and cold drinks.

"I'm not sure you can afford us, Roscoe," I tried to tease him. "We about finished off your cooler."

"Nor you I," he quipped, taking a humongous bite of his fourth sandwich.

We had expected to earn a little money on the road, mostly by lucky chance or pleading with the gods of easy fortune to guide us, but we never considered that guys like Roscoe were loose on the highways. It was because of him that my perspective about traveling would eventually change, and by the end of this trip the idea of home became of renewed importance to me. It was also because of him that easy fortune would not be in our future. We were about to be offered some hard, dirty work, by one I fondly came to know as, "The Second Greatest Man in the World."

"You men didn't tell me where you are heading? All I can gather is that by the direction you're parked, it ain't south." Roscoe had a trained eye for such things and even made this sound funny.

Rick waited for me to respond first, still mindful of his blunder with Carmen.

"We're on our way to Canada to see what all the fuss is about," I said, without fear of any prying and at ease in the long miles that now separated us from Carmen. "We figure on taking four or five days and do some searching around. If we stay gone longer our parents will have the blue meanies or the Black Panthers looking for us."

"Yeah, I thought you two might be in search of life on the road. I did it myself once, when I was about your age. Now I just drive it and do my real searching at home."

"What do you mean by that?" Rick asked, sharply, the way one does when unexpectedly put on the defensive. I thought the same way. At first, I thought it a callous remark, intended as criticism.

Roscoe detected this and quickly redefined his meaning. "Oh, don't get me wrong, meant no offense by it. The road isn't a bad thing. Hell, I earn my living by it and got no complaints. And there are some valuable lessons to be learned out here. What I meant is that I search at home for the deeper meaning of things. Everything I am lives there and there lives everything I am. When I was young, I had to wander to survive, in search of work, and I lost my home and everything that it meant to me. Then I found it again, one I built myself, and it's there that my heart and soul searches for the meaning I can't find out here or anywhere else." He paused for a moment to gauge our reaction to his earnest sermon, but we just sat there like knots on a log.

He tried to find a different way to reach us. "Like a circle is the way I think about it most, where the best stop is the final stop back home. The home that a person wants and needs to come back to. Life is like a circle that should always lead back home. That's all I mean." I was moved by his sincere conviction and believed that he believed all these things. But, at the time, I didn't think he could possibly be right.

Roscoe was on the part of the circle that he most desired and needed, and we were on the part still untraveled and untamed. Although I tried to understand the meaning of what he said, I can't say that I actually did. He was a wise man of the road and trying to hint at what both of us would also come to believe, in due time, but for now the message made little impact. Just the same, in our usual, polite style, we nodded our heads in some agreement with him, thinking this might somehow make all of us feel better, even if we didn't really understand him.

When he was finished, I stated an objection, anyway, the only one I figured the more experienced Roscoe couldn't criticize. Nonetheless, in a curious way, I already valued his judgment and just wanted to throw some prideful static at him. "Well, we haven't seen the circle," I said, adding, "I'm looking to draw my own conclusions. Why should I believe what the guy in front of me says? A man should see his own country, up close and in a personal way, and not just look at pretty pictures in a stupid magazine." I thought this summed it up—and so did he.

"You put it well, I think," Roscoe replied, in a gentle manner. "A very understandable viewpoint, indeed." He would say no more about the subject for now, except, "So, do you got enough to see it with any class?"

"Well, no, to be truthful. But we figure to earn a little money," I fired back, a little too aggressively, feeling unintelligent and ashamed, still convinced that the color of money would magically materialize for us, somehow.

"Well, then, I think I can help you out with that, if you're not afraid of a little hard work."

"We're not afraid to work hard, man," Rick said, perhaps too bravely, having little idea of what awaited him in the arms of one Roscoe Van Hamilton.

"And you, Rusty?"

"He speaks for me, well enough."

"Good, then it's settled." He finished his sandwich and stood up to stretch. It was time to move on.

We followed Roscoe northwest for three hours, mostly on slow, winding roads, meandering our way to his home near the Smith River, within spitting distance of the Oregon border. We had been hired to unload 15,000 pounds of furniture. It's the hardest day's work I've ever done. Rick too. Roscoe stopped for chocolate milk first: a king's ransom.

[3]
SUGAR AND SWEAT

Far Northern California in redwood country is a climax of extreme beauty. If I thought it true only because I'm native to the state, I would tell you. More probably, I would put it this way. Doesn't everyone think that his or her home state is the best? Of course, and they are almost always right. Some states have the best mountains, other states have the best lakes and rivers and forests, and then there are the states with the best parklands, wild lands and wetlands, and, quite naturally, there are the states with the best cities, ports, people, and pride. We all brag about it: home!

Roscoe had a little brag in the pot. Having built his castle near the river run and a pretty lake, he and his family set up house and pursued the western life. His small ranch and the surrounding area were spectacular.

"I've seen places in West Virginia that come close to matching this, but I reckon we are going to stay here for the long run. Isn't that right, Rosie?" Roscoe placed his colossal paw over his wife's delicate hand, patting and rubbing it briskly, in affirmation of true love. Then the two pecked each other on the lips and just smiled. It was a truly warm and touching scene, and with the smell of banana pancakes enveloping the kitchen and the syrupy laughter of children sweetening the air, an ideal moment that we all shared. This was our breakfast hour with Roscoe and Rosie, and their five young children peppered us with questions when Roscoe was silent. One query reminded me of our arrival the night before, which had taken place in the following uncertain mood and manner.

"Man, it's sure dark here. Spooky, too," Rick said, with some alarm. "I hope there ain't any wolves close by, Cosmo. I've heard of wolves eating people, in a pinch."

I looked him up and down in the dim light of the car, measuring up the prospects. "Are you kidding? No self-respecting wolf would eat your scrawny carcass."

"That's right, Cosmo. They probably don't like dark meat, anyway. No one does. Aaaaah!" He abruptly reached over and grabbed my cheek, pinching it hard, the way he does the poor, miserable fish, squeezing it tight with his iron fingers. He does it all the time, and it hurts like hell. "Aaaaah! But I bet they like white meat like you. Aaaah-haaa!" he cried, again, delighted by this little feat of physical abuse, further proclaiming that I had tender, fresh cheeks, the kind wolves enjoy the most, especially topped off with a little glass of chocolate milk. "Aaaaah! Cosmo, if the wolves don't get you, his little boy will!" It was his way to harass me, but he paid for it.

"Hey, man, watch it! You're going to get us into a wreck." I slapped his hand away and in the same motion latched onto his long chest hair. It resembled a bushy tarantula, by anyone's measurement, antennas bursting from his open shirt collar, sniffing the air. It's the most impressive, full-flowing stock of black chest hair I've ever seen. Oddly, lots of women are turned on by it, I've noticed, the mere idea outrageous and queer to me, one of bare chest. Whatever your preference, it made a dandy target. I yanked hard, the way he had done to my cheek.

"You bastard, Cosmo!" He retaliated, pinching my cheek again.

"Damn it, Ruiz, knock it off. I'm trying to drive here. Quit acting like a crazy fool! You are going to get us killed."

"Then keep your hands to yourself, Cosmo!"

"I'm just checking the spider's temperature. The wolves might want him for dessert. God, what a hairy sucker you are."

This brought him back to his original concern, which died in the next moment—apologies to the wolves.

"You can stop being so spooked now. I see house lights ahead."

We pulled into Roscoe's wide driveway, with a special section made for T-Rex. Getting settled in, we made it through the warm summer night sleeping on Roscoe's living room floor.

Breakfast over, Rosie made for the kitchen sink. It was time to go to work.

"I'll help you with those dishes, Mrs. Van Hamilton," I said, and I really didn't mind. I was quickly reminded that there were bigger things on our plates.

"The hell you will. We got work to do!" Roscoe slapped my back, playfully, and I felt the vital organs inside me collide together. At 6 feet 2 inches, I was just a rag doll when swatted by this goliath. As noted, he was an immensely powerful man, standing 6 feet 8 inches and weighing 335 pounds, as I came to know. There are foothills in West Virginia that aren't as big.

"Don't kill the boy before you even get him out there!" Rosie exclaimed, panic stricken, very aware of the possible repercussions of Roscoe's playful banter.

"Naw, Sugar, it's just a love tap to get him loosened up," Roscoe assured her, mischievously eyeing Rick as his next victim, winking at him and the children, simultaneously, while crouching in a bear's charge. Mr. Ruiz lost no time removing himself from the table. The kids, all of us, found a new source of laughter.

We were soon outside, and I will never forget my first good look at daytime in this part of the world. Not 200 yards away were redwoods as wide and tall as skyscrapers. The vistas had sung for us—but not these big daddies. They sing for the clouds and not mere human droppings on the ground. Roscoe gave me the OK to look around, and I was immediately drawn to them first, soon standing at the base of one 20 feet wide, measured in strides. It was perhaps 300 feet tall. I paid due homage and reverence to all of them, humbled to think of my relative insignificance in the natural world. In this marvelous kingdom of giants, I understood where I ranked, and it was best to watch my step. To them I was no more than a speck of bothersome mortal curiosity, leaning presumptuously against their mighty trunks and reciting nonsensical poetry to them, the quality not worth hanging at the base of their massive boles. Despite going unnoticed, I stood before them in great veneration and divine respect. There is little that is more overwhelming than one's first encounter with a mammoth redwood tree and a crowd of its bodacious buddies. From a spiritual perspective, the only thing I could compare to them were the times I've stood very high on the ocean cliffs of the Western Continent, gazing upon Mother Pacific. They deserved the awesome esteem that she did. Simply put, redwoods are righteous representatives of nature's conspicuous glory, dignified American giants and icons, and though for the most part friendly, they wish for us to keep our place and let them keep theirs.

"Cosmo, are you going to stand there all day and chirp like an English poet? Man! I've never seen another like you. Cosmo the nature boy, the landscape lovechild, creation's cream puff. Now stop it and come on. Aaaaah!" Rick had his own distinctive way of viewing things.

"You just have no appreciation for God's miracles, Ruiz. And what do you have against English poets?"

"They're not American."

"They don't chirp like birds, either."

"Maybe, but they still shit like them, and if you stay standing there long enough, Cosmo, you'll be as full of it as they are."

"I suppose you have a real reason for being here, knucklehead?"

"Yeah, you idiot, Roscoe said it's time to go to work. Let's get moving."

"OK, but just one more English poem."

"Shut up, nature boy. Just break a leg, will ya!"

Really, is there nothing at all that won't finally break your heart?

Roscoe wasn't taking our short delay to heart. There was some minor damage to his trailer. He was busy fixing it.

"Yo, Roscoe, where are you?" Rick called out.

"Here I am, men." He appeared from deep within the trailer, having crawled the length of it from the opposite side. "The first door is busted. This is the only way I could get in here. What do you think?"

We thought it must be a trailer fully loaded, top to bottom, with other people's household junk. We were right, except nothing resembled junk, each item individually and expertly wrapped inside its own super thick, jumbo cloth pad. These heavy coverings were the color of puke-green and each one wide enough to swaddle the Great Lakes. They clung tightly to whatever was hidden inside of them and were secured by elongated, brawny rubber bands, on loan from Paul Bunyan, no doubt. Everything was stacked snugly from floor to ceiling and together formed a solid wall of impenetrable fabric. There wasn't an inch of wiggle room between anything. It was remarkable. What great men can do such things?

"Bet you've never seen something like this, have you?" Roscoe was proud of his craftsmanship. He should have been.

Both of us agreed, "No, never." Was it really furniture or just a vast wall of green cloth?

"The greatest man in the world taught me how to do this. It's most like putting a heavy puzzle together, piece by piece, so that nothing moves or shifts. No damage in my trailer, men. One can develop a skill for it with hard work and practice." Roscoe batted his fist on the padded wall to show us that nothing could be disturbed until he was ready to disturb it. Grandma's china was safe in Roscoe's trailer.

"What do you want us to do first?" I asked.

"Well, the first thing we need to do is prep the trailer. You two grab the walk board. You'll find it underneath the trailer, on the right side. Then we'll start unloading. I want you to put everything on the grass, gently, and don't unwrap anything. We'll be putting it back this afternoon. And don't get my pads dirty!"

It all sounded simple enough. Still, we were already exhausted four hours later, the sizzling air and the scorching summer heat assaulting us, not to mention that Roscoe was a nonstop and tireless worker. The sweltering ordeal reminded us that furniture is often quite heavy, especially if it happens to be oak furniture. Yes, it happened to be oak, every piece of it. Lucky us. To make our burden worse, the pads began to get slippery from the sweat pouring off our hands and arms, and with no other sure method of gripping any object firmly, our every move was filled with dicey adventure. Just the same, the biggest problem was the troublesome difference in height between the two of us. Thus everything had to be carried at a lopsided angle, putting more weight and stress on Rick. To adjust for my height, he was forced to dig his forehead into each pad to keep from losing his step and balance. The result was a nasty red spot that developed on his brow, one that resembled a melted scarlet crayon on a butter dish, mixed with plenty of dirt and anxious poop. Poor boy, I thought he looked stricken, ready for bed and a hospice nurse.

Roscoe's watchful eye and encouragement kept us going throughout. He was a benevolent taskmaster. "Nothing to it, men. It sure is hot, but I think we'll whip it. Hard work is God's work. I think we about got it now!" Roscoe would sing this song each time we started unloading a new tier of tricky green surprises. It took hearing him recite the same refrain five more times before we stopped believing him.

"Roscoe, you said that the last time and the time before that and that," Rick complained, good-naturedly, glistening buckets of coastal sweat dripping from his brown skin. "How many tiers of this stuff are left, really?" It was a question born from a telekinetic desire to more easily move the core mysteries of life, in this case furniture, without the use of physical force. We both were getting plenty weary.

"I'll tell you what," Roscoe said. "You jump on the ladder and hand things down for a tier or two. I'll help Rusty."

Rick readily agreed but vaulted back to my side just as smartly. Roscoe had tricked him, edifyingly so. The temperature inside the trailer, near the ceiling, was 10 degrees hotter than what we endured on the floor and outside. Prior knowledge can be greatly undervalued.

In the end, it was one of the most satisfying days of hard work I've ever done. We unloaded 15 tiers, each averaging 1,000 pounds, and then reloaded them, all in a total of 11 long, brutal hours. And—for what? It was for the shining privilege of discovering a lost gemstone, a treasure bartered away long ago in selfless love, finally returning home to its rightful owner. It was Rosie's satin walnut Steinway, a melodic opus, a musical masterpiece celebrated home, and the most stunning baby grand piano I've ever seen. Roscoe was more of a king than we ever could have imagined, and we were his allies in chivalry, grand knights in this dazzling display of how the crown jewel of love always seems to circle back to the place it began. We were eyewitnesses to a giant of human compassion jousting for the affections of his pretty queen, one who loved him enough to have traded away her cherished piano. It was a grand ransom to set her king free, more than 14 years earlier.

Roscoe slowly unrobed the gorgeous piano for us to inspect, and we gaped and fell about the trailer, then consented to his demand that we swear a knight's oath of secrecy. The magic of the moment had all the charm of an Arthurian legend. Finally, he covered it again with the soft pads, gently and covertly, and with our loyalist help delicately rolled it outside. Then he tiptoed to the front door, very slyly, an Excalibur man, calling out sweet nothings to the mysterious Lady of the Lake. After a short, suspenseful prelude to the music that was to come, Rosie finally emerged with baby Lisa in her arms, the suckling child still in diapers and crying her own soft melody.

"What is it, Roscoe?" Rosie half barked, sweetly irritated. She even smiled when she was annoyed. Then she spied the two of us drenched in the sweat of our labor and industry, showering pity on us. "Oh, my! Don't you two look done for. Land sakes, are you trying to grind these boys to dust, Roscoe?" She was accusatory, sidestepping the big beast to get a better view of his wreckage. "Well, don't fret none boys. Lunch is almost ready. I'll be back in a few minutes to save you from the mad maestro." This time she examined Roscoe with a kind of parental discontent and demanded of him again, "Now, what is it, Roscoe? I'm very busy."

"Just got something I'd like you to see, pretty pumpkin." He hesitated for an instant, smiling goofily at her, prolonging the intentional tease. At the point when he knew she wouldn't tolerate his nonsense any longer, he undraped the piano in a deliberate, unhurried manner. "I hope you like it," he said, coyly, winking at us and smiling broadly at her, "'cause I ain't taking it back!"

One year my three sisters pitched in and bought me a new bike for my birthday. I was a young boy, and it was the first new one I ever owned. I was so surprised that I couldn't speak to them for 10 minutes or more. I just stood there, gazing, thrilled and shocked silent. I still get choked up about it, their kindness undeserved, and Rosie was displaying all the same symptoms. Still, her adorable silence couldn't stem the tide of angelic tears that rolled like radiant diamonds down her soft, blush cheeks. With unmatched elegance, she slowly tiptoed around the heavenly music box, staring in stunned disbelief. She finally stopped when she stood in front of the ivory keys, caressing them with trembling fingers, smiling at Roscoe in the sort of passionate love gaze that melted my heart to wax. Now and again, she would try to speak, but all that came from her quivering lips were the murmurings of some unknown, secret language that only she could decode. Roscoe giggled at her, nervously, as if to say that he really understood. A few more minutes ticked away in this endearing drama of love and surprise. We waited in nervous expectation for the dam to burst and the tears to explode. Gracefully, she held firm, not wanting to unravel in front of us. At long last, she sat baby Lisa on the grass, and with moist eyes and fragile arms hugged her husband, whispering something delicate into his ear. All was well—the king was on his throne.

I think there are special moments in life, without which nothing else is worth living. I know I would have unloaded and reloaded five furniture trucks to see this miracle, and from the look on Rick's bedazzled face, I thought he would too. Heretofore unknown to us, Rosie was an accomplished piano player, from the time of her childhood, and years ago allowed Roscoe to trade the Steinway for T-Rex to help secure their future. The baby grand, old, cherished, and beyond the value of mere money, was once owned by her grandfather and then her father. For her to part with it, in the way she did, was a confirmation of love's devotion that Roscoe carried around with him to every state in the union. I had no idea that we would be lucky enough to stumble upon such a wonderful occasion, aching muscles or not. While I watched Rosie beam in disbelief and supreme joy, I remembered what her husband had said to us at the rest stop, "Life is like a circle that should always lead back home." An important part of Rosie's life had traveled the full circle and was now here, where it belonged, back home. Roscoe lived what he preached.

After lunch we spent the long afternoon and early evening reloading the truck, a much slower and painstaking process than unloading—and that was that. And I don't know who these gutsy men are that make a living like this, day-to-day, but without them no one is moving safely anywhere.

Music and mirth filled the air that evening, after a scrumptious dinner. It would be our second and last night with Roscoe and his family, and they spared no expense to make it a good party. The children pinned up balloons and paper streamers in the living room, kitchen and hall, and the two oldest girls, not yet in their teens, made a luscious chocolate cake and dared me to gulp it down with chocolate milk. After speeches all around—Rick was very funny—it was time for *The Rosie Show*. Even so, first came more soft tears of winsome bliss, the kind that always have a way of infecting the mushy among us. Rosie's girls caught the happy disease and joined in with their mother, and it was another few minutes before the music started.

Well, you know what? Rosie rocked. She could play upbeat, grease lightning piano licks, remindful of southern rock bands, and toe-tapping boogie-woogie that had all of us stomping our feet in delight. Then she skillfully and artfully switched to soulful blues melodies, and I was reminded of how my mom loved to listen to them. To everyone's surprise, except Roscoe, she also displayed her gifted talent and knowledge of show tunes, Rodgers and Hammerstein stuff, of which she played an enchanting version of, "Oh, What a Beautiful Mornin," from *Oklahoma!*. She said it was her favorite musical and kept staring at Roscoe during the rendition, dedicating it to him for what he had done today. Finally, she played and sang a beautiful hymn that she composed herself, as a teenager, an endearing tribute to her grandfather, a man of the cloth and good book. She would end each remarkable performance by apologizing for being a little rusty, "I'm so sorry!" It was sweet of her, but no apology was needed.

Obviously, beyond her humility and womanly grace, she was exceptionally skilled and creative, and it was wonderful to see the expression of surprised revelation that glowed like wildfire on the faces of her excited children. They were learning something completely new about their mother, and they were digging it. Two of the children—baby Lisa and one of her sisters—were too young to have known that their mom was such a fine musician, and the other three had only listened to her play softly in church. That was fine, but now they were hearing the flip side of her considerable holiness. Mrs. Van Hamilton's music is how I've always thought of it. She seemed to autograph each tune with her own individual style and sparkle.

It was late in the evening before the party died down. How strange it was to see Rosie back at the kitchen sink, cleaning up our slop. She should have been asleep in a castle, in a bed pillowed with roses. Naturally, Roscoe was of the same opinion, and she finally relented to his sugary demands to stop and rest. The energy extracted from the both of them on this day would have collapsed the average man or woman. Nonetheless, they would be the ones to wake up first in the morning and begin the process of life all over again. Roscoe would be back on the road and Rosie back to the care of her children and the six-acre ranch, "Where it's plenty big enough to have horses," her oldest daughter would always say. We would be back on the road to Canada, with time on our hands and our pockets full.

~~~

PART 2

At breakfast, before our sad farewell, Roscoe and Rosie shared a little of their life story with us. By the time they were finished, I knew I couldn't wish to find better Americans anywhere. The following is how they told it.

West Virginia is famous for its great coal producing supremacy, and Roscoe loved his home state. He might have stayed to work and die in the coal mines, as did generations of family members before him, but his desperate need to find work coincided with a severe decline in hiring. By the time he was 17 and ready for service, West Virginia's unemployment rate was the highest in the nation and climbing. Complicating such matters was the steady onset of technological automation in the mines, and this situation had the consequence of further reducing the workforce, so it was easy for Roscoe to read the handwriting on the wall. The result was that he ended up on the highway to New Orleans, a universe away for a young kid. His flight from the safety of family and friends had been carefully planned, a job in the *Big Easy* promised through an acquaintance of a friend of a relative. When he showed up for the interview, "The Greatest Man in the World" thought there must be some mistake. He had not been forewarned of Roscoe's size and mistook him for a much older man.

"Lord, the coal mines can't use your help? I believe you could brace up a mountain by yourself, in a pinch," the great man said. "No shit, son, are you really just 17?"

Seventeen soon turned into 21, and by that time Roscoe had fallen in love with the moving and storage business, taking to it faster than he might a coal miner's daughter. The daughter idea had also occurred to Rosie, who promptly married him before it could happen. As I listened, I was humbled to realize that Roscoe was so far ahead of us in road scholarship. He had abandoned West Virginia with self-survival in mind and left the goal of a mere joyride to someone else. Then, abruptly, in the middle of his entertaining story, Rick interrupted, asking if his great stature had provided him with more confidence to take on the challenges of the road at such a young age.

"Well, let me put it this way, men," Roscoe responded, changing unexpectedly into a quiet, priestly narrator. "When you are big, other people tend to leave you alone, mostly. If you're VERY, VERY big, they tend to leave you alone and get away from you as fast as they can." Then with the shrewd craftiness of a snake in hiding, he slyly motioned for Rick to lean a little closer. Unbelievably, my unsuspecting friend obliged him. Roscoe looked him squarely in the eyes and began with a hush, "But when you are as big as me, they can do neither, BECAUSE NO ONE EVER ESCAPES THE MAD ROSCOE!" Then he jumped at Rick in a fearsome, mock attack, rattling the table and chairs we sat in, and in a flash all bedlam broke loose. It even startled the two family hounds, one breaking for the screen door and the other for the nearest bedroom. From the momentary, ghastly picture of horror on Rick's face, one could guess that my good friend had received his answer.

When all was calm again, Rosie explained that she was first attracted to Roscoe by his good sense of humor. When she met him, she was still living with her mother, a widow of considerable grit and fierce independence. Shortly after her father died, Rosie's mother took boarders into her home, and to further supplement their income, Rosie gave piano lessons to an enthusiastic and growing number of students. One day Roscoe showed up and rented a vacant room, proceeding to ignore Rosie for days, too shy to approach anyone.

"God, she looked just like a lump of sugar," he would inject sporadically, interrupting her in midsentence, but it was worth the guff she gave him just to say it.

"Now, Roscoe, hush up. It's my turn! Well, I finally had to walk right up to the big goof and stare him down, just to introduce myself," she said, in fond recollection. "I then asked him point blank if he was a man of any brains or just another pretty face on the loose. Now, my Roscoe, as you know, is not cut from the general cloth of men," she continued, looking at us for confirmation. We agreed with a nod. Her short pause allowed Roscoe to interrupt again, eager to recall his answer to her very first question.

"I don't believe I'm either, Miss," I said. "But it'll take you having dinner with me alone to prove that the one doesn't matter, and the other one is a work in progress!"

"Oh, Roscoe, darn you! I was going to tell them!" She slugged him in the arm for cutting her off, adding with an excited laugh, "But he wouldn't tell me which was which!" Then she finished with the punch line that she first intended to use, "Well, as long as he's still working on it, whichever one it is, that's all that matters. If the big dope can hit five hundred, I'll keep him on my team."

She knew about baseball, too?

"Ain't she a lump of sugar?" Roscoe said, beaming when she was done.

Despite their informative and fun account of things, the one question they wouldn't answer was how they got to California. They insisted that it gave us a reason to return, to ask them again. Is this a great country—or what?

Roscoe had a few final words of advice and caution for us, as we prepared to leave. "I want you two to be careful, wherever you roam. As I said at the rest stop, there are lessons to be learned on the road, but I'll add today that not all of them are good. Ya hear? Come back on the circle home, if you can. It was our pleasure, and we won't forget you two. The Mad Maestro has spoken!"

"Everything is going to be fine, Roscoe," I said. "If it keeps going like this all that can happen is we'll be tired and rich."

"Don't worry, Roscoe," Rick added. "I'll always be there to save him. I always am. Ain't that right, Cosmo?" He shoved me in the shoulder and laughed.

"Yeah, I'm for that, Mr. Ruiz."

"Well, just keep an eye out for things. The unexpected, especially." He escorted us to the Princess, shook our hands, holding them for a long minute, in an intimate gesture of friendship, then wished us God's speed. Rosie and the kids each hugged us, inviting us to come back soon for more music and cake—minus the hard work. Both of us were for that.

By the way, it was Roscoe's 13-year-old son, Frankie, who loved chocolate milk. I took him for a wild spin in the Princess. When we left he asked to go with us. It would not have been a good idea, all things considered.

[4]
LOST CHILDREN

I'm providing the following information for any map lovers out there. I know some will be curious about our specific route, and that's fine, but we didn't really have a precise itinerary. We had a final destination in mind, with a reasonable timetable, but the path we took getting there wasn't marked in red and blue ink on white paper. Just the same, you gotta love the colors.

We left our hometown heading northeast on Highway 80. Then we followed Highway 505 to Highway 5 before cutting directly east on highways 32 and 70 to the Plumas National Forest, truly a heavenly place. From there we turned back to the northwest, seeing a fair slice of Lassen National Forest, before merging back onto Highway 5 and eventually meeting Roscoe near the charming town of Yreka, California. We followed him due west, to very near the coast, finally ending up on his lovely ranch near Highway 199 and the Smith River. That's accurate enough, I think. Had it not been for the summer season and the subsequent light-soaked days, plus meeting Roscoe, it was perhaps more than a day's journey. Yet we accomplished it all without a map, and the idea of using one never actually occurred to us. Now that I've taken the plunge with you, I'll do my best to provide brief updates.

Roscoe had been more than generous with our pay, and we thought ourselves well-off and ready to travel in relaxed comfort. That's not to say that we had been overly worried about a lack of money. In fact, we planned to park the Princess, if we fell short of cash, hiding her safely somewhere near the Canadian border and then proceed by thumbing a ride into our auspicious northern neighbor. It would be mostly for the experience of it, long-distance hitchhiking not yet on our resume as veteran road warriors. One thing is certain, we hadn't thought to consider whether or not the good folks of Canada might think we fell short in some more important matters. That's for later. For now, we had some jingle in our jeans, and the feeling of well-being that it gave us helped to heal the physical soreness it cost us.

"Hey, man, I bet Roscoe is laughing at us right now," Rick said. "He probably thinks we're crashed on some beach, too exhausted to move a muscle."

"Yeah, and the big bear would be right about that. I wonder where he is now."

"Somewhere on the road, Cosmo, like us. Learning lessons."

"Or giving them. He sure is sentimental about the road home, isn't he?"

"Yeah, he sure is. Hey, I'm hot. I'm going for a swim." An excellent swimmer and bodysurfer, Rick was in the water in 30 seconds, only his head visible to me now, trying to catch a wave. They were small and he was out of luck. Returning, he plopped down next to me. I handed him a cold soda from our cooler with ice. We could afford it now.

"I thought you were tired?"

"The water is refreshing, Cosmo. It's good for the tired bones."

He was right. I took a relaxing dip myself, and by the time I returned he was asleep on his towel. I kicked hot sand on him.

"You bastard, Cosmo!"

"You better hope I don't do it when you're with your girlfriend."

"At least I can get one, and I don't have to go to Canada just to get a feel!"

"I should have never told you that story, dopey boy."

"Everybody in the world should hear that story."

"Maybe they will, someday. I'll be sure to write it where I come out the hero."

He lunged at my cheek, barely missing. I went to grab his bushy tarantula, what he deserved. He was too fast, kicking sand on me first, hitting me squarely in the face. "Take that, hero!" He jumped up and sped down the beach.

We had been bantering about for most of the day, now resting on a hot, white beach in Southern Oregon. I tried with dull and tired eyes to appreciate the pristine nature thriving around me. Oregon, so far, was a jeweled lady, with Mother Pacific adorning one side and an exquisite timberline on the other, not a mile from the beach. The sand was as white as I've ever seen it, pure, and not the grayish color of beaches back home. I was thinking about these things when Rick returned, feigning repentance. Something was bothering him. He plopped down.

"Hey, man, do you think the people in Oregon are going to be as cool as we are?" He asked. I swear he was serious.

"What a boneheaded question. Why would you think not?"

"Yeah, I suppose it is dumb to think that people are somehow different here. After all, it's still America. Isn't that right, Cosmo?"

An absurd question on top of an inane one deserves no answer. I ignored him. Just the same, I was sensitive to the real substance of his concern. We hadn't seen another Hispanic since leaving the Bay Area far behind. That troubled Rick. Still, it was an insignificant issue in the America of my mind. I would not have thought to fear one of my brothers. God forbid that one of them should fear me. If the womb begins the game in the same color for all of us, why bother about meaningless details, especially skin pigment.

"I said it's still America, right? Isn't it? ISN'T IT!" His insistence on an answer was accompanied by another hardy kick of hot sand, splattering on my peaceful, reposed chest. That did it! He would get the whole enchilada he deserved.

"YEAH, RIGHT! IT IS STILL AMERICA! But don't ask anyone around here such a moronic question, for God's sake. These fine Oregonians will think we're some kind of California aliens and chase us both butt naked into the ocean!" Inspired, I saved the best for last. "Only then will they see that your ass really is white, like theirs, and you're just as much an American as they are. But then it will be too late because the sharks will have us. And brother, if you kick sand on me again, they'll bury your white American butt right here—in white Oregon, AMERICA!"

My theatrical retort relaxed him a little, and I was pleased to see it. He rolled on his back, laughing hardily at the idea of his butt being the thing to get him out of a sling, instead of getting him into one. He said he saw the obvious logic in utilizing his fleshy mounds as the great equalizers, since most Caucasians identified best with this section of their anatomy. Before I could leap the great divide and really murder him this time, he kicked hot sand on me again, speeding down the beach once more, stopping at some distance, mooning me! No sacrifice is too great for a friend in need.

Late that afternoon we got serious and dragged ourselves off the beach, heading up Highway 101, north. Oh, man! I almost forgot to say. Just as we planned to leave, a black, three-legged Labrador Retriever appeared from out of thin air. From nowhere! We had been sitting comfortably near the water letting the waves brake soothingly over our sore legs, talking about our next stopping point. Then, suddenly, he appeared behind us, barking with much persistence and authority, hopping up and down like a three-legged Olympic athlete. Alarmed, we jumped to our feet, not knowing what to think or do about such a freaky surprise. However, we were in no real danger. This was just his standard way of saying hello. Still, it was only the beginning of our fascination with him. To keep pace with the normal course of things in this part of the world, he was built like an ocean boulder, and the big guy was easily the largest Lab to come across my path. He even carried his very own play stick. Go figure. It was a long, round piece of driftwood, moderately thick. He had worked hard to first gain our attention and was now dropping his prized possession and quickly snatching it up again, over and over. He was making a point, but we were still rather startled, so it took a minute to understand what he wanted. It's a tossup as to whether a real alien—happening to arrive on this spectacle at this very moment—could have guessed the smarter of the two breeds displayed before him. The whole scene had taken us so off guard that for a few more seconds we remained dumbfounded, asking each other all the questions one would ask about such a thing. I'm embarrassed by what he must have said later to his other dog friends.

"Yeah, they're plenty big enough to play with but altogether witless. I almost lost my voice trying to communicate with two of them. But they can throw a mean stick and that's what counts!"

So we threw a mean stick again and again. He wouldn't get tired. With only three legs he could outrun the waves and outlast us, and he acted exceedingly displeased when we stopped for a moment, looking for a lighter stick. When we found one he snubbed it, bringing back the one he brought. I guess if one has a favorite stick, he has a favorite stick. I imagined that this wasn't an isolated experience limited to us. Surely other people have seen such dogs—and own them, too.

That was the bigger mystery. How were we to account for him? He wore no tag or collar. We searched up and down the beach and then hiked to the parking lot and found nothing. Not a single vehicle in sight, save the Princess, and by looking inland we could see that there were no homes or buildings in the area. It was then that I suggested we might take him with us and inquire at the nearest town. Do you know what? I think the big guy must have sensed my plan. Mysteriously, by the time we returned to the beach, he had disappeared in much the same fashion as he showed up—and the stick, too. Puff! We couldn't find him anywhere.

We later told an older man about it, when buying gas, and although puzzled like us, he said there must be a logical answer. How dull and enslaving that sounded. This dog was magical and no logic could explain him. We vowed from then on to keep him a secret. I think that's the way he wanted it.

"Coos Bay, Oregon, two miles to the next exit." Rick interpreted the sign for me, and it was a relief to both of us. Road grime had bonded with sand in our hair and clothes, making a hot shower and a clean bed sound like the stuff of kings. Naturally, we felt like kings must feel when they have the world at their feet and treasure in their pockets. For now we lacked nothing and would go another night without unrolling our sleeping bags on the hard ground. I thought it not right for the reason that it derailed the adventure of roughing it. Rick said that was crazy talk. Of course, it was. Hadn't Roscoe roughed us up enough, already?

We rented one room, two twin beds. Well, at least my feet would only stick out three inches. "Man, America can't be full of nothing but midgets, can it? Who do they build these beds for, anyway? This is a real crime scene." It took some of the luster out of my kingdom, and the king in me was upset.

"Quit bitching, man. It's better than the hard ground."

"That's easy for you to say, Ruiz. I'd have to put stilts on your legs before you could even stretch them out."

"So, sue me. Can we go eat now, or do you want me to call the cops for you?"

Yes, a hot meal to restore some luster.

~~~

PART 2

Honestly, what do you think the odds were against us finding a Mexican restaurant that served genuine south-of-the-border cuisine? Fate threw back the curtains of heaven and rained down angelic, authentic tacos and burritos so hot and spicy that we were positive the devil had been hired to do the cooking. We gorged ourselves on these and more, flour tortillas and refried beans and luscious tomato slices oozing with pink passion, and we even found room for an enchilada or two. It was the best one could expect at a Mexican feast. We downed them all with fiery hot sauce brewed out of thunder and lightning, and the inferno scorched our tongues and smoldered in our bellies. Rick bragged to me that the food at his father's restaurant was better, but he wouldn't boast about it to our waitress.

"You two boys are going to bust a gut! My Lord. Where are you putting it all?" It was her, and she thought we must be eating our last supper.

"We're afraid it might be our last good Mexican food for a while," Rick answered, politely. "We're going to Canada."

She was a petite, pretty lady, maybe 35, dark brown eyes and long brown hair, streaked with premature gray. Rick's answer sparked her further interest in us. "You don't say? I hope it's not army trouble?" She asked, her tone now one of motherly concern.

"No, of course not," I said. It came out too conspicuously. "What I mean is that we're not running from the draft or any such thing. We wouldn't do that."

"He's right, Miss, we would never do that," Rick confirmed, thickly saucing his next taco and rather unconcerned by it all.

"You wouldn't? Why not? Lots of boys are going there now, and I don't blame them. It's a terrible war, and we shouldn't be there." She appeared disheartened by what she must have understood to be our misguided patriotism or a boyish disregard for losing our lives in a dubious cause. The country had long been divided about the Vietnam War and a great number of Americans, especially the young, were at the forefront of opposing it. Personally, I was a bit ambivalent, confused about why some Americans believed we were heading for national destruction by fighting a senseless and unwinnable war, while others believed we must do everything we could to stop the world from being overrun by communist devils. On the one hand, I thought it right that patriotic sons and daughters should be willing to die for the things they cherish— the things they swear to honor and protect. On the flip side, I had watched with horrifying dismay how the long years of war raged on with no apparent end in sight. The death toll of young American men had grown to a staggering number, and the weekly body count was in the hundreds. Still, I had to admit, I was on my way to college and not war, and this fact made it easy to be stuck in the middle, unclear of where I really stood on the matter. I knew Rick was also uncertain about how he viewed the war and how he thought about those escaping to Canada to avoid it. He had already been disqualified from military service because of a mild physical abnormality, one of his legs slightly shorter than the other. This caused him to walk with a minor limp and was enough to keep him out of the army.

"Well, if you two end up there, keep your heads low. We don't need to lose more precious young men. It's much better to have lost children in Canada than dead ones in Vietnam." With that she put her hands on our shoulders and told us to be safe in our travels. She was leaving her shift now and another waitress would help us from here.

We needed no help polishing off our plates, and no meal was ever better. I suggested that we might visit Rick's great ancestral homeland someday soon, and if we found it as much to our liking as this place, we would conquer it, growing fat on salsa and chips and dying of old tequila.

"And young senoritas, too," Rick added.

"What?"

"And die of young senoritas, too."

"Oh, yeah. I'm for that."

After returning to the motel and watching TV for a few hours, Rick was fast asleep before his head hit his pillow. My bed was not only short but extremely lumpy. It was as if the day crew knew I was coming, and there would be no comfort given to foreign-bound traitors, real or imagined. I got up after tossing and turning for an hour, got dressed, and walked out into the warm, delicious air.

The full moon on this night in late June was awesome. Huge and hanging high over the city and bay and ocean, it was God's lighthouse to guide the stars on their safe journey throughout the dark cosmos and illuminate the paths of his little children on earth. The resident gatekeeper of this responsibility was the Man in the Moon, and he accepted it with a smile on his face. His smile guided me to a street in Coos Bay that looked similar to many in my hometown.

How reassuring it is that all American shipyard towns seem to look the same. The buildings and homes near the piers and loading docks are always the oldest and best, and they proudly guard the coast and let foreign admirers see them first. Of course, being the first to be built in these places of great water commerce, they are meant to stand until the final pallet and forklift load of cargo, of endless variety, especially lumber, is loaded and then shipped across the vast oceans of the world. The people living in them sleep little, not resting until the grand vessels of the globe are safely moored and secure, and then daybreak starts the vigorous work all over again. They are sublime and lovely, constructed of sturdy stock and inhabited by sturdy people. I liked Coos Bay. It reminded me of home— where heroes live.

I know there are other splendid and pretty places that can rightfully boast to be the greatest in America, we've already covered that, but for sheer grit and guts, I'll take the shipyard crowd any day. I'll admit to being biased because I grew up in the same kind of place, and I suppose that I don't know any better, but is there any better way to know? I'm not kidding, where else can you find a city or town of men and women who will not dare to own more than one real suit between them? In fact, most shipyard towns are places where nearly all formal occasions are celebrated in wool shirts and plain cotton dresses, and there is never an accordion festival to spoil the day. They can outwork you, outsmart you and outfight you.

It was in such a prideful and homesick mood that I entered the Late Night Café, open until early morning, so the sign read. This homey place fit in well with my prodigious admiration for Coos Bay. It was large and aged and stout, and it featured broad picture windows that faced the street and bay. The thick walls were lined with old photographs illustrating the town's long history, all of them marked by the day and year they were taken, and each one identified the men and women who appeared in them. I took a few moments to study some closely, curious about the lives and events they framed. History has always fascinated me, and if it is told in photographs, so much the better. On one side of the building a dozen circular dining booths could be found, most of them with sickly cotton protruding from their cracked vinyl seats. They were far beyond the needed time of good repair. A haggard and lonely-looking elderly man, with a gaze of stifling despair covering his wrinkled face, sat in the far booth stirring his coffee. A younger man, probably in his late 20s, sat at the counter, a massive mirror attached to the wall behind it. This antique object of reflective light was some four feet tall and perhaps 30 feet long, covering the wall's entire length. People sitting in front of it could see everything that moved behind them, missing nothing. I've seen comparable mirrors in cowboy movies and TV shows, and I suppose they have saved many a bad hombre's life, the ones obligated to always watch their backs.

A capacious kitchen was located just beyond the far end of the counter, with its wide swinging doors pinned open. I could see only one person there, a very big and tough looking man, likely in his 50s, wearing a stained apron with white T-shirt, white pants, and a dark blue cap that swayed lopsided on his head. It had "Navy" etched on it, so I guessed him to be an old sailor cook. He also sported a long and heavy white beard that needed a good trim. If there was ever a surrogate for a hard-bitten Santa Claus, it was him.

I acknowledged the young man at the counter and sat down a few seats away. He suddenly got up and slid behind it, asking what I'd like to order. I soon learned that he was a regular at night and sometimes helped out.

"Just coffee, thanks," I said.

"You got it. Give me a minute, and I'll make a fresh pot."

"Sure, why not. How about some water while I do?"

"Coming up, one water."

Coming in were four local dockhands, bursting through the door with great fanfare, tumbling over each other and laughing their way gaily to the booth nearest me. The last one made a point to nod at me, smiling broadly and winking. It was an invitation to stay put and enjoy the show. I had no place else to go.

Then they unexpectedly became as quiet as church mice trapped in the pews of a stern pastor, and I glanced around to examine what reason might lead them to adopt this new piety. My eyes landed squarely on the reason, just in time to hear it quake. It was the sailor cook and the Navy was firing its big guns.

"I won't be having any horseplay tonight, gentlemen," growled Big Jack Stockbean, proprietor and night cook, as I learned later. He followed up this resolute command with a determined, lethal stare, one worthy of an angry battleship, his head cocked like a 30-ton anchor ready to drop. Having made his point, he purposefully returned to doing whatever he was doing in the kitchen, mumbling something about nonsense and folly. By necessity, his back was now exposed to the playful villains. It was the opening they needed. They immediately launched into a raging stream of unbroken groans and targeted complaints, loud criticisms labeling Big Jack a killjoy and a spoilsport, a curmudgeon who would have them dine in graveyard silence. Big Jack, not intimidated in the least, was obligated to turn again and issue a second warning that also achieved only momentary success. In another minute they were back at it.

"But Beanie, you've got to hear this one. You absolutely must! And it can't be told without laughing," said the most bombastic of these brawny men, looking over at me with a gleam in his eyes and then back at his friends. More laughter. These four must have been an invincible, nightly farce, because Mr. Beanie soon gave in.

"If the kid at the counter and John want to hear it, then go ahead," he said, with tired exasperation, shaking his head and giving me a quick, apologetic glance. "But I don't have time for your foolishness. Keep it to a roar, gentlemen."

"Thanks, Mr. Beanie," I thought.

What follows was their madcap story, but I doubt you will believe it. I'll tell you later if I did.

None of the four had actually worked this day. Only minutes after clocking in they were summoned by an agitated dock foreman and told to grab as many shovels as they could carry, then proceed at once to the local police department. Their instructions would be forthcoming upon arrival. They had no idea what was required of them, but the rumor hinted of a terrible accident, and all hands were needed on deck. As in most places, locals are seldom asked to mobilize in such a breakneck fashion unless something dramatic or overwhelming has occurred. In this case, and from the rest of the story I was about to hear, the town and Oregon were a safer place for it. After the dockhands got their commands and arrived at the scene of the calamity, solemn discourse and fearful speculation turned quickly into hilarious disbelief. They were immediately confronted with the undisputed realization that America's nuttiest professor had come to live and thrive in Coos Bay, Oregon.

"Professor Dynamite" is what the outlandish men named him, and whenever he was prominent in the account of the story—which was always—they howled with boundless joy and unrestrained laughter. They applied special emphasis to the pronunciation of the six syllables making up his name, and they took sheer delight in singing them out, all together, in perfect, ringing harmony. Over and over they squalled, "PRO-FESS-OR DYN-A-MITE! PRO-FESS-OR DYN-A-MITE!" It was rather loud and nerve-racking, as one might imagine. Just the same, they were entertaining and as the silliness continued, I realized, with some culpability, that I wanted to find out more. Then the wacky and weird narrative rapidly turned bewildering and absurd, and I secretly scolded Big Jack for not standing firm with these overaged hooligans. Yet they insisted that their incredible tale was not a fictional gag and if we didn't hear it from them, we surely would from someone else—and not as believably.

OK, then, a massive male sperm whale, 60 feet in length and weighing 50 long tons, had unfortunately managed to beach itself very near the city. The whale was dying and its fate settled. It would have to be either hauled away or moved offshore. Unluckily, the county public works department was unavailable to offer timely help, whatever it might be, and the Oregon Highway Division also refused to provide immediate assistance, swamped for a time by its own heavy workload. The owners of the local maritime companies, the other logical option, were scurrying to meet a bone-crunching summer schedule and likewise denied swift aid. So it appeared that there was simply no way of quickly removing the carcass from the beach, and the hapless whale would rot where it was. Pitiful.

The professor sympathized with this pitiful nature of things, and he deemed it vital that the poor guy be moved or done away with—without delay. The harrowing problem had to be fixed before tomorrow morning, by any means possible, extreme or otherwise. According to him, such an appalling environmental disaster put the public at great risk, this section of beach used heavily by them. The concern had to be faced head-on, and he kept repeating that speed was the order of the day. After all, only God knows what kind of dreadful diseases one might catch by stumbling across a decomposing dead whale. Except he never bothered to explain the extreme measures he had in mind, only that such a cataclysm screamed for drastic and decisive action. Professor Dynamite was a decisive man, and this grand leadership quality, known to all, convinced the town populace to adopt whatever measures he thought appropriate. Apparently, it didn't occur to them that the professor's radical solution might explode the difficulty far beyond all good reason. It certainly did explode it, and these goofy men were jubilantly pleased to tell us about it.

I won't identify the whale whisperer by his real name, but I will say that he wasn't really a professor, at least not presently. He was a county supervisor and a former teacher at the local junior college. I suspect that he will now and forever be referred to as only Professor Dynamite around these parts, but who can predict what legacy will haunt a man.

His solution? He would blow it up! And he did, using more than 500 pounds of dynamite and making six attempts. The logic behind this detonative act was solid from a purely academic perspective, but from a practical viewpoint it created more widespread challenges. Whale flesh was blown more than 800 feet away, large chunks of it landing in the beach parking lot, where the cleanup crew had gathered. A 400-pound hunk destroyed the windshield and roof of one car, and several other pieces did significant damage, including breaking an arm of one volunteer and the foot of a teenage girl. Predictably, this led to a number of heated verbal exchanges between the helpers and the professor, and at one point he was forced to physically defend himself, the father of the young woman decidedly displeased. It took the efforts of a few of his more loyal constituents to save him from being lynched by the volatile crowd.

Just the same, the deed was done and the subsequent mess a bigger problem than the first. Still, the ever-resourceful professor was not deterred, appraising this new trouble as only a temporary setback and one that actually provided him with more powerful ammunition. With his new firepower and his influence as a government official, he unilaterally persuaded the National Guard, located in Portland, to send help. Being good and supportive National Guardsmen, as one would hope them to be, they immediately dispatched a large helicopter to lift the whale and move it offshore. However, when the aircrew arrived there was nothing much left to move. In fact, the eager but confused pilot hovered too low while trying to examine what part of the remains could be transported, and the sheer force of the ship's whirling blades further scattered the gooey mess, splattering whale blubber across every inch of the pristine beach and soaking the volunteers. This only heightened their already tall anger, and a number of fistfights broke out, the professor suffering a broken nose!

The regretful but amused pilot then left for home, but on the way radioed the state police, reporting a series of explosions on a beach in Coos Bay, and at least one casualty—the whale. Having little more information to act on, they responded without hesitation and in great force—ready for anything. I wondered just how much pertinent information the pilot actually did give the state police and how my friends seemed to be so well-informed about it. I couldn't imagine that he really would omit important aspects, as they claimed. Anyway, if he did, I hope no harm came to him, and he got a whale of a promotion.

Whatever the case was, the professor, broken nose and all, was obligated to explain to the perplexed police all the parts the pilot apparently left out. According to my friends, he suffered a breakdown at that moment, and his cockamamie explanation got him and six others handcuffed and arrested. Furthermore, the lot of them were now locked up in a jail cell at the same police department it all started at—a short 16 hours ago. Between their squeals of delight, they declared that the professor had not only underestimated his charges one time, but he had done it twice, and the second time would result in even more grievous misfortune for him. He would be released in the morning only to find out that he would have to ride on the blown-up shoulders of their fame! I wasn't sure what they meant, and their earsplitting laugher momentarily prevented the punchline. It soon came, and it seemed the realization of it was almost more than they could take.

Not two hours ago, the four of them, they proclaimed, excitedly, were interviewed on local and state television for a firsthand report of the bloody demolition. In all the confusion, it seemed that news crews had been alerted to a possible enemy invasion at Coos Bay—the explosions being heard for miles around. Factually, even if it was previously unknown to me and most others, Japan had bombed Southern Oregon in 1945, so such things were not an off-the-cuff mystery.

When the excitement from this error faded, and to put a positive spin on an otherwise madhouse story, a few clever news people decided to make these four rugged dockworkers local heroes, reporting that they showed up courageously for what they thought might be a real coastal invasion. At the opening sounds of the explosions they were the first there. The American shipyard worker! Within days of the Fourth of July. Brilliant! Whales be damned! There is a nation to save.

That's it. They were thoroughly convinced that by sunrise Coos Bay would surely bask in worldwide fame, and the four of them would be forever hailed as patriotic, brave men. Fortuitously, the congratulatory cards and letters and the offers of paid television interviews, movie deals, autograph sessions, and book signings would explode. "Get it? Explode! Lord God!" they howled. "If we play our cards right, we will soon be American champions and rich men, and the professor will be the dynamite guy responsible for it all!"

Then they launched into another round of howling and laughing and celebrating his name, whooping at each other, overcome with delight. They were much too excited to go to bed, they asserted, so the Late Night Café was the best place to show up and rehearse the glory that would soon be bestowed upon them. They would stay here until the bars closed, retelling the story to a larger crowd and wait to glow in their fame on the morning news.

"And Beanie, we just want you to know that the Navy decided to stay out of it, and that's just one more reason to be proud of that boy of yours!" Poor Mr. Beanie.

So there you have it, and I know what you're thinking. "Not a chance, not in America. Colossally stupid shit like this doesn't happen here."

In the end, they had made me thoroughly dizzy, and I could relate to why Big Jack found them intolerable. As I got up to leave they stopped me and said, "Hey, kid, be sure to tell everyone you see about the whale of a story you heard here tonight!" More raucous laughter and it came at my expense this time. It was just the kind of circus atmosphere Roscoe had imagined: a real barn burner.

At first I didn't believe a single word of it, but it was completely true. Rick and I watched reports of it on television the next morning. Still, there was no mention of what the funny pilot might have really said, so I think they made that part up.

I don't know what became of Professor Dynamite, but I'm alarmed to think that he may have been re-elected. Americans delight in a good joke, and such a man adds color to the dull moments of our lives.

Finally, after Rick had seen and heard the story, he had but one question, "Why do white people think that the solution to every problem is just to blow it up?"

[5]
THE DUNES

Upon leaving Coos Bay our northern journey kept us close to the Oregon coastline for another 40 miles, and we were surprised and delighted to come upon the Oregon Dunes National Recreation Area. It was the kind of righteous place the two of us had no idea existed in America.

The Dunes, as most casually refer to them, are the largest expanse of windswept coastal sand dunes in North America, and beyond their span of significant distance, two miles wide in several locations. The most spectacular areas house the individual mountain dunes that often rise 500 hundred feet above sea level. These formidable mountains of pure white, shifting sand—at times so close I could reach out and almost touch them—brought to my mind's eye the thought of giant sand tsunamis rushing to overtake us, sweeping us away and gobbling us up without mercy. Egad! It was a bona fide revelation to find out that sand monsters are actually real and alive and flourish so fearlessly on the beaches of Oregon. I thought they existed only in chilling bedtime stories, like the ones conjured up by my older siblings to scare the hell out of me, keeping me awake on the edge of my seat. Yet here they were, more frightening than the scariest legends about them, stirred to fury at the first scent of us, their jagged crests whirling angrily in the gusty winds, hideous maulers in constant lookout for defenseless victims to snatch up and eat. Wonderful. I reminded Rick of this reality each time he sought refuge behind one of their bloodthirsty summits. "Ricky Ruiz, you're going to get eaten up one of these times. The sand monsters will get you!"

"Man, stop with the jokes, will you? Can't you let me do my business in peace?"

"No! I can't believe that a little hot sauce could do this to you. You are a sorry excuse for a Mexican and an embarrassment to a proud heritage."

"I'm not taking a crap with my Mexican part, Cosmo. I'm doing it with my Caucasian part. You said so yourself. Remember?"

It was a short-tempered reply, so I remained quiet and watched him once again trot hurriedly across the dunes, disappearing behind one of the citadels of vicious, blowing sand. He wasn't gone as long this time. When he returned to the car, I asked if the worst was over.

"I don't know. But I want you to stop driving so fast. The bumps in the road are killing me."

There were no bumps in the road, and I wasn't driving fast. I leaned toward him and studied his ashen face. It was ghostly, flush with sickness and bodily misery from last night's uncontrolled feast. "Man, you really do feel bad, don't you?"

"Yeah, Montezuma's revenge is the real shits, Cosmo. How come you didn't get it?"

"You can't get it in the States."

"Get what?"

"Montezuma's revenge, you fart brain."

"Who says?"

"I says! You have to go to Mexico to get it."

"Mexico? I thought you said Oregon was in America?"

"Shut up, Don Quixote, or I'll sic some windmills on you!"

I was very gentle with him, but within 10 miles it was the *Aztec two-step* again, and he did this little dance at least three more times before we got a break.

Not long after, we arrived at our new locale. It was a rest stop, containing a park and clean toilet facilities. Rick would be more comfortable here and safe from my jokes, especially the certainty of a monstrous death. We entered by an expansive entrance, newly paved in shiny asphalt and painted with glossy-white directional stripes, identifying which lane accommodated the type of vehicle one occupied. A wide variety of the usual sort were in view, including several large and expensive recreational vehicles, all of which appealed greatly to my sense of adventure and relaxed freedom. Once parked, I was comforted by the sight of numerous eighteen-wheelers, like T-Rex, most of which were driverless but with their diesel engines idling. It was a pragmatic and common practice of truck drivers, though it didn't bode well for the air.

Close by, a spacious, well-configured park struck me as an unexpected and miraculous amenity. It was a mystery to me how park officials did it, but the entire area was carpeted in thick, neatly manicured grass: a luscious green oasis floating perfectly atop a shifting sea of imperfect sand. It featured a half dozen oceanview perches, perhaps 20 feet high, and all of them arranged around a large, two-part platform. This platform, itself elevated a few feet above the grassy sand and some 40 yards wide, pointed proudly in the direction of the ocean. In addition, there were bright green signs surrounding the main deck, strategically placed in order to inform visitors about the amazing and incredible geological properties of sand and more sand. I was enchanted to find out how sophisticated sand could be. Who knew? In fact, I'm one of those people who actually find pleasure in reading these types of message boards, so the fine-tuned efforts to make me a happy sightseer were not in vain.

After 30 minutes of browsing and reading, trying especially hard to keep from eavesdropping on the conversations of other travelers, I walked back to check on Rick. He was asleep in the backseat of the Princess and resisted my attempts to arouse him. "Well, you're no good to me now, tiger, sleep well." Trying not to disturb him further, I grabbed a beach towel and made out for the ocean.

I soon discovered that the good folks of Oregon had also thought to enhance this small portion of God's heavenly kingdom by carving out a well-marked hiking trail, one that encircled the resident sand monster and met its halfway point at the beach. I sought it out by walking in the proper direction but quickly reversed myself and proceeded in a counterclockwise manner, desiring to read and study the faces of my fellow wayfarers. Of course, this forced them to sidestep past me. It was cheating and a little pretentious, I know. Still, it was natural for me to want my eyes to seek the fruit of my heart's desire, which is that no person should remain a stranger to me in such a friendly place. A look and a smile, and you're my instant pal. If that's a backward way of approaching it, then it matched my direction, and the two fit comfortably together.

I stumbled first upon a number of older people strolling gingerly and chatting gaily in groups of four or five at a time, all of them conservative in both demeanor and dress. Most took the time to say hello. On one particular occasion a finely groomed gentleman, struggling a bit to maneuver his cane through the thick sand, reached out and grabbed my arm to steady himself.

Then he excused himself with a hearty "thank you" and patted me firmly on the shoulder to signal that he was OK, and his balance had returned. I never actually saw his face clearly because his head was permanently tilted downward at a sharp angle, but his voice was kind and full of genuine gratitude. His wife was golden and lovely in her advanced age, and I couldn't help but think that their years of long journey together must have been great ones. They moved on happily, walking with the same footsteps of wisdom and experience that older people always seem to possess, and for the first time I was alone on my journey.

As I neared the beach, two young girls, about 13, scrambled toward me in a much hurried fashion. As I turned to let them pass freely, I offered up an enthusiastic greeting. Nonetheless, they elected to ignore my friendly gesture, acting indifferently toward me, seemingly puzzled that I would speak to them at all—or perhaps that I even dared. Still, once safely past me they broke into delightful girlish giggles, an unrefined acknowledgment of me, but a delightful trademark of the universal friendliness and bashful charm of young girls. In four, perhaps five years, their youthful chimes would fall away silently, and they would blossom into the glorious national flowers that can only be grown here. Yet, I was still deflated somewhat by their initial rejection. Instead of looking at it reasonably, I was afraid that they somehow found me unworthy. It's only when I'm overtired that I start second guessing myself in such a way. I decided to just ignore it and not be so sensitive. After all, to them I was nearly a grown man, and near-grown men are not of great interest to teenage girls, save dads and money. It did rattle me a little to think that I was fast outgrowing my youth and the young people I best related to, with budding adulthood destined to finish the race for me, once and for all.

I was relieved when finally reaching the vast beach, and the ocean was as impressive as I've found it anywhere. I fixed my attentive thoughts upon the gently breaking waves for a fair amount of time, as one might do for a good friend in need of close scrutiny. They rolled in lazily, flirtatiously caressing my feet and ankles, gently tumbling over the sand the same way a shy boy gently tumbles over his first kiss. I soon found a secluded spot 200 hundred yards from where the trail met the beach, and with nothing but time and sun and sand to occupy me, I fell into a deep and haunted sleep.

Traveling with me on the dream train was a repulsive image of a dead sperm whale being blown to smithereens. Chunks of disgusting flesh rained down upon my head and shoulders, the smoldering slime dripping from my face and hands like melting wax. I was nauseated, but to my great liberation they disappeared in a final blinding explosion of searing light and heat and smoke. When the hot fog lifted, there appeared before me a brigade of ferocious, three-legged dogs, nipping viciously at my heels and ankles, causing me to fall flat on my face. The angry hounds then slung sharp, thorny sticks at me in a sadistic effort to shatter my knees and slice my legs, carving up my flesh the way a butcher slaughters his fresh meat for the day. Struggling back to my feet, I grabbed one of the spiky weapons and whirled around insanely, in violent circles, defending myself from attacks in all directions, begging for assistance from two young girls who suddenly passed by. They just giggled and laughed at my dreadful plight and uncaringly moved on. Then the biggest and most crazed canine assassin moved in to finish the kill, but when I lunged out fiercely at him—hitting him squarely and dead on the head—they all evaporated into thin air. It was short relief because taking their place was a demented, wild acting horde of sadistic men, prowling menacingly all about me, howling as they lit sticks of dynamite and threw them at my face. The flash explosions burned and blinded and choked me, and there was no escape from this hell. One of the men suddenly tried to force a lit fuse into my mouth, while the others pinned my arms and feet tightly to the sand and cheered him on. I felt it was the end!

Then I awoke to a rude, firm kick in the ribs, jumping up with such a fright that Rick raced backward several paces, yipping at me in mortal fear. "Rusty, take it easy, will you? It's just me!"

"My God! What a hellish nightmare. Where are we?" I was serious. It was a scare like no other.

"We're on a beach in Oregon, and we need to get going. I want to make Cottage Grove today. But you had a bad dream, did you?"

"Yeah, a vast understatement, Ruiz. God, I swear I'll never go to sleep on a beach again, not if I live to be a 110."

"What was it about? The way you jumped at me, I thought you might have been running to escape an axe murderer."

I was too weary to relive all the graphic details, so I just highlighted those I could articulate without becoming ill. Recalling any part of it was terror enough. "And what about you, my sickly friend. Are you feeling better?"

"Yeah, right on. I think it's all finally out. I'm good to go, if you are?"

So, with a rough morning behind us, we loaded ourselves into the Princess and made our way inland. Our final destination today was Cottage Grove, Oregon. Rick was intent on surprising an old friend.

~~~

PART 2

Our unexpected encounter with the dunes, and all their mystical allure and wonder, led us to make a slight navigational error. We had driven too far north, and to reach Cottage Grove we needed to travel east to Eugene, Oregon, then backtrack south for 30 minutes. That aside, the trip inland was pleasant, and I was beginning to think that every new inch of this magnificent state was fighting hard to outshine the last, the earnest contest staged for our pleasure alone.

Such were my sublime thoughts as we moved at a moderate pace toward the heart of the Beaver State, along the line of Highway 126 and the great Siuslaw National Forest. The heavy hand of sweet solitude and beautiful desolation was but yards on each side of the Princess, and it made me sad to think that I might never travel this way again. I decided not to gamble and painstakingly seared into my memory the picturesque sights and musical sounds that helped usher us along this salient roadway. On occasion, I asked Rick to pull over so that I could stretch my long legs and breathe the unspoiled air, excitedly searching the skies for one of the many solitary eagles we had spotted along the way, sailing majestically atop the highest drifts of cloud and wind and timberline. It was an enchanting drive.

Such a leisurely tempo into Eugene took a few hours to accomplish, and once there it was disheartening to participate again in the sprawling commotion of a large city. Our part in the melodrama was to move slowly through the scene of Eugene's late afternoon rush hour. I couldn't compare it to the snarl of steel and rubber that smothers the freeways around San Francisco and Oakland at quitting time, but there's a definite stop-and-go stage to it, and we were two of the unlucky partakers. To ease the fumy boredom, I began to point out cars with license plates that identified some yet unvisited state. Most carried young families, likely on vacation for the summer. I called out their places of origin to Rick to inspire him to play an old game that I learned as a child, while on vacation with my own family. I instructed Mr. Ruiz that his part was to respond with the most appropriate words, in his learned opinion, that best described the state.

"Texas?" I quizzed him, a real softball to get him warmed up.

"Forget the Alamo."

"Try to be nice, will you? Colorado?"

"Pretty girls."

"Vermont?"

"More pretty girls. The ones not living in Colorado."

"Is it just that you can't play the game correctly, or are you trying to show off your ignorance for the fatherland?"

"OK, Cosmo. Cows!"

"Cows? How do you come up with cows? What's wrong with something like magnificent forests, maple sugar or magical lakes? What's the matter with you?"

"Why can't I say pretty girls and cows but you can say magnificent forests and magical lakes? You're a romantic dope —and that's what the matter is."

"And you're a horny cow. Let's move on, shall we? Nevada?"

"Blackjack."

"Iowa?"

"Potatoes."

"That's Idaho, dummy."

"Oh, that's right. Sorry Iowa."

"Well? Iowa, what about it?"

"Let's see. What's in Iowa? I can't think, offhand. Give me a minute."

As his imagination flew to hover over the golden fields of dreamy Iowa, a voice as fresh as an Iowa honeydew morning brought us quickly back to Eugene.

"Hi, there, handsome. Are you two heading home?" The voice was that of a vision from heaven, driving a 1965 burgundy Mustang convertible, the top down. Her three companions were equally angelic, their tanned faces and bright smiles aimed at my open window in curious, kind greeting. Unfortunately, my heart was so overloaded by the sudden, unexpected jolt of such a miraculous moment that it raced to collide head-on with my brain, and they both shattered into 100 pieces. I was rendered dazed and virtually speechless.

"We saw your California license plate," She said, trying me again. "Are you two having enough fun?"

"Who, us? Do you mean us?" I fumbled badly trying to get out just this much, and my bumbling breakdown prompted knowing, playful laughs from all of them. My humiliation and embarrassment were complete. Before I could recover enough to say something clever and witty, the spirit-filled driver turned to her friends and said, "Oh, he's cute and shy, how adorable."

Then traffic suddenly sped up in their lane, and to keep pace they quickly advanced several car lengths ahead of us. I could see that their bumper sticker read, "University of Oregon, Go Ducks!" When I fell from my cloud of befuddlement, Rick was there to catch me, and the landing was rough.

"Way to go, stupid. Don't you know they were flirting with us?" he growled, an incredulous stare of disapproval contorting his bronze, sunlit face. One might have thought I just threw away the very treasure he had hoped to discover on this trip, and we would never be this close to it again: pretty girls. "Look, Einstein," he continued, "I'm going to try to catch up with them. If I do, then I want you to yell out that we need help with directions. Maybe we can get them to stop. Can you handle that?"

"Stop where, man?"

"Any dang place off the freeway will do! OK? And don't act like an idiot again. You'll blow it totally for us."

"Do you think they thought I was an idiot?"

"No! They thought you were a cute, shy idiot. Man! Did they have to spell it out for you? You just sit there and be adorable, and let me do the talking this time."

Alas, such romances are naturally fleeting by uncontrolled circumstance, and soon a semi-trailer truck moved into our lane and blocked all sight of them. Then, in a minute more, the traffic started moving rapidly, and they were forever lost to us.

"They must have gotten off at one of the exits," Rick said, overcome with genuine sadness and dismay. "Well, nice going sheriff. You let the thieves get away again."

"Thieves? What are you talking about?"

"The thieves that were about to steal our hearts, man. How could you blow it so bad, Cosmo? You stupid schmuck!"

"Gee, Rick," I pleaded. "Give me a break, will you? What did you want me to say? They caught me by surprise. I'm not exactly the gangster of love. I think that's you, Romeo."

"You could have said anything but what you did," he complained, in final, bitter frustration. I slumped low in my seat, a failure.

Rick had been my best friend since we were both 11, a loyal comrade in our common struggles against the ravages of worldly chaos and the evils of bad men. So it was with thoughts of such loyalty, and years of youthful friendship, that I swallowed my well-deserved medicine and didn't let on that his harsh words stung like darts in my ears. Admittedly, my lack of street savvy pertaining to women, in close-quarter interactions, had been a hindrance to him before, and I felt doubly miserable for costing him this shot at singing out his hot Gregorian love chants. They were the carefully crafted and rehearsed songs and poems that he had made up for just such occasions, delivered in his manly voice and masterful cadence, which the girls always swooned over. Master Rick—as I hinted at on the way to Roscoe's house—was a genuine Casanova or a near carbon copy, and he had closely studied the art of romance and was pretty good at it. The real gangster of love, one might say. So we drove on in silence and detachment, which were my lesser punishments, and I hoped that Cottage Grove might provide me with an opportunity for redemption. My own city upon a hill.

"This is it, man, we're here. Right on! Far out! Groovy! I'll be crapping in a brass toilet tonight." Rick erupted, slugging me in the shoulder—not gunning for my cheek—which told me things were getting better but not completely settled between us. Just the same, he was wildly enthusiastic about finally arriving at the place we always intended to visit. He would finally get to see Wesley, his old-time buddy.

"It looks nice," I added, perked up myself by his sudden turn of mood.

We exited directly onto Main Street, optimistic, intent on taking the town by storm. Our first order of business was to get the lay of the land. So we cruised around the heart of the small town and some pretty neighborhoods, snooping about like hunter-gatherers on the prowl for the very substance of life: Cottage Grove.

The aging business district, a well-kept and comfy replica of what is fairly commonplace in our own neck of the woods, reassured us and boosted our confidence that it's an America of cohesion. It was a grainy portrait of old-school USA, its commercial center having the flair of nineteenth century design but populated by new cars and late model trucks and shiny people, and the new competed nicely with the old. The overall charm and appeal of the small, rustic homes, dispersed among shady streets and sunny avenues, painted a vibrant picture of how middle-class Americans live and stay connected to each other. The small and lovely American town.

At last, we stopped and mingled with a bevy of friendly denizens, young and old, and saluted all with our own youthful brand of patriotism, often having to duck under Independence Day banners that hung in business doorways and on street corners, announcing the coming Fourth of July. We confirmed in our hearts that Oregon, indeed, was still in America.

"Man, this place is too cool, ain't it?" Rick mused. "Look at all these old buildings and great homes. Just like Wesley said, he's living in the real red, white, and blue."

"Yeah, the place is a national treasure," I added. "Tocqueville would be proud."

"Who?"

"Tocqueville, he's French."

"You read French dudes now? What the hell does France have to do with this place?"

"Nothing, I suppose. He was just a brilliant fellow who was intrigued with America, pea brain. He's dead. He won't bother you."

"Oh, too bad. He would have liked it here. By the way, did you see all the babes walking around, Cosmo? You adorable schmuck."

"Leave me alone!"

"OK!' He trotted off, a horny cow in search of girls and pizza.

While I waited for Rick to fetch one—a pizza, that is—I strolled down the sidewalk and noticed that numerous professional people had conspired to buy and inhabit many of the best and oldest homes on and near Main Street. One was now likely to have his teeth filled in the exact spot where Granny once baked the chocolate cookies that gave him the cavities in the first place. I viewed this practice with some regret but reasoned that it was no more than a new generation grubstaking on old ground. Progress, they call it. Just the same, it was a handsome and comfortable town, and I was glad to be here. As well, Rick was glad to be here, pizza now in hand.

Besides the welcoming warmth and attractiveness of all things old and new, we soon drove by a massive lumberyard and sawmill on the west side of town. It blanketed the landscape for nearly two square blocks. This armada of wood and more wood began with a modest storefront and reception area, but once past these, we came upon a humongous, steel-gated entrance. Behind it, inside the main yard, we could see an impressive display of enormous, open-framed buildings, cascading one to another in perfect alignment, all constructed of massive steel columns and iron girders the size of battleships. An ocean of lumber was stored in each one.

It's also where Wesley Warrens worked. Unfortunately, we missed quitting time by almost two hours and would be forced to track him down at home. The honorable Mr. Warrens was Rick's childhood buddy, but I didn't know him. His family moved away from our hometown a few months before I met Rick. They had been pals and running mates well before my time. Apparently, the relationship had been a close one, and Rick was anticipating a joyful reunion. Regrettably, when swimming at the beach, where we encountered the dog, he left the directions and phone number to Wesley's house in the pocket of his shorts, and they were smeared and unreadable, along with his driver's license.

"Well, what do we do now, Goober? Did you maybe think to ask him to place lanterns in his window, one by land and two by sea, like Paul Revere?"

"He's not as clever as that, Cosmo, and it ain't nothin' to start a revolution over. We'll find him. Let's go ask someone."

"Like who? Nobody's here. Can't you see that?"

"What I mean is that someone in town has to know him. Let's cruise back and check it out. We can even stop at a park. I think I might have his address in my luggage. I'll look for it."

We first checked a telephone book. On cue, he wasn't listed. Luckily, we soon found a pleasant park three blocks off Main Street. It was of good size and impressive design, surrounded by an artful circle of very old, lovely, and plump oak trees, nearly bumping up against each other as we passed between them. It was a soothing enclosure of warmth and comfort. After we found an open spot, Rick began to rummage through an old suitcase he had slung haphazardly to the ground, cursing his misfortune. He couldn't find Wesley's address.

I left him in his distress, unable to help much, and strolled leisurely through the park. It was filled with the sights and sounds of children playing, young parents relaxing, and enamored couples in love, walking and talking, holding hands and kissing. There was even the occasional group of friendly old men playing chess and checkers and horseshoes. Some of them just sat and read the newspaper or fed dried bread to the birds, enjoying the lazy ease of a fine summer evening in Oregon. Now and again, one would lift a bottle to his lips, holstered in a brown paper bag, taking a sharp swig and giving a sweet sigh of forbidden pleasure. There was no alcohol allowed in the park, so the signs read, but the discreet and respected patron could get away with it easily enough. These men were of such respect, and no one seemed to mind. It was a genuinely romantic scene in a play about mainstream America, and I was proud to have a small part in it, the sentimental dope that I am. Just the same, sundown was beginning its evening march, and twilight would soon draw the curtains on this theatre of enchantment. My new acquaintances were beginning to wander off, a few at a time, in their quest for home and hot dinners and soft, clean beds to accommodate the coming night.

When I returned, my irritated friend was still sweating over Wesley's address. He really was mad at himself. He moved about quickly, back and forth, hesitating a bit with each step, returning to curse and kick the suitcase, swearing up and down that he had a copy of Wesley's address in it. "How the hell does something like that just up and disappear? I know I had it written down," he kept repeating to himself—and now me.

"Calm down, man," I tried to console him. "We'll find him, eventually."

"Yeah, I know, Cosmo. I just can't believe it. I know I had his address in my suitcase. Now it's not there. Dang it!" His frustration peaked, giving it one last kick that sent it sliding 10 feet away, slamming shut by itself, as if to provide the exclamation point on his annoyance.

"That's funny," I said, grinning at him. "I guess that closes the case on this mystery." I took a swipe at the pizza box sitting on the grass, still unopened. He kicked my hand away. It hurt a little. "Don't eat that, Cosmo!" he cried. "I bought it to share with Wesley."

"We're never going to find him tonight, and I hate cold pizza." I replied, ready to give up the search, even if he wasn't. His temper tantrum had been unpleasant to watch, and the endless, fruitless searching just deepened his depression. It was beginning to spread to me. I told him it was time to end the madness.

"No, man, I'm sure it's in there, somewhere," he responded, in another round of huffing and puffing, fetching the suitcase and starting the search again.

"Come on, Ruiz, how many times are you going to look through the same stuff? This is really painful to watch."

"You're right. The hell with it. I give up. Damn it! I would have liked to have seen Wesley tonight." He gave it one last kick for good measure. "Give me some of that pizza."

"Just don't eat Wesley's part."

We finished Wesley's part and the rest of it, then decided, as a practical matter, to sleep in the park and seek him out at work in the morning. Then like a frying pan had struck him in the head, which is what he needed, he jumped up in celebration, grabbing the pizza box and tossing it like a Frisbee. "Oh, man, I got it! Yes! Right on! Yeah! He said he lived in a trailer court." He stood in place, dancing a little jig that reminded me of Roscoe's dance by the river.

"That's helpful. Do you remember the name of it?"

"No, I don't. But my genius tells me there can be only one here."

"Yeah, man, but it's getting late," I argued. "We better ask someone quick; it will be dark soon. I'm not driving all over this town at night. It'll make me and the cops nervous."

We began our new search at the Post Office, back on Main Street, accosting a frail, elderly man, a raisin-dried gentleman searching wildly in his shirt pockets for the key to his mailbox. "Oh, no, not this again," I thought. He took the time to help us, anyway. It was the town he had spent his life in, and he was proud to let us know that he knew her better than the back of his hand. Between his mirthful finger searching of all important things not there—he had actually forgotten the key—he managed, using a sort of Oregonian sign language, to direct us to a small trailer court on Washington Street. "Just one right and fast left away. That's it, boys. Nothin' to her." He was a kind old fellow. When he found his key, I hoped his mail would be good to him.

He was right, there was nothing to her, and in no time we were there. Except when the manager pointed out Wesley's trailer, on cue again, he wasn't there. Worse, this cranky woman with parachute hair and painted on eyebrows, thick as black moons over Miami, behaved as if she didn't care for Wesley very much. It was plain to see that if we were his friends, then she didn't like us much, either. After some minutes of us parked in front of his place, she snuck up on us and pointedly asked us to leave. "I chain the driveway at nine, every night," she announced, holding up and rattling her keys like gilded weaponry. "You might want to come back on another day. I keep the hatches closed tight here." With that, she walked away in a huff, saying no more, as one does when fully expecting the issue to be settled.

The voice of authority had chased us back to Main Street. Still not fully integrated with our new surroundings, we took a few minutes to cruise about town, aimlessly, before heading back to the park. It would be our first night of sleeping on the hard ground. It had been a long and intense day, and Rick was too weary to wrestle any longer over Wesley. Thank goodness.

All thoughts fuzzy, we slipped into our sleeping bags and pondered the night sky. Heaven's prosperous black cosmos was filled with dazzling silver stars, the kind of sparkling diamonds that adorn the fingers of well-heeled women. The Big Dipper was still the bear he has always been, and the Little Dipper chased after him, close on the heels of his singular grandeur. Their charge tonight was to keep my unexpected loneliness on the mend, I decided, celestial guardians to watch over the night, steady and sure, to be there to comfort me should I suddenly wake up. Isolated, road weary and a little discouraged for the first time, we fell asleep expressing our opinions on all that passed for life on the road, good and bad. We thought we had learned much already. The last thing I heard was, "Man, Wesley sure would have dug the pizza." Rick was the sweetest guy, always trying to feed somebody.

[6]
KIMBERLY

To keep pace with yesterday's stream of disordered events, I felt a rather starchy kick bounce off my butt. "What the hell is he doing up so early?" was my first thought, my second was of his death. "You better knock it off, Ruiz. If you do that again, I'm going to get out of this sleeping bag and kick your fanny all over this park!"

This thing called life is full of surprising variants. This was one of them. Another firm poke, right between the ribs this time—it was meant to hurt a little. "Wake up, young man, you can't sleep here."

I hate adrenalin, especially when it comes courtesy of the police. Before my eyelids popped open, I was standing at attention. "Sorry, sir," I said. "Our mistake." The other part of our mistake was still fast asleep, oblivious to the whole commotion.

"Roust up your partner and gather your things, quickly," the officer said, slipping his nightstick into its holster and adjusting his gun belt. "I need you to get moving fast, so that I can. If I hurt you, son, I'm sorry," he added, sincerely. "Light a fire now, OK?"

The early morning sun, at his back, was momentarily blinding, obscuring the finer details of his face, but his voice sounded young and eager and devoted to the steadfast rule of law. "Yes, sir," I assured him, trying to sound alert and decree abiding. "I'll wake him right now. It won't take us but a moment. Very sorry."

"Well, you should have read the no loitering signs, but I suppose no harm is done. Does that Camaro on the street belong to you two?"

My vision clear, I could finally distinguish the sharp features of his face, even younger than his voice. He was impressively tall, an inch above me, with muscular arms attached to broad shoulders and long legs, all packed into a neatly pressed uniform. He was kind but resolute in his behavior: a man who knows what he's about and what he was born to do in life. Such men really exist and make the ladies sigh. "Yep, is that a problem?"

"No, I just wanted to tell you how much I admire it. It's a stick, right?"

"Yeah, and packing a 327 but not stock. I changed the pistons, camshaft and carburetor, and I added some other goodies to help out."

"Horsepower?"

"Well, near 375, give or take a few, about 100 over stock. My brother-in-law helped me to reshape her. She holds her own pretty good with the fat boys, especially out of the hole."

"Yeah, it sounds like she would. Very good. Well, as I said, you two need to get moving. And keep the speed down while you're here. I don't want to write you a ticket, should I see you again."

"Yes, sir, I understand."

It was that fast, and I thought he must be a fine gentleman, still young and mindful enough to have put himself in our position, and to have asked me casually about the Princess was a real plus. I watched him walk smartly to his patrol car, parked directly behind her, assuming he had already checked my plates and found me clean. No matter, such moments still bring that adrenalin thing to bear, and I hurriedly put on my shirt and shoes.

Lugworm remained horizontal through it all. His peculiar brand of morning doltishness, twisted so deeply within his bag, resembled a pile of disfigured, gypsy laundry. "Hey, Rick, get up," I said, leaning down and lightly shaking his shoulder, not wanting to startle him the way I had been. Usually, I wouldn't have cared, but my manly worth was still down from yesterday. Rick had taken the time to remind me of my blunder with the college girls, a number of times. So he warranted a gentle touch. "Hey, Sweet Pea, wake up. The cops say we gotta get out of here. We're loitering on the grass, breaking the law." Nothing. Lazarus must have been easier. I shook his shoulder a little harder—and then harder still. His head bolted out, a round fired from the Bismarck, and the grumpy little fireball was ill-tempered, indeed.

"What? What cops? This better not be a joke, Cosmo! Damn, man, what you doin' up so early?" The bag swallowed him up again.

"You better listen up, grouchy Groucho, and take a gander over there. See him? See? Now, come on. He isn't kidding around. We gotta go."

"Damn it. All right, but give me a minute."

"You know, Rick, you're starting to become a real bore."

"Yeah, yeah, Rusty. You might be right about that. Sorry. I think I'm still a little frazzled from my fight with Montezuma. Plus, the pizza didn't seem to settle well."

"And lost love?" I asked. I should have left it alone.

"Well, you were pretty stupid."

"But right now I'm smart enough to get out of here. Let's go."

"Yeah, I'm for that. Let's go."

We collected ourselves, in short order, wobbling like winos to the car. As soon as the officer observed us driving away, he waved, flipping a fast U-turn and heading off in the opposite direction.

"Tinhorn," Rick judged him.

"He's OK, just doing his job."

"But, man, I had another two hours in me. What time is it?"

"You know I don't wear a watch, and what does it matter? Let's find Wesley or let's find Canada."

We found breakfast first, and it renewed our spirits for the task at hand: finding Wesley at his place of employment. The food at Kate's Diner tasted 10 times better than it would have, had we not spent the night sleeping on the hard ground, breathing in the cool night air that stripped our bellies clean. Rick started to head for the car before I was ready. "I'd like to get cleaned up now," I said. "This place ought to do it."

"No, man, it's not even eight yet. We might catch Wesley at home," Rick said. "We can clean up there."

I still took the time to wash my face and brush my teeth in the restaurant's tiny bathroom, while Rick paced outside, impatiently. My hair was dirty, and I needed a shave. Otherwise, all in all, I felt good and ready to resume my worldly struggles. One thing though, I dreaded meeting Wesley for some unknown, intangible reason. I just had a bad feeling about it. Maybe it was because I swiped his best friend, and I thought he might resent me for it. That was fine, but for the pleasure of it his life should be shortened. The guy bothered me immensely, and I had never met him. After I exited the bathroom, I took a pathetic shot at flirting with our pretty waitress, but she just laughed back. I found Rick in the driver's seat.

"You're driving?"

"That I am, Cosmo. At the rate you're moving we'll never get there. Can we go now? And you don't look any better, either."

"All this hurry from the guy who wouldn't get out of his sleeping bag?"

Within five minutes we had arrived at the trailer park, the chain down and our path clear. Wesley's abode, on the right and the first in view, was a decrepit eyesore. I felt sorry for him and ashamed of myself for so quickly prejudging Rick's friend.

Anyway, at one time a happy jacket of blue paint covered the slender shoebox, a thinly framed single-wide trailer. Sadly, that was eons ago, and the ravages of time had since peeled it to the bone. Only pale blue teardrops were left to cry out now, a handful of cheerless, mournful blotches somehow surviving in this iconic shape. I cried right along with them. I remembered back to our arrival the previous night, when we found no one, and how the pitch of darkness had disguised the worst of this loathsome place. The long list of the trailer's scant attractions featured the complete absence of a front porch, the shabby front door in ruins, cracked and weather beaten. Above the door a thin and gaunt covering of brittle awning shifted and swayed, lurching precariously even in a mild wind, secured only by two badly frayed ropes attached atop a drooping and unsteady roof. The whole assembly might come crashing down at any second: casualties would be taken. Wesley was obviously not a handyman. Beyond these afflictions, two old wooden chairs, most of their back slates broken or missing, stood guard in the small front yard: grizzled, grand knights, sentinels of bleak house. To access this palace one was obliged to maneuver over a series of crumbling cement stepping stones, nearly buried in dirt, and grown over with spotty, puke-colored grass. The rest of the gritty yard was bare and brown and lifeless. From what I could see this place served no good purpose to anyone, beyond a debate over bad taste and good riddance. On the barely marginal upswing were several young rosebushes, arranged carefully in front of the trailer's meager slab foundation, a sweet, tender attempt to grow some happiness. They spoke of a woman. Still, even lovely rosebushes couldn't hide the stark, thick covering of blight and poverty that encircled the place. Nothing here inspired a sense of joy or good fortune—or even a reason to get up in the morning. The idea of a warm and fuzzy reunion escaped me.

"Hey, Cosmo, what's keeping you? Stop spacing out on me and go knock."

"No way," I said, taken completely off guard by the demand. "Aren't you going to do it? You're a crazy man if you think I am. He's your pal."

"No, man, com'on, do it. I want to surprise him. Go knock. See if you can get him to come to the car."

"How?"

"Tell him you need a jumpstart or something. Ask for directions somewhere. Tell him you got a map in the car."

"You and your directions, man! He's likely to think I'm crazy and shoot me."

"I'm going to shoot you if you don't do it. Go on!"

I got out, reluctantly, and made my way toward the door. I decided to let Wesley in on the joke, thus turning the tables on Rick and adding more intrigue to the reunion. However, before I could follow through with my traitorous scheme, I was interrupted by an inquisitive, musical voice, carried on the waves of the bright morning light.

"May I help you with something?"

I turned to see who it was, spotting a vision of beauty 20 yards away, young and petite and tanned, and she was dressed in baggy pants and a checkered, oversized shirt. She was also standing in the presence of the trailer court manager, the older woman who had been our rude welcome wagon during our first visit. The domineering hostess also occupied a large and fashionable mobile home, the exact opposite of what stood before me. I felt as if I had circled the dark side of the moon and was now smiling upon the flourishing earth again.

"We're looking for Wesley," I called back, motioning for Rick to fall out and provide me with his needed expertise. The young woman seemed to sense my anxiety but didn't say anything else. She waited quietly for us to approach her. Within a few paces of where she stood, I could see that she was extraordinarily pretty, with an easy smile that quickly melted away my previous thoughts of dark trailer park despair. I let myself bask in her delight. Rick muttered something to me under his breath, indecipherable, but I was fairly certain—from my own increased heart rate—that it was the same thing I was thinking.

"Hi, we're looking for Wesley Warrens. I'm a friend of his," Rick said, extending his hand to her. She took it, a bit hesitantly, and then mine, in turn. Though small and delicate, she was surprisingly strong and displayed a vigorous handshake.

"I'm afraid he's not here right now," she said, seemingly embarrassed. She looked directly at me, in a probing stare, to see if I had detected her guarded discomfort. I smiled and diverted my eyes away from her. "I'm his wife, Kimberly," she added, her voice cracking slightly.

"Oh, great," Rick exclaimed, his enthusiasm for the moment causing him to miss the signs of her distress. "Maybe he told you about me? I'm Rick, from California. We grew up together."

"No, I'm so sorry. I don't believe he did," she said, now as equally embarrassed for him as she was for herself. It was one of those awkward moments that nobody reacts to very well, so for a few tongue-tied seconds none of us knew what to say next. I then made an attempt at a formal introduction of myself, just to break the silence. It came off comically, at best, and caused Kimberly to laugh and smile curiously at me.

"Don't worry about him. He's a moron," Rick said, coming to her aid.

"Thank you," I said.

"Glad to help, Cosmo."

"Well, I'm very pleased to meet both of you," she replied, now grinning brightly at us. Our easygoing attitude seemed to encourage her to accept us as friends, and a new strength came to her voice. "This is Irene. She runs the place."

Irene gave us both the "once over," and I wished I had shaved. Then she swiftly brought Kimberly up to speed on our prior visit. She also displayed a commanding and forceful manner that left no question about who was in charge here. It made me wonder what might happen to those who trespassed on her dominance. She was the sort of person who always makes other people feel like convicted criminals—just by being in her presence.

"I'm sorry that I wasn't here to help you last night," Kim said, after listening carefully. "Maybe I could have saved you some time and trouble. At least I could have given you some information."

"No, it's no trouble," Rick said. "I just thought he was expecting me, that's all. I wrote him that I might be here about this time. You said he was gone? Will he be back soon?"

"It's not likely," Irene broke in, her voice crisp and terse. "And if he does come back, I hope someone takes him to the woodshed and cuts his balls off!"

Such a showstopper stunned me, as one might easily guess, and it turned Rick to solid stone. Kimberly came instantly to the rescue, "Oh, no! Irene, please don't! They have nothing to do with it!"

"Well, I'm just saying what should be said, that's all," Irene countered, her verdict of speedy justice for the vile Wesley consoling her. She stared steadfast into our eyes, as if to cement her official decision.

"Gee, if there is some sort of trouble, maybe we better excuse ourselves," I offered, apologetically, stealing another quick glance at Rick. He was mummified. Preempting me, Irene promptly turned and stepped inside her front gate, disappearing inside the huge trailer, without another word or kind farewell. The three of us remained silent until the door closed firmly behind her.

"I'm real sorry, guys. She's just upset," Kimberly said, her eyes now moist but thankfully tearless. "If you wish, you can come to my trailer. I'll make you some fresh coffee and explain the best I can."

"I'm the one who is sorry, Kim," Rick finally said, suddenly back in full command of himself. "We didn't mean to come at a bad time. If you rather not bother, we can just be on our way. You don't have to explain anything."

"Is it really that obvious," she tried to joke, but we wouldn't laugh at her. "Oh, please, I can't let you two leave without at least a cup of coffee. You've come a long way. I will be happy to do it."

Of course, we accepted her kind invitation. Once inside her small kitchen, I struggled to straighten out my legs underneath the heavy kitchen tabletop that folded down from one of the trailer walls. I wondered if this was how she got her strength.

Kimberly quickly made herself busy. In a nervous but quiet method she proceeded to load the coffee pot, collect three cups, and then cream and sugar from the preposterous thing that passed for a refrigerator. Then she smiled warmly at us and excused herself for a few minutes inside her bedroom, just a few paces down the narrow, dimly lit hallway.

Rick, sitting next to me, was still shaken by the sudden

downturn in events. Thus he remained very quiet, only smiling at me dejectedly, raising and dropping his arms in a sign of frustration and utter disappointment. He could not have been more defeated and appeared to me as one betrayed. He placed the palms of his hands on his temples, staring down at the table.

I filled the strained silence by examining the areas of the trailer I could see. The living room in this small prison was furnished spartanly, featuring a beaten-up and scratched television sitting in one corner, propped up on garden bricks, its tinfoil rabbit ears able to connect with world events and nonevents in black and white only. Next to it were two homely chairs, one a beige leather recliner that was on its last legs, literally, and the other a large brown beanbag chair, one of its seams beginning to fail, so that it leaked tiny beads of Styrofoam onto the carpet. This same carpet, possessing barely a hint of its once vivid colors and creative flower designs, ran throughout the trailer, and in several places it was worn completely through to expose the metal floor. Throw rugs would have helped immensely, but they were obviously an unaffordable luxury and of minor consequence in the scheme of bigger troubles.

Paradoxically, this sad home was as clean as Kimberly could possibly make it, easily rivaling the diligent care my mom takes with our own home. Military clean is how I've come to know and define it, where even the nonexposed surfaces of most things, hidden from normal view, shine like the sun. What furnishings can't accomplish with fluff, God's little worker bees, like Kim, accomplish with sparkle. Moreover, the entire inside had the sweet, delicate smell of fresh vanilla, the same pleasant aroma that radiated from Kim. I first noticed it when I walked alongside of her to the trailer. Suddenly, a stimulating thought about my own future matrimonial bliss overcame me. If Kim, or any other woman for that matter, treated a derelict trailer with this kind of loving care and attention, making it smell and shine like a king's castle, then how much better must she treat her man? Wesley must be a fool, I decided, like no other. I was both anxious and afraid to hear about him, trying not to speculate to myself about why he had gone missing. Irene might be right.

Kim soon rejoined us, this time with her long black hair arranged nicely around her tanned shoulders. Gone was the straight ponytail that had swayed so lightly in the wind, bouncing along buoyantly with the beat of my heart. Lord, if she was pretty 10 minutes ago, she was just stunning now. She had also exchanged the baggy pants and large shirt for an attractive pair of shorts and a feminine navy blue top, with gentle, white doves painted on it, pointing skyward. If I could have taken their place, I would have flown away with her at once.

I watched her closely as she put the finishing touches on our fresh coffee. When she finally made her way to the table, her arm accidentally brushed against mine, and she momentarily let it linger there. I felt the exhilarating surge of excitement that comes at such a hopeful moment, when a man is thoroughly enchanted by a woman and wonders, by what miracle of chance or fate, how he might get even closer to her and stay there. I've fallen in love before at first sight, but it happened to be with my seventh-grade science teacher. A failed experiment.

Now sitting directly across from us, Kim began the conversation by asking a series of questions about our recent travels and Rick's relationship with Wesley. I thought it sweet and brave of her to show genuine interest in us, not trying to rush into the more pressing subject at hand. Still, there was little question that Rick was eager to know the whereabouts of the elusive Wesley. She let us carry on at some length, paying courteous attention to our disjointed account of events and how we planned to enjoy ourselves in Canada. Being such an attentive and gracious audience of one, she gave me the opportunity to study her closely when Rick was talking.

Her brown popcorn eyes, buttery and soulful, were crowned by perfectly crafted eyebrows, the exact pitch of her black hair and shaded over by long, natural eyelashes, curved into a flowing symmetry that duplicated the soft lines of her fresh, olive-brown face. Her delicate nose and ears and finely shaped cheekbones, like crescent moons, accented the same perfect design of her mouth and full lips, and the result was a picture of near flawless beauty. Her only visible blemish was a small but noticeable scar on her lower chin. I found out later that it came from a fall, as a young girl, while riding her bicycle. I imagined her no older than 20. It would have been very embarrassing for me if she could have read my mind. I was definitely not the first guy to have this kind of reaction to a real angel, at first sight and greeting. I was sure of it. And a married angel, no less. I must be the devil, but I didn't feel like him.

"Well, it might be difficult for you to hear," she finally said, speaking in whispered tones, and more to Rick than me. "Wesley has been gone for six weeks. I think he has left for good. I'm pregnant, you see, and he didn't want a child. He wanted me to abort it and I refused." She spread her elegant fingers across the tablecloth, timidly, trying to flatten out the creases that formed sharp folds in the linen, but they wouldn't disappear on her like her husband.

Rick and I couldn't look at each other. I couldn't look Kim in the eyes. In fact, I wished to be blind. Unlike our conversations with Rosie, this was a deeply painful moment that we were sharing with her, and it came to us without proper warning—save Irene. It cut out my soul and tore through my heart like a buzzsaw, ripping them both to pieces and casting them away like so much chaff in the wind. I didn't know what to say or what to do, and sorry is truly a sorry word. It was Rick who finally saved us from the suffocating silence.

"The bastard."

"Amen," I added, softly. Three short words that summed up all that was needed to say, and neither one of us were sorry about them.

Kim stood up quickly and moved toward the sink, her back to us now, not wishing for us to see her cry. It gave us the chance to look at each other. Rick's face was ashen, drained of all its natural color that usually lit up the world in bright tones of friendly goodwill and affable easygoingness. Except this wasn't good and it wasn't easy. I didn't say anything to him, just shook my head in that universal acknowledgment and tribute to what might have been—and what should be. I thought of the Zodiac killer and how he was still on the loose in the Bay Area, wishing he was having his way with Wesley right now. We reap what we sow.

Then a knock at the door, and isn't it odd that such a simple, mundane thing should offer the three of us access to the perfect avenue of escape. Kim moved hastily to answer it. It was then that I first noticed the slight bump on her midsection, a telling reminder of the unfinished business that Wesley left behind. Never mind, the baby would be the glorious miracle that God would give her to finish the business.

"Hi, Bonnie."

"Hi, Kim. Who does that gorgeous car outside belong to? Oh, please excuse me. I didn't know you had company." Bonnie eyed us suspiciously, a bundle of beehive hair and overdone makeup, yet still attractive in her bright summer dress.

"It's OK. These guys are friends of Wesley. Come on in, and I'll introduce you."

"No, I can't. I have to run. I'll be late for work. I just dropped by for a minute to let you know of some good news. I think I found a car for you. Oh, hi guys. I'm Bonnie. If I had time, I'd stay and interrogate you." A much needed laugh. We didn't mind that it was at our expense.

"What did you say? What car? Whose car?"

"My neighbor says a guy at my church has an old car that he wants to give away. All you have to do is pick it up. If it runs, that is. I forgot to ask him that part. I just spoke with him briefly on the phone this morning. But I have the guy's number and address. We can go over after I get off work. Unless these two gentlemen want to take you?"

"Oh, no. I couldn't ask them to do that."

"Sure you can," I chimed in.

"Really?" Kim said. "You would take me?"

"Be glad to."

"OK, then," Bonnie said. "Here's the guy's information. Well, gotta run. I'll call you later."

"Oh, you can't. I had to shut off the phone. I'm late on the bill, but I think I can pay it next week."

"Darn it. It's always something."

"Yeah, that's for sure. Anyway, these two nice gentlemen are Rick and Rusty."

"Hi and bye, Rick and Rusty. Thanks a lot. If you lay one hand on this girl, I'll have you both beheaded." Another needed laugh and we didn't mind paying for this one, either.

"Bye, Bonnie. I don't know how to thank you."

"No thanks needed. I'll check in on you soon." With that, the bundle of Bonnie was gone. How beautiful are the feet of those who bring good news. It was the first time I saw a real, hopeful smile on Kim's face. The light was shining through the door, illuminating her black hair and slim figure, creating a faultless outline of God's cherished gift to mankind. Goodness me, she was beautiful. I changed my mind. This was the finest trailer in the universe.

"If you two don't mind, I'm going to run over to Irene's trailer and see if I can use her phone. You really won't mind taking me?"

Does an angel really have to ask anyone anything twice?

"Yes, go ahead. I mean no—yes—no. Yes, we won't mind taking you." I was excited for her and us, and it showed. I blubbered it all out badly.

"Go ahead, Kim. It's OK. He's still a moron."

Then the first relaxed, genuine laugh of joy came from her, as she laughed at funny Rick laughing at me. I didn't mind if it was at my expense, alone.

Before we left the trailer I borrowed pen and paper from Kim and scribbled my folks a short letter, informing them that the two of us were fine and not to bother having my brother alert his police friends about us. My brother's best friend was a deputy sheriff. I figured if I was playful and pushed the onus onto him, as a sort of joke, it would bring a smile to my mom's face. It was time to lessen any tension I might have caused. I added that we had made some money working, had a safe trip, and we were presently helping a lady in distress, hoping that tidbit would also help. I had no worries about my dad, but a son shouldn't mess with his mother.

~~~

PART 2

We let Kim walk to the front door alone. A middle-aged woman answered, speaking with her briefly before stepping outside to get a better look at her and us, I guessed. Then Kim motioned for us to join them. We quickly made our way to the porch. "This is Mrs. Clark," Kim said. "She is the wife of Mr. Clark, the nice man who has the car. Mrs. Clark, this is Rick and Rusty, two friends of mine." It was a relief to now be her friend and not one of Wesley's, who we weren't. Mrs. Clark smiled broadly, shaking our hands. Her palms were a little wet from washing breakfast dishes, and she still held the moist dish rag in her hands. She promptly led us to the backyard, where not one but three old cars crowded the grass and fence line, and from the many assorted car parts scattered about, I figured her husband to be an auto mechanic. I was right.

"There she is. Not much to look at, I guess, but it is yours for the taking. I don't think it runs right now and will need a little work. But my husband, Bill, says it won't take much to get her up and going. He just hasn't had the time."

Not much to look at? Wow, I might have teased Mrs. Clark had I known her better. It was a fabulous red and white 1956 Chevy Bel Air, the body straight and the paint not badly faded, and I couldn't believe Mr. Clark was giving it away. The only downfall—in strict, car-dude terms—was that it was a four-door sedan. Most of my friends would die for a '56 Chevy, but it would have to be a two door. Kim walked around it excitedly, examining the prized trophy, while Rick and I opened the doors to get a look inside. It was what we expected, a three speed with a column shifter, and the interior had only one small tear in the upholstery, on the driver's side. We quickly popped the hood and also found what we expected, a small six-cylinder engine that produced 140 horses or so. It was just enough for Kim to get around and not hurt herself or anyone else. The tires weren't bald but close to it, and one hubcap was missing. All in all, a nice deal for free.

"What do you think, guys?" Kim asked, beaming. "It is cute. Isn't it?"

"I'll say," Rick said. "Let's see if it will start."

Nothing good, dead battery. There was likely more trouble to come. Kim appeared a little deflated, a short sigh coming from her.

"Don't worry," I said, touching her gently on the shoulder. "It is nothing we can't handle."

Within 10 minutes we had the battery pulled, and Rick was taking it to an auto parts store to see if it would hold a charge. Kim had gone with him, needing to get to work, having a part-time job at a local bookstore. She walked the mile each day from her trailer.

Upon Rick's return, I told him the grim but fixable facts. "It looks like she needs new points and plugs, and the wires need to be changed. The entire ignition system might need to be replaced. She also needs a new fan belt, but the hoses look fine. I'm not sure about the carburetor. The oil is filthy, and the tires feel like chucks of driftwood, but the brakes have another 10,000 miles in them. We're sure to hit a few snags we don't expect. What do you think? One long day?"

"It could be a longer list, I suppose. But they tell me the battery is toast, Cosmo."

"Oh, great."

"Maybe if we swing a deal here and there, we can afford to help her," Rick said, in his undying valor. "Yeah, I think we can do it in a day."

If one can't be anything else, he can always be a gentleman. The task cost us half the money we had, but the deed got done. I sent Rick to fetch four used tires, a new battery, and the other parts we needed. In the meantime, I stripped out the wires, pulled the plugs and drained the oil. Mr. Clark had a tire changer in his garage—a real godsend. It took all morning and a long afternoon, but we shined like heroes. Mrs. Clark fed us a hefty lunch during a delightful break, showering us with praise and good conversation.

Kim was standing nearby when the Bel Air fired up like a new car. I drove it slowly to the street, having to be careful of the narrow path between Mr. Clark's fence and the sidewall of the house. Kim had gone inside with Mrs. Clark, finishing up the paperwork that would soon make her the legal owner of a fine Chevrolet. In a minute more, she hurdled down the steps of the high porch like a professional sprinter, running to where we stood. It was pretty darn good for a pregnant lady. "This is just so wonderful. Thank you both so much!" She squeezed our hands and hugged us, hopping up and down, joyfully happy. "But I don't know how I'm going to pay you back." The issue of money made her anxious, and I tried to help.

"We always do this," I joked. "On a daily basis, don't we, Rick?" I was touched by the rare combination of joy and despair that came from her, at the same time. The car meant freedom and independence, and it would provide an easier life for an expectant mother with unpaid bills. A really big deal to her, in other words. We got the happy and sad girl calmed down, convincing her that room and board in her trailer tonight, and perhaps again when we got back from Canada, should fit the bill. We needed a good halfway rest stop. She was overwhelmed by our generosity and agreed to our terms, which she said were too much in her favor.

"Not at all," I responded. "I think we're the ones coming out ahead."

"Then I think I know how you can square it with me, Rusty Anderson," she said slyly, teasing me, the subtle charm of it catching me by surprise. "I don't know how to drive a stick shift—but I bet you can teach me!"

"Fair and square!" I added, pleased to be the target of her joke, at any expense. I was in love. In one more day it would be returned and change the entire course of my life. Yes, life is full of surprising variants.

[7]
TEACHING KIMBERLY HOW TO DRIVE

Fixing Kim's car earned us a place to sleep and dine: barbecued burgers, chips and soda, all supplied by Bonnie. She showed up a few minutes after we arrived back at Kim's worn trailer, and it was easy to tell they were good friends. It was a fun time cooking and eating outside in the magnificent summer evening. Bonnie was eager to know all about us and our travels, so we shared the story of our memorable beginnings, including our good fortune to meet, "The Second Greatest Man in the World." I told her a whale of a story too, but she didn't believe a word of it. "The Japanese bombed Oregon? No, that can't be right. How ridiculous."

At one point I drove her back to the market to fetch more snacks. She insisted on paying us for the money we spent fixing Kim's car. I wouldn't take it from her.

"But you must take it. She won't be able to pay you for months, if ever. You know that, right?"

"No, no, it'll be fine. She's giving us a place to sleep, and we're getting dinner from you. It'll all break even in the end.

Besides, we had a little money when we left and earned a pretty good payday unloading furniture."

"You guys are angels dropped right out of heaven."

"Well, that must be true because Kim also said it about 50 times to us today. Please don't worry about her. We said she could repay us in full by letting us sleep at her trailer, as I mentioned, and again on the way back from Canada."

"OK, Cosmo, you win. It's Cosmo, right?"

"You can call me Mr. Cosmo."

"You're not only cute, you're adorable."

"You haven't been the first to say that this trip."

It was getting late before the party broke up, and Irene paid us a visit soon after Bonnie left for home. It was time for her nightly chore of chaining the front entrance, which she had left open an extra two hours for Bonnie. There was another way in and out, but one had to drive to the back of the park. Kim was inside, vacuuming the front room. She wanted to provide us a clean floor to sleep on. Of course, it was already spotless, but men must let women do what women do, and it doesn't include taking advice about housework from them.

"I don't allow any alcohol outside, gentlemen," Irene announced, knowing we didn't have any. Authority must say what it must say.

"We only drink sodas. Neither one of us drink alcohol," I said, a little too defensively. It was a generally true response, if not altogether accurate. I sometimes told people what they wanted to hear.

"Well, just so you know." She marched away, in paratrooper style.

"Que amiga tan rara!" Rick said.

"Exactly, whatever that means."

When we got inside Kim had already arranged our sleeping bags on the floor and was busy brushing them clean. The top she wore hung a little loose, and I inadvertently caught a glimpse of her apple-shaped breasts, just for a second, quickly diverting my eyes. Oh, boy, there wasn't anything about her that wasn't perfect.

"There," she said. "I hope you two will be comfortable."

"This will be fine, Kim," I said. "Like kings in a castle."

"Well, I don't know about that, but at least the police won't bug you early in the morning."

It must have been about three in the morning when I awoke to use the restroom. When coming out I heard the faint noise of tender crying coming from her bedroom. I stood near to her door listening and hating myself for doing so. I started to knock gently, stopping just in time. I stood there for another moment or two and didn't hear her again. I walked very quietly to the front room and slipped into my bag, unable to sleep. I almost cried myself, choked up for her, unable to comprehend what kind of monster would leave this beauty and his unborn child. I wasn't ready for the altar, but I thought about just asking her to marry me and let me love her madly, wiping away all her tears. It would be as Saint John said, "There will be no more sorrow, crying or pain, for the former things have passed away." I finally fell asleep and purchased another ticket on the dream train. This time it was tanned girls in convertibles, sand monsters who wanted to eat me, married angels who smell like vanilla, mothers who slayed their youngest son and truck drivers who run over and squash estranged husbands on the lamb. Then I woke up, laughing this time. Thankfully, it was not as bad an assortment as the day before—but still a dynamite dream. I hoped the crying had stopped for her.

The next morning was a Saturday, and Kim cooked us a delicious breakfast, including hot coffee brewed with egg whites, a recipe learned from her dad. The plan was for Rick to help

Bonnie set up new bunk beds for her children and for me to teach Kimberly how to drive her car. It had all been arranged last night, and during this time I could tell that Rick and Bonnie had hit it off. She was a young divorcee with twin boys, and she was perhaps three years older than us. That would make her 21. I've heard about older women who go for younger guys. Kim, herself, was actually only 19, a year younger than Wesley. Rick had always hung out with older guys, a habit learned from befriending his brother's buddies. It wasn't really unusual for older women to be attracted to him. He could be very mature and persuasive if the situation called for it. If the situation was love, he was at his best. I was always intrigued how Hispanic men, in general, seem to grow up faster than their Caucasian counterparts. I'm not sure why that is, but it seems to be the case.

Well, the debonair Ruiz and the black Princess were soon off to save the swooning Bonnie and her twin hellions, for better or worse, and better is what he said he expected. It left me alone with Kim for the first time.

"Can I help you with the dishes?"

"Sure," she said. "I'll wash and you dry."

I jumped at the chance to stand close to her, thinking I would volunteer to dry a battalion of Marines' dishes for less.

"So, do you think I should name him?"

"The baby? That's the usual thing to do."

"No, silly boy, I mean the car. I decided that he is a male, and I'd like to name him *The Prince*. Then for a while I'll have a prince and princess parked in front of my trailer. What do you think about that?"

"I think the prince is a sly guy, moving in on such a beautiful princess."

"And he has a handsome friend who was a big help to him yesterday. Did you know? I think he's a prince, too!" She looked me directly in the eyes and didn't take her stare away. It was now or not at all. I dropped my towel and cupped her small, delicate face in my trembling hands and kissed her passionately. She let me. Holy smokes, God runs a fine universe at times and knows how to move things along! She tasted like ripe strawberries, is the best way I can describe it, her warm breath and moist mouth succulent to savor and inhale. Once bitten, I thought it would be impossible for me to get enough. I moved my lips to the base of her little ear and down the side of her soft neck. Then she suddenly and playfully pushed me away.

"I think that's enough for now, Mr. Anderson. We can't have a prince losing his head over a married and pregnant lady, can we? The kingdom will suffer a scandal!" She turned slightly away from me, giggling and sighing deeply. It was the same sense of joy and despair that I had noticed yesterday. The two mingled together were charming but difficult to reconcile. Then she suddenly turned back and grabbed me, kissing me teasingly this time but not letting it persist. She ran her hands down the front of my shirt until she reached my stomach and then gently pushed me away again, tending quickly back to the dishes, acting as if nothing had happened. A wide, grinning smile covered her face, and it was a pleasant and satisfying thing to see, a perfect crown on more than a perfect princess. I was captivated by her and just stood there for a delectable moment, smitten, thoroughly dumbfounded by love. It is a fine, mysterious feeling.

"The prince is at your command," I finally said, reluctant to resume my chore of drying dishes—long live the Marines.

Teaching Kim how to drive was almost as much fun, not all things being equal, naturally. I was impressed by how fast she caught on, and it surprised me a little. I remembered how nervous I was when first learning and how my brother made it a point to laugh at me. She was doing as well as I did, big brothers be danged.

"You're doing great, Kim. Press the clutch down, shift, back up, pick up some speed, now clutch down again, shift, clutch up. Way to go!" Of course, there were the usual engine stalls and lurching accelerations and decelerations, now and again, and downshifting was a little challenging for her. The steering wheel was a tad too big at first, but she finally got comfortable with it. Within two hours, all things considered, she was doing pretty well. We were on a country road and passed more than one farmer or rancher. Many took the time to wave at us and smile knowingly, seeing the erratic movement of the car. It was fun and having a pretty student made it more fun.

Cottage Grove is famous for its covered bridges, and we stopped at one to rest and goof around, walking and talking and holding hands. It had been an ideal start for us, and all was right with the world. How can one explain such a turn of events in the lives of two people who two days ago didn't know each other existed? It's impossible, really. All I knew is that I was with a charming young woman, who was also smart and brave and funny in gracious way. It was hard to believe my good fortune. Is this what love is supposed to be like? Does it just happen to arrive one day, no warning, no preparation, no announcement, no kidding? Yet here it was, suddenly upon us —and that was that. We had no complaints.

We walked along the bank of the north fork of the middle fork of the Willamette River, or some long name like that, having fun trying to say it five times very fast. We could only do it three times without slurring our words, laughing and joking about it, experiencing the joy and bountiful hope that is carried along on the wings of new beginnings. We stopped a few times on the river's edge, where the high brush was the color of golden brown, and where the evergreen trees served as a natural picture frame for the charming white rapids, rushing and rolling along. The electric sound of abundant life buzzed and hissed all around us, nature's pleasing symphony. At one point, we startled a bevy of quail, and I thought of my friends who like to hunt and cook them, all claiming they taste a lot like fried chicken. The air was as crisp as fried chicken, filling our lungs with the saccharine sweetness of a fine Oregon morning, and there was no finer morning to be in love.

When we got back to the Prince, Kim removed a soft blanket from the backseat and spread it upon the lush grass, beneath a large and vibrant hemlock tree, where a variety of birds claimed residence, not all of them happy to see us. She had packed a lunch of peanut butter and jelly sandwiches to bring along, plus chips and cold soft drinks. We ate and drank slowly, watching the crows and blue jays and sparrows—and others I couldn't identify—fly to and fro among the thick branches. Kim was afraid of dragonflies, and I had to defend her when two large ones whirred close by. We thought they might be associates of the huge bully crow that barked loud displeasure at our arrival, eventually calming down, realizing we meant it and its kingdom no harm. It soon ignored us, tending back to the business of bossing around any of the other birds it could. Another dragonfly zoomed close to us, and I told Kim how much I loved them because they're so beautiful. She said it was OK, as long as I loved her more. Wow, music to my ears. Oh, yeah, and I assured her of it.

"So how long do you plan to case out Canada, Cosmo?"

"You can call me Mr. Cosmo."

Kim laughed. It's always worth a laugh if done right. The timing and delivery are important. "The pregnant lady will concede to formality, Mr. Cosmo. Now, as for my question?"

"No set amount of time, I reckon. Still, we can't be gone too long. My folks will have the blue meanies looking for us."

"You should have told your parents you were leaving. Your mother is probably blue in the face with worry."

"By tomorrow she'll have your sweet envelope and know everything is fine."

"I hope you're right about that, Mr. Cosmo."

"Oh, I think it will settle her down. But you are right. It was a spontaneous decision, and it is the perfect excuse."

"Yeah, why is that?"

"My mom always told me that she likes spontaneous people the best, and she thinks they are the most interesting people to be around."

"Like when you spontaneously kissed me?"

"Only partly. I wanted to the moment I saw you."

"Oh, so you planned it?"

"I only kiss while drying dishes. So it came naturally. By the way, it would have helped me out later if you hadn't brought these paper plates."

"Well, maybe I can fix that. You can kiss me over paper plates—too!"

So I did, again and again, and thought it should be the name of a love song. She tasted liked peanut butter and jelly this time, but she never pushed me away. It had been the kind of morning and early afternoon that no lovers want to stop experiencing— not ever. We talked and laughed some more, kissing for another half hour. I was very careful to stay away from the subject of her lost husband, and she never cared to mention him. I sensed that we both wanted to think only of the future.

When we got into the car to leave, she held up a small mirror to my face, teasing me about how red my lips were from kissing so much. I didn't know that happened, but sure enough it did and looks very funny. Kim's were the same and we joked about it all the way home. Moreover, she only stalled the car twice.

Rick was still gone, and Kim complained of being a little tired. She asked if I'd mind if she took a nap. While she did, I walked the grounds of the trailer park and couldn't help but notice what I had first decided was true. Kim's trailer was the least fashionable here. I soon came upon a middle-aged couple trying hard to hang an American flag on their porch roof. The gentleman's wife was attempting to hold the ladder for him, but it was a cheaper brand of flimsy aluminum, and she was having trouble keeping it steady. I offered my help, of course, and my heartfelt and patriotic gesture was eagerly accepted. The Fourth of July weekend was approaching fast, and we found common ground in all things American, chatting for some minutes about them. Later I came upon a woman about 30, walking her dog. "Is that your cat, Miss? That's the ugliest cat I ever saw."

"It's a dog. It's not a cat. Is there something wrong with your eyesight?"

"Sorry, that line comes from a famous novel. I thought maybe you knew it."

"I don't read."

"Oh."

She moved on, muttering something about stupid kids. Stupid? The last time I heard I was cute, adorable, and an angel who dropped out of heaven. Some people are just scandalous and can't take a joke. Oh, well, I decided to cut my losses and go back. When I arrived at Kim's trailer the Prince and the Princess were parked next to each other. Rick had just gotten back and was still sitting in the car doing nothing.

"It looks like you are sitting there doing nothing, Romeo."

"Oh, man, I got into a fight with Bonnie."

"A lover's quarrel? So soon?"

"Man, those darn twins of hers. They wouldn't leave me alone. Every time I turned around one of them was tugging at my knees or trying to untie my damn shoelaces!"

"When they get older they tie them together."

"What?"

"Nothing. Sorry to hear of your troubles. Did you get the beds put together?"

"Yeah, that was the easy part. The hard part was trying to kiss Bonnie. Every time I went to try it one of the brats showed up again. I yelled at them and told them to go take a nap. Man, it didn't go over well. Bonnie got mad and kicked me out."

"Kids are overrated, eh?"

"Not around here, apparently. Did Kim learn how to drive?"

"Sure did, a real natural. She taught me a few things too."

"Yeah? I bet you tried to kiss her, didn't you?"

"She's married and pregnant, Rick. Are you crazy?"

"You're stupid, Rusty."

"You are not the first to say that this trip."

"When it comes to the ladies, you are just no good."

That night, our last night, Kim cooked us a delicious pot roast with mashed potatoes and French bread, courtesy of Irene. I suddenly had a new opinion of Irene. Then we watched a few hours of TV, but I watched Kim, mainly. She laughed at the stale jokes on a few sitcoms, and then we all watched Walter Cronkite deliver the nightly news. It was all bad and featured the daily body count of dead American soldiers. It always made me feel ashamed that I was ducking the war and heading to college. It also made me angry that we were still fighting this senseless crusade. When would the insanity end? When would my brothers and sisters come home and parade down Main Street, proud and safe? Not this Fourth of July or many more.

When Rick fell asleep, I knocked on Kim's bedroom door.

She cracked it open and smiled at me. Then she opened it wide and let me in. "You can't make love to me, Mr. Cosmo. But you can stay and hold me. I would like that."

I did. Again and again I refused to let her roll over so that her back was to me. She giggled each time and said that pregnant women like to turn over a lot. "It's sometimes hard to get comfortable," she explained.

A few hours later it was equally hard to go back to my cold sleeping bag. Luckily, I didn't dream this night, but they couldn't scare me now, anyhow. The only fright I had to worry about was Kim Warrens and what would become of her without Cosmo to guard her life. I felt like the angel who fell from heaven but very much wanted to fly back and take her with me.

We left after a late breakfast, noon closing in. Kim and I sat at the kitchen table and talked while Rick loaded our personal belongings into a washed, stunning black Camaro. He was being a gentleman and knew how and when to make himself scarce, in the name of love.

Kim was sad and nervous and funny, all at the same time. She asked me a series of rapid fire, sincere questions, as if she knew there was scant time to fit them all in. Where did I come from? Why did I care about a pregnant girl who could only be a burden to me? How could I make her fall in love with me in only two days? Was this all just a dream, and would I forget about her as soon as I left, never to come back? Finally, "I'm just so mixed up, Mr. Cosmo, there are so many questions and always something new to cry about." I was both troubled and tenderly amused. Hidden beneath her worry was a definite uplifting tone in her voice, during these uneasy minutes, when she was talking so fast and thinking beyond the next sentence. I could perceive her new self-confidence, and it betrayed her fretful anxiety. She really knew all the true answers anyway, and that is surely why she didn't give me time to react fully to any of them. Sometimes a woman just wants a man to listen. So I did, finally embracing her closely and promising to return soon.

A last hug and a goodbye, Kim refusing me a farewell kiss —at least on the lips. "No way, Rusty Anderson, not until I see you again! You see, my fine prince, if you don't come back then I'll have had the last laugh." This was a smart woman.

So it was at Kimberley Warrens' trailer.

[8]
THE RESTLESS OREGON TRAIL

This morning's drive was going to be lonely. It was now my turn to ask distressing questions about the true meaning of the miracle that just occurred, as both Kim and I saw it. What was supposed to happen now? Why didn't I stay at least one more day? What would be the best way to dispose of Wesley's body should he try to come back and reclaim her? I didn't spend a lot of time on that one, thank God. Except the next one really puzzled me—and a few more after it. What the hell was she doing with a loser like him, in the first place? How the heck was she going to be able to afford to take care of her new baby? If I don't come back to save her, will she divorce Wesley and then marry the first wife beater who comes along, if he can put food in the kid's mouth and decent clothes on all their backs?

So many questions and always something new to cry about. Isn't that what she said? Goodness, how many of life's questions will make us cry when we finally do get an answer? But love doesn't cry over silly questions about itself, does it? No. Love is just love and something we relinquish all of our collective logic to, trying to get out of its way at the same time. When we are successful, the result is often blissful tears of joy that we don't have to cry about. I suspect that we all have this funny notion that we control the heartstrings of love, but nothing can be further from the truth. Love does exactly what it wants to do and lets us have control of nothing. What else makes our lives purposeful?

I was still trying to unravel the riddle of love and all the crazy questions about it, when a grizzled stranger came to save the day and to distract my restless mind. One Jimmie James Jesse Jackson, and a fine man he proved to be when all was said and done. Of course, this conclusion occurred to me much later. At the moment, he scared the hell out of me.

"Come on, Rusty, pull over and pick him up."

"Didn't your mother tell you not to pick up hitchhikers?"

"Come on, pull over and give the poor guy a ride. He looks like he needs it."

So I did, despite the acute reluctance I had for the idea. This guy, to tell you the truth, didn't inspire immediate trust in me. He was shirtless, heavily tattooed, unshaven and dirty, and sporting dark sunglasses, so his eyes couldn't be seen. It's the eyes of people that tell a big part of the story about them, I've learned. Are they glassy? They are probably high on drugs. Crazed? Then pull away fast and keep driving. Lonesome? Sometimes they just need a hug and some friendly company. Bright-eyed and sociable? The ones who can generally be trusted not to murder you in your car. Homesick? They are often military people and usually the best passengers. In the end, the most telling look is the soulful look. It's the look people have that says they are of great experience in the fine art of living, and they have more to share with you than they have to take away. My mom has this same look about her. I think I mentioned it already. If not, she got it by growing up as a Great Depression Era child, forced to mature early. So it wasn't until one

Jimmy James Jesse Jackson approached Rick's window that I saw the same soulful look in his eyes, sunglasses politely removed. I was greatly relieved—but the subsequent conversation ruined it for me.

"Nice car. From California, eh? How far north are you two gents heading? I'm hoping for a ride to Seattle."

"We can take you to Seattle, mister," Rick said. "But we plan to move a little slower soon. It might be a day or so before you get there."

"If you are Seattle bound, then better late than never is something I can live with. Yes, sir. I can put my duffel bag in the trunk if it makes you feel better?" A sensitive question, one that comes from an experienced hitchhiker. Everyone knows that threats come from oversized bags and the nasty things that are reported to come out of them.

"You don't look like an axe murderer, mister. Just toss it in the back seat," Rick said. "If you turn into one while you're sitting there, just go for my blond friend's neck first, will ya?"

That made Jimmie James Jesse Jackson laugh a little, and he replied, "Be my pleasure."

Swell.

When the would-be axe murderer got in, perhaps 30 or so, I could clearly see the number of interesting tattoos that decorated his entire upper body, front and back. On his left forearm was a powerful purple dragon racing upward toward his shoulder, breathing out red-hot flames that exploded into bursting streams of immoral scarlet, covering his well-formed bicep, thick and muscular from years of lifting weights in prison. On his chest was a pretty lady, riding happily on a beer bottle that thundered rapidly skyward. She was holding a smaller beer bottle high in her left hand, in a sacred assertion that her charge in life was to fly to heaven and offer God a glass of beer. I bet he might take it too, on a hot day in heavenly Oregon. On his right forearm were the initials of his name, JJJJ, in large letters about three inches high, a swaggering and artistic tilt to them. Needled next to them was an eerie outline of a large gravestone that turned out to be a tribute to his father. On his back was just one massive tattoo, a beautifully stunning depiction of an American Bald Eagle in all its patriotic glory and perfect form: claws curled in wartime ready, fierce black eyes scanning for prey, its countenance one of determination and victory. I also noticed later that when Jimmy raised his arms the wings of this proud warrior spread full, taking flight, making for an impressive visual portrayal of this American champion on the fly, battle bred and invincible. It's an image we have all grown to love and admire as our own: a nation's symbol of fierce independence. I liked it very much. The eagle settled in, we were off. Then Jimmie James told us about Jesse Jackson, and vice versa, and much of it was of boundless interest.

"I hail from North Carolina originally, gents, but I've lived and worked in most all parts of this great land. Hell, when I wasn't much more than a kid, my daddy and I were roaming through these parts picking apples. But it's been a few years since I've been back, and it's nice to see it again. Yes, sir, it's nice to be free."

Jesse—he asked us to start calling him that—hadn't always been free. I forgot to tell you that burned into the very midst of his impressive tattoos was a grisly scar: a long swirling river of rotted flesh erupting from the center of his hard stomach, then rippling hideously upward to the apex of his left shoulder, the exit point of the large caliber bullet. This grim trophy was the result of getting shot while trying to rob a fur store. The furrier was faster on the draw than Jesse and more serious about it. For all his trouble, it only cost him a decade in San Quentin Prison, California's notorious castle by the bay.

In fact, he had just been released a week prior to meeting us and hoped that a future life in Seattle, with his sister and her four children, would be a good start and bright beginning to his new found freedom. He added humbly that he was clean of bad habits, a much more mature man now—and ready to have a real crack at life. That was that and I believed him. He wasn't an axe murderer at all, just an American man born at the wrong time. It was a dreadful time that saw his mother die giving birth to him and his one-armed father, often sickly, unable to care for him properly, thus dragging the both of them from state to state, looking for enough work to keep a roof over their heads. Jesse had high hopes for himself as long as his dad was around but then—bang! His dad suddenly died. He was 19, alone, confused, desperate, and soon involved with the wrong group of fellows. Before he knew what hit him, he was in the slammer, shot, near death, out of luck, out of options, and heading for three squares a day and probably the best accommodations he ever had. Welcome to America, Jimmie James Jesse Jackson. I never got tired of saying his name. His sad and soulful story of the American dream derailed held me spellbound and in marked sympathy for him. He even made me forget about Kim for a few hours, which only produced a further sense of overall melancholy in me. I was alarmed to realize that she had escaped my mind so quickly. I was in this type of glum mental state until we reached Tumwater, Washington, home of the legendary Olympia Brewing Company. We took the first exit in.

"So this is where you planned on slowing down the trip? Great, I bet I can get a free beer in here."

He did. We toured the brewery with a group of other people, maybe 12 or so. The company's slogan was "It's the Water," and we must have heard it repeated cheerfully 50 times or more by this group, all from the same family and spanning three generations. They got the biggest kick out of it. It was likely a common gag here and so dumb that it ended up being funny just because it was dumb. We always laughed with them when they said it, but only because they were having such dumb fun laughing at it first. We enjoyed their company, and they didn't seem to care if we looked rather like an odd threesome, very taciturn, and just interested in watching them and listening to our tour guide. Our silence wasn't really intentional. The three of us, taken individually, were moderately quiet.

Anyway, the real point is that the tour was much more fun and interesting than we ever imagined it might be. The only real downer in this 90 minute event was not being old enough to be served a free beer at the end of it. Still, Jesse got three, one of his own and two from a few of these same family members, the ones who didn't drink but gave him their vouchers. No one seemed to mind, so good for him.

Upon leaving the tour, the three of us wandered down an alluring dirt trail that ranged for a great distance in front and away from the brewery, leading to the narrow but lustrous Deschutes River. Its distinctive appeal featured a series of gentle rapids and sublime waterfalls, a cascading show of potent beauty that gushed and slowed and gushed again. Our eyes delighted in its grandeur, and I now saw the reason for the company's slogan. It was a darn good one. We would stop often to drink and refresh ourselves, struck by the loveliness of the thick but placid woods that framed the river, including all the other marvelous sights and sounds that nature was providing free of charge. Now and again one of us would jokingly call out—in honor of our friends—"It's the water!" Then we all laughed about nothing all over again. One time, Jesse spontaneously stripped bare; then using us as lookouts, he took a long shower in one of the smaller falls, even washing his clothes. He said it made him feel great to be baptized in such heavenly water, even if it was used to make beer, adding, "It only proves that God must enjoy a good beer, now and again, don't you think, gents?"

It was akin to a spiritual cleansing for him, so he bathed in some irony and good humor, and kept repeating that it was just fine that such a godly cleansing should come in the nick of time for his arrival in Seattle and a new life. It warmed my heart to listen to him, a man long plagued by bad luck but now full of soulful hope for the good things that a bright future might bring. He also spoke kindly about how lucky he was to have our company and help, not expecting either. What a sweet guy he turned out to be, and I couldn't picture him locked up in a prison cell. I stopped counting the number of times he thanked us for trusting him, a rough looking man who stood on the side of the freeway and watched despondently as hundreds of drivers passed him by. Then I thought about how Rick had insisted that I stop for him and how close I came to be counted among the others. We finally sat down in a cozy area by the river, Jesse behind a bush until his clothes dried, and watched the little darling pass us by, gently and sweetly. It was an enjoyable two hours of sharing more relaxed conversation and undisturbed laughs.

Soon after, the three of us slipped out of the park for a few minutes to secure a safe place for the Princess and gather our gear and some food. We then hopped the fence back in and made ourselves comfortable at a predetermined place. It was just far enough down river so that we weren't trespassing on the brewery. Nonetheless, we all felt the uneasy pang of guilt people experience when they are unsure if they are breaking the law or not. The entire area may have been off limits to overnighters. I didn't want to be rudely awakened again, as I had been in Cottage Gove. Still, the place was so magical and enchanting that the three of us decided it was worth the risk. In respect to this, we settled down to a purposely quiet evening of eating French bread, a fresh loaf we had purchased earlier in the day, plus hunks of tasty cheese and plenty of cold drinks. We looked forward to a safe and quiet night's rest. No one else was on this section of the river. It felt as if only we had been allowed special accommodations.

It was then that Jesse asked us to reveal a little bit more about ourselves. So we shared some of our personal plans we had mapped out so carefully. I was headed to college to study history and philosophy, and Rick was on his way to managerial training in his father's Mexican restaurant. Our otherwise mandatory military commitments had been eliminated, as you know. Anyway, Jesse showed great interest in all of this and asked many more good questions, and it was only fair that he should know as much about us as we did about him. Most of all, he was openly relieved to know that we weren't fleeing to Canada to avoid the draft. Just before falling off to sleep, Jesse told us more about his sister and their close bond. I was moved by his tender account and so was Rick.

We were up early the next morning, climbing over the fence before the brewery security guards arrived. In no time we were on our way to Seattle, Jesse cleaned and pressed. We had stopped in Tacoma to have the pressing done for him—and for us, as well. He wanted to make a good first impression on his sister and her children, and we were happy to help him do this. He would arrive at their house prim and proper and delivered in a new, killer-looking black Camaro. Jesse looked like a million bucks and acted like it. All in all, we were a rested and happy and excellent looking lot, men of real value, we thought. So did Jesse's sister, Jessica, who would later tell us so herself.

Jessica was born five years before Jesse but given up for adoption as a baby. It was a stroke of luck, all things being equal. She ended up in an immensely better environment, one immersed in ongoing positive support, and she was loved by a family that did all they could to assure her good future. She was college educated, gainfully employed as a successful real estate agent, and she had money in the bank. They were all good things, but what she never had was the chance to get to know her only real brother, although she knew of him. In a touch of fate and destiny, the officials at San Quentin located her soon after Jesse was first incarcerated, and she proceeded to send him letters, waiting patiently for him to return one. He finally did, and it was the formal beginning of their new relationship.

Jessica first eyed us from her enclosed porch, with pronounced curiosity, then recognized Jesse and bolted forth to greet him. She flew into his arms, embracing him in ecstatic joy, only releasing him momentarily to study his visage. Then she started hugging him again, jumping up and down and squealing his name in jubilant welcome. The tears poured down her cheeks while Jesse tried to calm her, himself overwhelmed by her show of loving affection. It was a festive moment, and Rick and I smiled from ear to ear. What was it that Roscoe had mentioned about the circle of life? When she finally composed herself from the shock of surprise and delight—the kind that only women can display at such a time—she shot a first peek at us. When she looked me directly and probingly in the eyes to examine my soul, I saw hers. It said all would be well for us here.

The introductions were brief but suitable. We could ask for last names again, later. For now, we were ushered into her home to meet her kids, three girls nine to 13, all lanky but pretty enough, and a boy, seven. They were all very polite and quiet while we fielded many questions from their mother, including why Jesse decided to startle her with an impromptu arrival. I imagined the true, underlying reason was that he didn't want to give her a chance to change her mind and deny him a new, promised home. Such things are the backdoor approach to good reasoning, of course, and can happen to people in Jesse's situation, when they feel inferior and suddenly unsure of the world around them. He had badly misjudged his sister.

Jessica had only met him face-to-face two other times, long ago, during the second and sixth year of his imprisonment, but she was fond of his weekly letters and occasional photo, which he sent her when he could. He had been shy and ashamed, discouraging her from visiting. He couldn't bear to have her look at him, viewing his broken life and dire prison surroundings, and it was worse with her husband. Nevertheless, she had obviously studied his face closely from the photos, and she had little doubt that this was her true brother, despite seeing him only three times in 29 long years, including today. Jesse was really 29, one year under the age of official axe murderers.

We had every intention of staying for only an hour and then be on our way. However, Jessica offered us 10 dollars each, plus free eats and a secure roof to sleep under, if we would help Jesse pull a troublesome tree stump from her backyard. The big thing was sitting, in all its rooted glory, on the site of her new addition to the house. She warned us it might take all day, then smiled hopefully and asked, "Would you two consider it?"

It really was a good tradeoff, we both decided, even if it did delay us for a day. We could use the money, of course, and then there was the free eating and comfortable sleeping, but mainly we accepted because it's impossible to refuse to help a kind woman in need, especially if we could. Whatever secondary benefits came from doing so were just a bonus.

It did take all day, seven hours, and it was a grueling job. The stump was wide and its thick roots extended like spider's legs in an uneven pattern all about it. The resulting sounds of mad shoveling and grinding, mixed with the human outcries of grunting and heaving, were the order of the day. Charmed, I'm sure. I've never been so glad to see something finally come loose from the ground.

We then spread out on our backs, relieved and laughing, joking about how Jesse had received such a brutal welcome on his first day in the great city of Seattle. We would need a hearty dinner and hot showers just to repair the damage we did to our bodies. All three of us had significant scratches on our hands and forearms, highlighted by a few swollen red welts. Our injuries came from tugging on the thick tree roots, each one determined not to give way. When they did break loose they came at us like slashing, cruel whips, oozing a cream-colored sap, a milky latex that was sickly looking and had an awful smell. I could only guess that it was a failed rubber tree experiment, but I wasn't sure and didn't even bother to ask. Our knees were also swollen and sore from the hours of kneeling in the moist dirt, where small, sharp rocks lived, digging deep into our flesh, making life generally miserable. About halfway done is when it occurred to me that I would have preferred to unload a furniture truck. I thought of Roscoe and his lessons and life on the road.

All of that wasn't meant as a complaint, just a somewhat detailed account of our troubles. By the time our heads hit the pillows that night, we had forgotten about them, mostly. Rick and I concluded that the probable outcome of Jesse's new living arrangement, for all concerned, was positive. Jesse was comfortable around the children, the oldest girl being the most talkative, and they, in turn, seemed to warm to him nicely.

Jessica expressed high praise for us, saying that she was very impressed with our willingness to work hard, and she would pack a hearty lunch and dinner snacks for our next day's journey. So, altogether, it did turn out to be a good tradeoff, and we were happy we stayed and showed our true grit with Jesse. In case you're wondering, the stump was buried too low to get a chain around it and thus pull it out by truck or car. We didn't have the former and the latter was no job for a princess.

At dinner, a funny and emotional bonding experience happened between Jessica's boy and his Uncle Jesse. The boy, Robert, a good name, kept squeezing the dragon's head inked on Jesse's forearm. This caused the red-hot flames to expand wildly and then contract and expand again, a thing of great admiration and excitement to him, and he just knew he had found his hero.

As we lounged in our sleeping bags that night, on Jessica's living room floor, I first thought of Rick. It had been an altogether backbreaking trip for him. He broke it moving furniture, broke both it and his wallet fixing a car, and then a hot sweat broke out all over him about Bonnie. When his luck went broke with her, he capped it all by getting broken up and bruised by a charming and wonderful woman's mad tree stump. He had suffered greatly.

Jesse was asleep in a daybed, about 10 feet away. The living room would be his sleeping quarters until the addition was built, his new bedroom. He was turned toward the wall so that his uncovered back was exposed, sleeping blissfully for perhaps the first time in many years, and he had proven his worth to his sister today. Tomorrow, and for many years in the future, he would get up early and try to do it again. The eagle had landed. I just knew it.

Jessica needed an eagle in her life. Behind her soulful eyes was a sometimes-shattered spirit. She had lost her young husband in a tragic automobile accident just two years ago. She had loved him deeply. The girls were lost without their father to do what fathers do for young daughters: fix and build things, mend and console them when they are hurt, stick up for them when they are in trouble, and—most of all—keep them warm, dry, safe, and loved, in a secure home with a secure future.

Precious Robert, the funny boy with a Tom Sawyer grin

and an immediate love for his uncle, also needed the influence of a positive man in his life. It was easy to tell by watching him hang all over Jesse's arm at dinner, giving him little peace afterward and asking all manner of questions, especially about sports and baseball and, "Who do you think will win the pennants and the World Series this season, Uncle Jesse?" It appeared to be love at first sight between the two of them.

As I finally began to drift off into my own restful slumber, I spotted a sailboat next to me, part of the thick carpet's design. It was a small vessel, manned by a young couple smiling at each other, obviously happy and in love, sailing to uncharted parts of their own paradise. My last thoughts before falling asleep were of Kimberly Warrens, and if her dreams would take her sailing tonight, and would the lucky sailor standing next to her be me? Then the smell of vanilla and the taste of peanut butter and jelly came to mind, and I was hypnotized to sleep.

The next morning was bright and sunny, and I crawled out of my bag and got dressed before anyone else was up. I was loading a few things into the trunk of the car when I noticed little Robert staring at me through an upstairs window. I waved at him but he didn't wave back. He only smiled and stuck the index finger of one hand into his mouth. It was a little boy's delightful way of saying hello and good enough for me.

Our last hour with Jesse and the family was spent enjoying a hearty breakfast of pancakes and eggs, and thick slices of ham and bacon, all of it swallowed with ice cold milk. It was fun and cheerful and a good send off. Saying farewell at the car, all of them gave us a big hug goodbye and welcomed us to come back when we returned from Canada. Two fingers in his mouth, little Robert whistled loudly at the Princess as we drove away, and I was elatedly surprised that he could do such a thing. I can whistle some but it's not my best skill. So little Robert had one on me, eh? Admittedly, while I was enchanted by it, I was also a little jealous.

They all watched us intently until we were out of sight, waving and shouting good luck, with the girls blowing kisses the whole time. God, I loved them. "Good luck Jesse and new family." The eagle had definitely landed.

[9]
CHILDREN OF A COMMON MOTHER
(OR TROUBLE AT THE BORDER)

Upon leaving the marvelous metropolis of Seattle—a city we didn't really see—but where it is always clean from the always rain, we learned, we soon spied upon Blaine, Washington. But first just another word about our departure from Seattle because it played a significant role in some other decisions we made later. When leaving Jessica's house we took a different route out than the one we took in, so we got a little confused by the direction we were heading. This mistake led to a few wrong turns and unnecessary detours onto unknown roads. After doing the same a few more times, including a "whoops!" encounter with a one-way street, we finally reached the Pacific Highway, or Interstate 5, heading for international stardom, as we figured it. Though we were laughing and joking and feeling all right, a bigger mistake had gone unnoticed. We would soon be enlightened.

For the moment, none of our happy banter outdid the cheerful charm that is Blaine. It was an old, small, sleepy seaport town, population 1,900, with all souls aboard, and all of them anchored by peaceful mountains to the east, pristine flatlands all around, and the incredible Canadian Cascades directly north. Last, but hardly least, the beautiful and pristine water of the Semiahmoo Bay was to the left, Pacific bound. A pretty place, in short.

Blaine is also the last town on the American-Canadian border. We had finally arrived at our moment of truth, hundreds of miles away from our dubious and headstrong beginnings: "Last round and last call, gents." We could turn back now and remain untraveled, unlearned, and uncultured dolts or press ahead into the land of the unknown, the unseen, the unexpected, the unimaginable beauty of picturesque British Colombia, Canada.

Oddly, the decision for me had been made long ago in the dark driveway of my home, when and where a girl I had been dating asked me, "Rusty, what exciting thing are you going to do this summer?" This happened about two weeks before I graduated from high school and too dumbstruck to find a quick and safe answer to such a daring challenge, I decided to invent one, on the spot—without much forethought—but with great self-confidence.

"I'm going to visit Canada, darling, and see what all the fuss is about!" That was my spontaneous idea—thanks be to my mother. So that's what I told her. And, as you know, it all happened well enough. Naturally, she was impressed and that's what I had been aiming at. What other boy could boast of such bravery and daring? In fact, she was so impressed that she let me unbutton her blouse, and it was the first time I had ever done such a thing. I later repented but still regretted ever telling the story to Mr. Ruiz, the moon boy of Oregon beaches.

I dropped Rick off at a small market to shop for a few odds and ends we needed, finding a place to park nearby, under a shady elm tree on a happy street. I got out and took a good stretch, enjoying the calm and peace of a sunny day in this appealing small town, its multitude of flowers, trees, green grass, and nice people sprouting everywhere.

Rick soon returned, loading groceries into the truck. I was amused by how tidy he was: The cooler loaded with ice and drinks was placed in the middle; the vegetables were stacked nicely to the left, and the fruit was carefully arranged to the right. The bread, triple bagged, was placed in the far back to keep it fresh, no room in the cooler. While I watched this intrigue go down, he suddenly started to talk about the events of the past nine days and how peculiar they were to him. He said he didn't know what to make of them all. How could a three-day trip to the border result in a nine-day odyssey, instead? A fair question and one that deserved a fair answer, so he asked me again. "Who would have thunk it, Cosmo? I figured three days max, after a day at Wesley's. Didn't count on any of this happening. What about you?"

If my girlfriend would have asked me the same question in the quiet dark, I would have nibbled on her little ear and whispered how reasonable it all sounded. "It was stuff made for international heroes and surely created from the providence of young, fearless adventure," I would have likely said. But Rick wasn't her, and his ear didn't appeal to me, so I took the more conventional route. "I don't know if I would give up any of it, macho man," I finally replied. I sometimes called him that. "The only thing I would change is that I wouldn't have waited until the fifth day to write my mom. Still, it could have been worse."

"So, Cosmo, what really happened with Kim? Tell me all of it. You've got that love look in your eyes, gringo, and you've been a little on the quiet side for a few days now."

"Oh, is that all you really want to know? Why didn't you ask before?"

"It front of Jesse or maybe his sister? Yeah, it might have thrilled Jessica to have you describe the steamy affairs of your love life in front of her children."

"Yeah, I see your point. That might have been awkward."

"Well?"

So I explained everything that happened as best I could, and he didn't laugh or cry. He didn't even mention my decision to fall in love with his otherwise best, old-time buddy's wife. The scandal in the kingdom and all, you understand. He genuinely liked Kim, and I think he liked the idea of her landing a romantic, ambitious, and loyal schmuck like me. At least that's what he said later, and he added so many other adjectives that I lost count, but I was glad to hear them, mostly. He asked one last question before we moved on.

"What tasted better?"

"What do you mean?"

"About kissing her, butt brain! What else?"

"Oh, yeah. Well, I think I liked the peanut butter and jelly flavor the best, but I'm not going to quibble over small details." I admitted to feeling a little lightheaded just thinking about it all.

"Yeah, I can see that in your face, Cosmo. You look a little lightheaded. I better drive from here.'

It was a dismal mistake but only the first of three in rapid succession. "OK, but be nice to the border guards. Pronounce every word slowly and clearly. I want them to hear that you aren't really a Mexican, but you just look like one." I couldn't resist taking the jab at him.

"All of this from a white boy who speaks only one language?"

"It's the language they speak, knucklehead. When in Rome, do as the Romans do."

"Rome is in Canada?"

"Shut up, Ruiz. And try not to be so clever with these guys."

It was too late. I had set his clever wheels in motion, and now they were about to run over both of us, with the Royal Canadian Mounted Police driving. Speaking of them, I presently gazed upon one, surprised to see him manning the crossing booth. I was immediately mindful of the beloved legends about them, and I probably shouldn't have been so startled to see him. These were the days when thousands of young American men were fleeing to Canada to avoid the draft, and Mounties sometimes filled in to help filter the traffic. It was one of those times.

"Good day, sir," he said to Rick. "What is your business in Canada today?"

A sensitive question, at most borders, and one if not answered skillfully is equal to turning on the stupid faucet: dumb quickly rushes out and drowns you, without mercy. Big mouth Rick proved the point—perfectly.

"My business is *SHOW BUSINESS!* Mr. Mountie, and I'm *SHOW* glad to finally be in *CANADIER!* What ya think about that?"

What an astonishingly moronic thing to say to any border guard, let alone an honest, fearsome, incorruptible, gentle champion like a Royal Canadian Mounted Policeman. The trap had been set. The cavalier remark didn't make our humorless Mountie laugh or grin. He didn't even break into a slight smile. In fact, his stern face grew sterner, and I could see the scarlet begin to rush into his cheeks. Then he asked to see Rick's driver's license and vehicle registration, sharply, in a scarlet-rush-of-the-cheeks sort of way. This was already looking grave.

Before Rick could finish explaining that the Princess really belonged to me, the annoyed Mountie was already shaking his head, hard pressed to read Rick's water ruined, indecipherable paper license and was now asking to see mine. I first handed him my registration papers fetched from the glove box. All manner of miscellaneous junk fell out when I opened it, hitting the floor and embarrassing me. I then reached for my wallet in the back of my pants. It wasn't there. "What the hell! Darn it! Oh, man! I can't believe this!" My show of exasperation was not intentional and only caused further suspicion.

Some of my friends have told me about the panic attacks their mothers sometimes get—I think you might remember me saying so—and how they usually get worse before they get better. I was experiencing the same thing or something close to it. You know, that burning in the brain one gets when first realizing that something terrible has happened. Of course, it wasn't the end of the world. It just felt like it.

"You said you've lost your driver's license, sir?"

"It seems I've lost my entire wallet, officer," I said, as regrettably as I could, still somewhat discombobulated. Isn't *discombobulated* a great word? It's less of a great thing to be, but I think it's a pretty great word. Still, the Mountie wasn't at all concerned about that, proving it by moving on quickly.

"I see," he said, smartly. "Then if you two really want to enter Canada pull through the lane and park on the left-hand side of that parking lot, over there. Do you see it?" He had stepped out of the booth and was pointing with a stiff left arm in the direction of a large, window-filled building. The lot next to it was lined with new police and immigration cars, most backed in to make a hurried exit easy. In fact, I noticed that most everything looked new. It was exactly how I might have expected our proud neighbors to behave, putting only their best face forward to greet strangers and friends and sometimes young American morons. "Someone will be with you in a few minutes," he snapped. "Move ahead."

We did and someone was. It took him three minutes, to be

exact. This someone was a youthful Mountie in his mid-20s—
he appeared to be—and still young enough to be able to relate
to us in a common language, as did the friendly policeman in
Cottage Grove. He had thick, neatly cropped red hair and a
ruddy complexion, and glasses that kept sliding down his nose
as he bent over to speak to us. "I understand you two want to
enter Canada but neither of you have proper identification. Is
that right, gentlemen?" He was as polite as the first Mountie,
yet without the stern countenance, just an inquisitive smile and
a direct demeanor. I liked him right away.

We agreed that everyone in the last 10 minutes agreed with
his basic analysis of things, in our most respectful American
way. In addition, being good patriots, we also explained the
extenuating circumstances of our international crimes: Rick
hadn't meant to go swimming with his wallet still in his pocket,
and I hadn't meant to leave my freshly cleaned one in Seattle. I
only cleaned it because during the long hours of our struggle
with the stump, I had forgotten it was still in my pants and
loose dirt had grimed it. I had already figured that a family
member or Jesse must have discovered it by now, all of them
surely distraught for my mistake, wishing that no harm might
come to me by it. It was my resolve to call them, but the idea
was of no profit, their phone number and address in my wallet.
I thought of returning to their house to fetch it, but I wasn't
exactly sure if I could find it again without the address. What a
mess. The young Mountie listened to us politely for some
minutes, and when we were finally finished, he just said,
"Please, step inside."

Within 30 minutes the mess was made worse. A call to our
hometown police department turned me up as "missing" and
the Princess as possibly stolen. This report was only a day old,
and it showed that my mom waited four full days before having

me listed as gone astray or lost or mislaid, however the Pink Wall may have put it. Rick wasn't even mentioned in the same report, at all. Apparently, Carmen followed his instructions, and his parents surely assumed their young stallion was whooping it up in Disneyland and spending way too much time and money. The latter of which he now had very little.

This news caused me much consternation, of course. Boy, did I look rather bad in the eyes of the law, my foreign hosts, whose worldwide reputation—when just saying their name— "Royal Canadian Mounted Police" puts them far above the standard of any counterparts in global jurisdictions. Swell. Shame encased me, and my excuses for my wayward human existence scored few points with them. Instead, they just wanted the facts, and they wanted all of them, or as many as they could get out of me in the peak business hours of the day. I kept expecting to be asked, "Just how bad are you two, really?"

Luckily, no one did, and no one forced either of us to call our parents. Still, they assured us that the news of our safe arrival in Canada would be relayed back home and in short order. A call would be made to our town's police department, with the guarantee that they, in turn, would place one to our parents, thus completing two-thirds of the optimum circle of good communication. Fine. I would let the men in blue tell them I was OK and let the information in my letter stand on its own, not received by my mom until two days after I was reported missing. Rationalizing it, I took solace in the thought that she never wanted me to be a momma's boy. She often said she despised sissy men and found them a waste of God's talent.

Just the same, my decision not to call them myself weighed me down, but I further reasoned myself out of it, sort of. I used the backdoor process, the one I thought may have afflicted Jesse, but soon realized that we humans decide—sometimes for better or worse—to just leave all good reason out of it, front and back doors closed and locked, and just try to find another pathway into, "The House of Good Intentions Gone Bad." If I couldn't clearly understand why I was doing the things I was doing, and making the decisions I was making, why then should I always be expected to use good reason in the first place—about anything? No joke, isn't it highly unreasonable to expect people to act within their own good reason about everything they say or do, all the time? No. There will be costly mistakes. Nonetheless, it seemed to me that I had won the battle of the mind, decisively and fairly, but then, just as quickly, the battle would turn against me, and everything I had done—or will do—now sounded very ill-conceived. These nagging, guilty thoughts are what consumed me for nearly three straight hours. I had managed to perplex myself to no good end, and it was a joyless ride.

"I can write another letter!" The idea had an immediate soothing impact. "Right now, right here." It will be received by my mom in a stylish, brave and forthright RCMP envelope, and the excuses flooding out of it, those ordinary, watered-down excuses, tasteless and unpleasantly swallowed, will miraculously change into barrels of righteous fine wine, right before my mom's eyes. Wow! Jesus had little on me. It will be a miracle. She will know that I am being watched over by real men, suddenly growing solemn and breathless just thinking about it. "He's in the best of care now, and everything will be all right with my boy!"

OK, I suppose I should be honest with you. I was just too much of a coward to make the call. A thoughtless schmuck. Still, I found enough courage in my schmuck-ness to approach the only female version of the rugged, dashing men in red serge, presently on duty. To be more accurate, she was an immigration employee and not a Mountie, women yet to fill their ranks in these days. She was dressed in a gray, tight fitting shirt, and a dark blue skirt hugged her slim waist perfectly. Beyond very young and eye-catching—I guessed her to be about 25—she possessed the prettiest and whitest teeth of anyone I had ever seen in my life. They were a main attraction on a long list of main attractions, which included shoulder length brown hair, straight and thick, and dancing softly around her neck when she spoke or moved her head. Her eyes were big and brown and serious, but kind and intelligent, and her face was clear-skinned and radiant, with full cheeks and refined lips. She also possessed long, polished fingernails, bright red and striking, the kind my mom and sisters would kill for. It was hard not to notice everything about her. I compared her to Kim and thought she was almost as pretty, easily passing for her older sister. She was busy typing and didn't bother to turn her head to greet me, but her kind voice betrayed her momentary impoliteness. "How may I help you, sir?"

I explained my goal to her, briefly, and within seconds the issue was settled, the necessary tools awarded me, the problem solved—and found out. She was not only pretty but very perceptive. I now lacked but one thing, a stamp to mail my appeal to the motherly court. I soon found one in a convenient vending machine, under a sign that read, "Please Don't Shake the Machines." I felt embarrassingly homesick because of how American that sounded. I then figured it to be a worldwide problem and felt better for us about it, but only for being as equally bad shakers as other people must be, not better. A sign right next to it read, "Drive Safely in British Columbia." It was what we had planned to do, if we ever got to see it.

Anyway, what I didn't know at that moment was that our problems were getting more complicated. A call had been made to the U.S. Selective Service System to check on our draft status, and it was going to take a few hours to receive a return call clearing us. We hadn't anticipated this. There was a war going on and nobody got a free pass.

What I did know was that standing upright on the wall facing west, so one could look out and watch all the cars steaming back into the United States, was an old, tall, and handsome oak bookcase. I love books. I really do. I read them so fast that my dad often warns me, "Don't bolt through your reading so excitedly, son. You'll miss the real essence of the story and how it is to be understood." I had no reason to mistrust my dad but kept reading fast anyway.

The larger point is that this bookcase was stuffed with treasures. It contained a 15-volume narrative of the history of the Royal Canadian Mounted Police and several books about a fictional character, one "Renfrew of the Royal Mounted," a boy's adventure series. The writing was quite good in both. Still, as interesting and informative as the history books were, it was Renfrew who captured my real attention. He was always doing something heroic—and never another man did I want to be. Titles and stories such as, "Renfrew Rides the Sky," "Renfrew Rides the Range," "Renfrew in the Valley of the Vanished Men," "Renfrew Flies Again!" all sounded thrilling and highly desirable to emulate. I thought right then that I might become a Canadian citizen, quickly join the Mounties and escape with Sergeant Renfrew into the wild of the Great White North. In no time I'd emerge a hero and be enshrined in a bookcase just like this one, right next to my mentor, so that young Americans like me can read about me and men like me, hoping they might do the same one day. Shamefully, it struck me as a little funny that I thought this way, knowing I didn't even have enough courage to call home.

I found a seat to write my heroic dispatch, the magnanimous Renfrew still burning fresh in my mind. It was a letter desk with a wide fold-down top, which was convenient and similar to the kind used in my high school. There were lessons to be learned in this building. Also, there was a post office drop box just inside the front door, another expedient perk for me.

In the end, I had been rather matter-of-fact with my mom, knowing for certain that she would have me cut directly to the chase. I explained what had occurred during the past nine days, how and why we managed to get ourselves into our present predicament at the border and what the near future held, I hoped, which was that I'd be back home in a matter of days. I closed with my sincere regret for causing her any grievous and unnecessary worry. I wanted her to trust that everything would be OK, and we planned to take every possible precaution and return safely: better, wiser, more experienced and worldly men. I would then, on bended knee, beg forgiveness for my rash, spontaneous departure, crying, "For the battle was ours, Mom, and victory was at hand!'" I hoped my final sentence would make her laugh, serving as a rallying cry to stop her from worrying.

Finished, I returned to Renfrew's wall, where the bookcase stood. I pondered, with some regret, all the cars streaming back into America. Had it all been a big mistake? Maybe it was the only question that needed to be asked. To no avail, before it could receive a proper answer, I was suddenly interrupted by Rick. He had been allowed to rest in the Princess during this time of uncertainty, minus the keys, of course.

"What are you looking at, Cosmo?" He was rubbing his eyes, overtired from his ordeals with furniture, diarrhea, a broken car, a nasty tree stump, little hellions, getting tossed on his ear, and now—in a very near moment—the nightmare of being a suspected car thief, possible murderer and kidnapper, potential draft dodger, and worse, just an innocent kid: an innocent Mexican-American kid, too naive and inexperienced to know any better. This was the worst kind according to Mountie Erskine, who had just stepped inside the building to surprise us with this new, updated, international news.

"You are free to move on, Mr. Anderson, if you wish. In this envelope is a temporary identification card, one issued by us for your convenience. There is also a copy of a certified criminal records check from your country, and I'm including a letter that Ms. Harris (the pretty secretary) is typing up now. It says you have been cleared for entry into Canada, but you are to return back here, promptly, in three days. We don't want you to run out of money and then have all kinds of bad things potentially happen. I believe that good neighbors should live in peace."

Sure enough, I believed that he believed it. Except the entire speech had an unreasonable quality about it. It appeared that Mountie Erskine struggled with the same problem that plagued me.

"Mr. Ruiz, we will be forced to inconvenience you for the present time."

"Why is that, sir?"

"There seems to be an immigration question, a slight confusion about your name. Apparently, there is another Rick Ruiz in your country's criminal database, and he's wanted for a number of felonies, including attempted murder, kidnapping, and carjacking. He fits your general description."

"The hell you say?" Rick responded in great, marked disbelief.

"Yes, but it is worse than that. He's also listed as an illegal immigrant from Mexico and has spent jail time in your country, twice already. He's reported to be armed and dangerous, and we would like very much to make sure you are not him. If you are, then just say so and we can quickly have the matter in progress and under control."

By God, he wasn't kidding. Mountie Erskine had been looking at Rick in a very guarded fashion, eyes locked on him, steady, unnerved, as in, "the Mountie who always gets his man" movies. It was more than a little disconcerting. Then, promptly, three more Mounties entered the building and quickly hovered around us, almost choking off the air. We were rattled by it all, of course. Mountie Erskine went on to describe the other Mr. Ruiz to all of them, so we got to hear it twice, and with each repeated allegation the noose got tighter around the neck of *my* Mr. Ruiz, who was suddenly very frightened.

So illegal immigration was worse than attempted murder, kidnapping, and carjacking? It sounded very much like a backdoor reasoning process to me, and it felt ugly to have these square-jawed, fearsome men, dressed in golden-yellow stripes and crowned by their gilded reputation, lose some of their sizable luster. I was no longer sure if I wanted to stay and become one. I guessed that Mountie Erskine (Sergeant Erskine) hadn't really intended to elevate any one of the alleged crimes above the others—except maybe the "attempted murder" part getting top billing. I was just overreacting, glad to think it for him. The idea of racial discrimination had been on my mind since our lazy afternoon on the beach in Oregon. Rick had mentioned his uneasiness an additional time, but I brushed it off as nonsense. Now here we were, and his worries were suddenly relevant, if not directly applicable to him, personally.

Abruptly, Rick was led to a confined room, escorted without restraints, not counting the three other Mounties who towered over and about him, Sergeant Erskine leading the charge. Can the color of one's skin, an inconvenient name, an inability to be properly identified, possible draft-dodging, suspicions of attempted murder, kidnapping and car theft, plus a friendly, albeit careless remark made to a border guard, get a person into this much trouble? How could we have come so far, so unknowingly, so unprepared, so unsuspecting of any such unreasonableness befalling us?

~~~

PART 2

The room Rick was led to had a glass front that extended from floor to ceiling, and it was used for official business, not to question foreign criminals or potential enemies of the state. Ironically, it had all the trappings of the most comfortable room here. There was a sparkling water cooler in the far corner, two more vending machines right next to it, a color television set, another handsome oak bookcase, and plush rugs softened the highly polished floor. All of this splendor was commanded by extravagant paintings of beautiful British Columbia gracing the four walls, each one dressed in an expensive frame. Furthermore, a long conference table, holding court prominently in the center, was equipped with a dozen lavish, high-backed leather chairs. I envisioned Henry Fonda standing at the head of it, starring in the movie *12 Angry Men,* and pleading with his fellow jurors not to condemn Rick and have him hanged straightaway. Rick sat in the first chair on the left side of the table, head down, in deep contemplation of Henry's appeal for his life, no doubt, agreeing that it was all just a big, unfortunate mistake, and if the panel of critics didn't mind too much, "I'll just be making my way now, adios!"

Finally, before barging in to console him, I thought of the comment and question he had for me earlier in the day, "Didn't count on any of this happening, what about you?" I'm sure my answer would have been different now, but I never got the chance to convey it.

"I'll have to ask you to remain outside, sir," the younger

Mountie said, the one who had first greeted us in the parking lot and whom I liked so much. "You will have a chance to speak to Mr. Ruiz, soon. Please, if you don't mind, sir?"

I just looked at Rick, giving him two thumbs up and my best James Dean nod of the head, which meant that everything would be all right. The notorious Mr. Ruiz may have been isolated and put in semicaptivity, but no one was being cruel or harshly interrogating him, nothing of the sort. It was just a place for Mounties to put people when they wanted to know where they were. In fact, all the other Mounties had recently gone home, including Sergeant Erskine, and I had not, at first, noticed the youngest hero. He had been sitting in a chair at the far end of the table, opposite Rick, with his own head down, reading a thick book. Perhaps Sergeant Renfrew had also gotten to him.

"Yes, sir," I replied. "I understand." It wasn't the truth but seemed like the best thing to say. I gave Rick one last affirmative look, adding a peace sign with two fingers and another thumbs up. His face looked like a basset hound's face, ears sagging and cycs droopy, his countenance one of sheer confusion and fright. My heart bled for him. Of course, he was completely innocent of any dastardly deeds the other Mr. Ruiz was linked to—but just to be suspected and detained because of them was a horrific experience. I had badly underestimated how really worried he was.

The scary ordeal turned out not to be as bad as we first thought. The good sergeant, and his trusted colleagues, guessed all along that Rick wasn't their "always get our man" man. He was only being detained long enough for them to be sure, in plush comfort, no less. What neither of us realized is that their actions were a subtle attempt to reveal this to him. There was another option available, a rather stark interrogation room, a bleak holding cell at the north end of the building. Comfort or misery, I didn't know what to say to him. What do you say to someone in this situation? Well, I'm here to tell you that I did the best I could—but in a minute.

Being a free man, able to roam this part of Canada without restraints, I stepped outside to check on another good friend. I can't remember how many times I might have already said, but I earned every penny to buy the Princess by the sweat of my own brow. It's not something I share to sound uppity or self-important. It's just a fact that speaks to the life lessons that my folks tried to instill into all their children. Anyway, when most of my friends were busy having fun during summer vacation, I would go to work on a farm in Northern California. I was always something of a hard worker and ambitious, and I came to trust and enjoy the company of the mostly Mexican field hands who worked around me. They were the kindest and most humble people I had ever met. I was only 13 when I started and the youngest tomato picker there. I was also an oddity, especially at first. None of these tough but caring men knew what to make of me, one so white and so young. Of the two dozen or so field hands I labored with, there were only two other Caucasian men. One was very quiet and gentle but the other harsh and bitterly suspicious. "You can't trust these damn Mexicans, kid, watch your stacks of tomatoes. They'll steal you blind!" It was his favorite thing to say.

Such accusations were pure hyperbole. Nobody ever tried to steal from me. Still, he gave me my first real lesson in racism, just for the sake of showing me that he could. Maybe he was envious, like me, because most of these men could fill twice the number of boxes we could in a normal workday. This very fact made me a better worker. I made it a goal of mine to try to match them. By the start of my third summer, when I was 16 and much stronger and faster, I did match them, box for box. Sometimes I would exceed them and my good amigo, Jose, a cheerful man in his late 30s, would shout out, "Goddamn you, gringo. One day you're going to make a fine Mexican!"

I had also worked at a gas station for part of my senior year, after school, and toward the end of this time I had earned and saved enough money from both jobs to buy her. So that's what I did. I walked into a Chevy dealership a few weeks shy of 18, quickly found the Princess, sitting majestically on the showroom floor, and just as quickly told the first salesman I saw, "I'll take her!"

"Sure, kid, I'll take one too," he laughed. "Listen, this is Saturday and we are very busy. Come back in a few years and we'll see what we can do. Have a nice day, kid. Talk to you later."

He did, very soon later. Because, of course, I couldn't have been more serious. I had $3,000 in cash on me, and I wanted to purchase a 1968 Camaro, a car I had read about and longed to own. Well, to make a long story short, I brought my father back to run interference for me, and we rapidly closed the deal. The last thing the salesman—the same salesman—said to me was, "I'll be a son of a bitch, kid. You sure surprised the hell out of me!" Surprises aside, within a matter of four hours, from first visit to last, a brand new black Camaro graced the street in front of my house. By the end of the day at least a half dozen of my high school friends stopped to ask me about her. They were gushing with envy. I let them.

That's pretty much the whole story, and if I've already mentioned it, then it's only out of forgetfulness that I do so again. It was a very thrilling day for me, one that came after three long and hot summers of working very hard. It was my mom who summed it up best when speaking about it to one of her friends, "If a boy has a fortune, I can't think of a better thing to do than spend it on a princess."

What does one say to someone in Rick's situation? By the second time I asked myself this question, I knew. I got my inspiration from the signs I saw earlier. So after a proper, "Hello, your Most Excellent Majesty" and bow to the Princess, I got into the passenger seat armed with sheets of blank typing paper and a black-tip felt pen. All of them were acquired from the alluring secretary, who didn't guess the reason this time. I proceeded to print a number of appropriate signs for this special occasion. At the moment, it was my only way to communicate with Rick. They read in the largest and darkest lettering I could draw, "Murderer!" "Kidnapper!" "Car thief!" "Draft dodger!" and "Mexican!"

When I re-entered the building, I coolly sauntered over to where he sat, careful to stand in a place where I would not be seen by the young Mountie, and held the signs to the glass, one at a time, so that Rick could read them. He broke into an immediate grin that warmed my heart to see. I further saw a new flash of life in him, identical to the one on the day we began this trip. It wasn't at all the face of a basset hound. Hooray! I held the signs up again, longer this time, pointing wildly at them to emphasize the point. He grinned wider still, and I thought his pretty smile good enough for show business. Absolutely, he just might make it in show business one day, perhaps right here in *CANADIER*. It could happen.

In the meantime, we waited to see what might happen first. A new shift had come to work, and by the way they treated us, I could tell that they had been well-informed. I was sorry to see Ms. Harris go home, as long as she was here it was a little softer place. Because she was a woman—and I think God's greatest idea—I felt more at ease. Kind and gracious women always seem to take the hard edge off a hard experience. Replacing her, and the others, were two tall and slim Mounties, agile and swift when they moved. I figured both of them to be about 35. Rick was still being watched after by the young Mountie, his shift overlapping the others by a few hours. We were now the only five in the building.

When not harassing and entertaining Rick, I killed time by more reading, including studying proud photos of Mounties that hung on the walls, the oldest one circa 1875. There must have been 100 such jewels, snapshots of bygone days, many taken with grainy black and white film, and all of them accurately depicted the long history of the gallant men. They have reasons to be proud of their long, illustrious heritage, and it really is an honor to be a member of their ranks. I could easily see that in the faces of the men in these photos.

A bit later, I got a little too comfortable relaxing on one of the many plush minisofas in this huge building, and I almost fell asleep. One probably knows what it's like trying to sleep sitting up. After your head falls over a few times, almost snapping off at the neck and dropping to the floor, it gets annoying, and it's better to try to stay awake. I walked outside to revive myself.

A mild, cool breeze blew in from the bay, refreshing me, reminding me of Mother Pacific swaying nearby, buoyant and beautiful, and how much I loved her. Border traffic into Canada had slowed to a few vehicles every five minutes or so. Of the six crossing booths available to traverse it, only two were now open and manned. At the moment, the two immigration employees who worked them were having a friendly conversation, one of them talking louder than the other, so I could eavesdrop from his end. They were discussing sports, something about bigtime hockey coming soon to British Columbia, and how they hoped it would result in a Stanley Cup Championship for the Canucks, the province's new ice heroes. Being a California kid, where the game isn't well known, I understood only the basic aspects of it. Still, I liked it and thought it must be fun and tough to be good at. Despite my lack of familiarity, I assumed it to be one of Canada's prized possessions and a valued symbol of its national legacy.

Beyond my great interest in sports, my real purpose and destination stood 175 yards to the south: the international "Peace Arch," built on the United States-Canadian boundary. It is an imposing, symbolic shrine to international peace between our two countries, and not a shot betwixt us had been fired in anger since the War of 1812. The towering arch is a lasting testimony to the idea that adults can, indeed, behave themselves. Moreover, I couldn't imagine, given our current relationship, America ever being at war with Canada, in spite of that war's English beginnings. Canada, after all, was now a helpful surrogate mother to tens of thousands of young Americans. It was also impossible for me to predict how this massive exodus, of mostly educated people, would affect Canada's culture in the years to come. I hoped the Americans now living here would be a good reflection of the fine nation they came from. Their new mother was willing to take a chance on it.

I walked slowly toward it, across waves of green grass, an emerald ocean creating a rich base of calm and comfort. It had been freshly cut and smelled like the grass smells in my own front yard, and the simple consistency of this somehow assured me that everything would be all right for us in Canada. The Canadian people had great sympathy for young Americans and although our age might solicit some mistaken first conclusions, we would be safe and welcomed here.

It was standing under the arch that convinced me I was unmistaken about this. It's not just its massive size alone that impresses one—67 feet high, 40 feet wide, and made out of reinforced concrete—but it is also painted a noble, arctic white, with inspiring inscriptions on its frieze that read "Children of a Common Mother" on the American side, and on the Canadian side, "Brethren Dwelling Together in Unity." I thought that summed it up nicely. They like us and we like them.

On my walk back, I stopped briefly at an enormous garden that decorated this area, examining a wide variety of attractive plants and pretty flowers, trying to remember the names of as many as I could. They included grace wards, impatiens, scarlet geraniums, calla lilies, gerbera daisies, roses of all colors and sizes, and yellow marigolds, all of them miracles of God. Still, my all-time darlings were the spectacular vincas, pure white flowers with bright red middles, which often come in the shape of a human heart, and the parallels to human love that they conjured up in me were instantaneous. They represent what the heart should be surrounded by: purity, the unattainable purity that we all wish we possessed. I was reminded of the wild flowers that Kim and I saw by the Willamette River, and then the taste of peanut butter and jelly came to mind. Moreover, the sudden aroma of sweet vanilla overcame me, and I could almost taste the sugary sensation of her full lips pressed hard against mine, her heart spiritual and pure, like the white vincas. They were the best thoughts of the day.

About two hours after our new Mounties arrived, one of them sat down at the secretary's typewriter and began plucking away, typing out directives to guide Rick's new freedom. He was soon finished and pulled the travel guidelines out with a sharp, military snap, folding them neatly and stuffing them into an envelope, identical to the one I had been presented with earlier by Sergeant Erskine. He then walked briskly into the room where Rick was being held, conferred for a moment with the young Mountie, addressed Rick, and in a minute more slapped the envelope hard on the table one time, as if to finalize the deal. He handed it to Rick and pointed him to the door.

That was it. We were officially free to go but with instructions to return to the border within three days. The way our hosts figured it, we had 33 dollars on us, so they divided by three and came up with 11 dollars per day, our daily allowance. I had no idea why they decided to use such an astute formula, but at the time it sounded reasonable to me, as long as we were free to leave. We decided against returning to Seattle to claim my wallet, but by making that decision we would be short 31 dollars, enough to cause us some big trouble—and soon.

We bolted from the building, happy, relieved, and anxious to get a healthier perspective on life. Our self-image was important to us, and we wanted to think of ourselves as decent people and not just two loose and bungling cannons, one alleged to have committed unspeakable crimes. We had our marching orders, and it was finally time to press on.

Before leaving, I reaffirmed my covenant with Sergeant Renfrew, and I thought once again that I might join him someday in the bookcase: an incorruptible, steely Canadian Mountie and his brave American sidekick, though different, still children of a common mother.

[10]
SWEET, TRAGIC JANE

Interstate 5 becomes Highway 99 near the border and led us directly into Vancouver, via Granville Street, across the pretty Fraser River. Our short drive was made just as night was falling, a warm ocean night, with the burning red sun sinking graciously behind Vancouver Island. We left the windows down to capture the soothing breezes coming from Mother Pacific, swirling about the car and caressing us gently on our necks and cheeks, then rushing back out into the unknown, unexplored Canadian landscape. Rick had been awfully quiet and I didn't blame him.

"I guess if you're going to break into '*SHOW BUSINESS!*' Mr. Ruiz, you'll have to change your name now, eh?"

"Yeah, I'm going to have to get a new sign maker too. You dope. What were you trying to do?"

"They didn't cheer you up? I saw you grinning. Everyone on the way to prison should be cheered up first. It's the Mafia's custom in America, you know?"

"This is Canada, Cosmo, if you haven't noticed."

"And a fine thing it is. America probably isn't a good place to be a Mr. Ruiz right now." I wasn't going to let up on him.

"I don't think the moon is," he said, dejectedly.

He wasn't finished eating his bowl of sour grapes. As I said, I didn't blame him. I changed tactics and did my best to smooth things out. I reached over very fast and grabbed his chest hair, yanking hard, "Oh, man, come on, cheer up. It can't be as bad as all that!"

"You ass, Cosmo! That hurts. Stop kicking a poor guy when he's down. All you white men are the same."

"Yeah, Custer deserved it. Ya think?" I shielded my cheek, laughing deliciously at him. "Just wait till you kiss your first Canadian girl," I said, figuring nobody can be unhappy thinking about kissing a girl. "You'll see. Your whole life will change." And it would and did, in a very weird and unfathomable way.

"I'm for that," he said. He didn't retaliate. He was thinking it over.

On Granville Street, the city built on good looks and logging was busy, cars streaming fast in both directions, all heading for distinct and different locations, except one: a black, mysterious princess. I was growing impatient to find a place to bed down, and Rick had grown quiet again, seemingly disinterested and still brooding. To express my haste, I developed the habit of making abrupt, very sharp left and right turns but always, always ending up back on Granville Street.

"You better slow down, Cosmo, and stop taking these turns on two wheels."

It's always when I'm the most tired that I readily adopt my worst habits and then try to defend them. "Just testing the pavement, convict, making sure it can hold down quality American rubber."

"Yeah, and if the cops catch us, Mr. America, they are

going to put us both down in a quality rubber room, reserved for crazy people. Now knock it off!"

It was very good advice because right then we came upon two new, polished police cruisers, both of them belonging to the beloved Mounties. I doubted very much if they wanted to see us again so soon. I knew Rick didn't want to see them. They were parked on busy Granville Street, the dashing men in red outside talking together. One of them looked sharply at our license plate as we passed by.

"Yeah, I see them, Rick, so take it easy." He was eyeing me critically.

"Just stay at the speed limit, Cosmo. These guys are everywhere."

He was right. They were everywhere, and we saw them everywhere we stumbled during the next three days.

Luckily, it only took another three minutes to stumble upon Stanley Park, a wonderful, huge squirrel factory, located very near a harbor and a nice bay, so they had the best of lives. We couldn't do any better, so we would join them tonight and maybe tell them a whale of a story about crazed professors, pregnant women to fall in love with, tattooed convicts on the mend, shy little boys, loyal sisters, and then Mounties at the border, and lots of other funny and interesting things. They would sit enthralled, captivated by us, two international men of mystery and intrigue. It would be a happy time for all.

"I'm happy we found a park so fast, Cosmo. Damn, look at the size of this sucker. It looks like it goes on for miles. Good job."

We parked the Princess on a well-lit street, lined with pretty Japanese cherry trees, and quickly got our gear, heading for the park. The tall downtown buildings, very close and on the left, displayed the same trademark signature of any big city: glass, concrete, and steel and lots of it. These ornate ladies sparkled tonight, like every night, their walls and windows to the outside world bedecked in the illumination of thousands of bright lights, so much so that one corner of the park shared vibrantly in their artificial glory. We could clearly see many people, couples mostly, of all ages, sitting on park benches and holding hands, some strolling sweetly and talking in whispered tones, eagerly planning for their own adventures in life, maybe. I hoped they would all be heroic and rewarding and that none of them would be strangers in exotic lands. Within feet of entering the park, covered in the dark anonymity that we so much desired right now, we were approached by two strangers, a young couple walking in the opposite direction.

"God bless you, young men. How are you two tonight?"

It was the kind of exuberant greeting and question that comes from a Christian man, this young evangelist exploring dark parks for souls to save, his angel of light by his side. I guessed them to be in their late 20s, nicely dressed, and they had a really clean look about them. It was the military-clean look that I talked about earlier. People can have it too. I felt dirty and misplaced standing next to them. They asked if we would stop for a minute so that they could chat with us. The offer was made in authentic good cheer and spiritual warmth, meant to convey that they were genuinely interested in us. Rick was from a solid Catholic family, and I was a Protestant, of fair standing, although both of us needed some spiritual improvement. No matter, despite how obscure and dubious our daily devotions might have been, we both believed in God and heaven. Moreover, we both believed in Jesus as the opening and closing act to cover our personal indiscretions. As far as I was concerned, it was my winning trifecta. So they ended up preaching to the choir, pretty much, but it was reassuring to hear again that God was in control of our lives, still interested in what we were doing and would always watch out for us.

We told them bits and pieces of our story, smoothing out the rough edges, taking into account their possible sensitivity. At one point the young man said, "You know, men, there is no shame in avoiding a senseless, unwinnable war, don't you?"

"We are not draft dodgers, sir," Rick answered.

"Well, I just want you to know how most of us in Canada think."

In the end, they thanked us for our time, saying an endearing prayer over us and blessing our trip. We both liked them very much, and I hoped they had believed Rick. He needed someone to believe in him today without the derailment of blind suspicion. It's nice to be trusted.

We found a beautiful red alder tree to sleep under. Along the walking path I had seen a sign that said the park covered 1,000 acres, and I believed it. It was easily big enough to get lost in. Once settled on the soft grass and comfortable in my bag, I could see a harbor close by, its watercraft for all occasions swaying and dancing in the glow of their own parade of lights, some green, some red, some blue, some white. This celebration to trip the light fantastic reflected brilliantly off the smooth, glassy water, and it was a delightful vision of what the day knows nothing about and wouldn't believe anyway, even if it was true. Like God, I suppose.

I thought Rick was asleep as soon as he zipped up his bag. Not so for me, I was still keyed up by the events of the day, and I gazed into the evening sky, comforted to find the North Star and the Man in the Moon safely where they were supposed to be. Rick suddenly rolled over, startling me, blurting out a question to something he had always believed. "How do we really know that God is real, Cosmo?"

"Oh, I thought you were already fast asleep, Ruiz, dreaming about kissing Canadian girls. OK, then, do you want the long answer or the short answer?"

"I want the right answer."

So the following is what I told him, and it was the long answer. Whether it was right or not was up to him to decide. "Got it, doubting Thomas. I will do my best to make it unproblematic, even for you." I tried not to sound too condescending, knowing how very bright he really was, but he was a step ahead of me.

"Just get on with the story, Cosmo, and quit stalling. I need something to put me to sleep."

"OK, then, listen up. We all accept the notion that love is very real and witnessed in the material world, in all manner of ways. Si, senor?" It was more of a rhetorical question, but I got an answer anyway.

"Yeah, yeah, I'm for love."

"I thought so." He had me laughing inwardly this time, but I didn't pause again. "And we all also accept the suggestion that love can't die as an absolute idea or real, substantial thing. If it happened to die—just one time—then it couldn't possibly be both alive and dead from that point on. This is pretty obvious, at least it sure seems obvious to me. I'm betting that most others would think the same way. But, eventually, the inevitable occurs and all people who love or are loved die physically. Then what happens to the love that was in them? One seemingly rational answer is that love continues to live, just not in them. It simply returns to its fundamental state as an absolute, undying idea, as I said. Or, secondly, perhaps it continues to live but only in others. Let's consider the consequence of all these things. Are you following along, Mr. Ruiz?"

"Yeah, I got it, pastor, keep talking. I'm getting sleepy."

"Then if love lives within a physical body and is itself not a material thing, then its real essence can be said to not only live in a physical body but in the mind's spirit. Therefore, Mr. Ruiz, if love in fact cannot die, and in fact simultaneously possesses a physical body and one's spirit, then even when the body dies, love is still alive within that person's spirit, despite the fact that we cannot then see either of them. So if we agree that love cannot die, and we agree that it lives in a person's spirit, as an absolute idea—and I think we all do—then we are forced to also agree that the spirit of a person cannot die either. How can something die without that which lives in it die as well, if in fact both are capable of dying? Because love is not capable of dying in a natural sense, because it is not physical matter, and the thing that houses the love, a human's spirit, is also not natural or physical, then we can only come to the conclusion that the spirit is not capable of dying either. I hope you can see the obvious logic in this point?"

He didn't really protest to anything I said, so I gave him the second round. "Then where do they both go? Well, religious folks, as the majority idea, say heaven or hell. They firmly believe that all this means that God must exist because to deny any of it is to actually deny the very existence of the idea or life of love. God set it up that way, both physical and spiritual. He's got love covered from both ends. Besides, if someone else is responsible for creating love, then I think we would have discovered it by now. The Hunk over the gunk, so to speak. And that's how we know that God is real. What do you think about that?"

"Where did you hear all this?"

"I heard it put that way by a seminary student," I told him. "A friend of my brother. It made some real sense to me. I never forgot it."

"And that's your answer, love?"

"Yeah, what else ranks as high, convict?"

"You're right, pastor, nothing ranks as high. I agree. I also agree that you are going to die a love struck schmuck. I swear.

My best friend, the lover boy, the love bug, the love preacher, the love struck schmuck! Man, Cosmo, Kim has got you thinking about nothing but love, doesn't she?" He gave a hardy laugh underneath the hardy stars, rolling over, chuckling. I heard him mumble, "Love is God, and God is love. What is love?"

"Goodnight, senor, unless you have more questions?" He was soon asleep and so was I. It had been a long, draining day, especially for him, but I was sure tomorrow would hold better prospects for us, making up for anything we lost today, which was some self-esteem and a little bit of our naive innocence. Losing the latter I wasn't aware of until later. But I knew that God would surely watch out for us. Hadn't I just stuck up for him?

~~

PART 2

Our plan was to spend a half day in Vancouver and then take the afternoon and evening to drive east to Calgary, Alberta, about 600 miles away. The sheer length of the trip would require almost eight hours, if there were long stretches where we could drop the hammer on the Princess, burning fast and free. We were up early in the morning to greet the bright sun, and Rick took the short walk to downtown on a mission to buy us coffee and donuts. I stayed behind to pack up and look around.

Last evening I had noticed another fairly large body of water close to where we slept, now walking the short distance to get the full picture in the streaming daylight of a blue sky, Canadian morning. It was Lost Lagoon and I thought a fitting name for a young, sad, lost American. That aside, it soon brightened me up to observe that it was shaped in the figure of an elongated human heart, pulsating with the blood of vibrant animal and rich plant life. The entire shoreline was covered in dense, thick green flora, and I guessed it to be a half mile long, 400 yards at its widest and 150 yards wide at its narrow end. The squirrels had plenty of neighbors, among them this morning were four raccoons, a mother and three spring kits, braving the sunlight, scurrying along the narrow shore opposite me and stopping every few yards to claw the moist ground for insects and fresh worms. Momma occasionally snapped her head up and sniffed at the cool air, eyeing with bad intent small birds that flew close by. Some of the larger birds, in good number, were the stunning, pure white mute swans and great blue herons—that have nature's funniest neck to brag about—if not the swan's great beauty. Canada geese and grey geese and ducks, in even larger numbers, flocked about other areas of the deep lagoon, milling around and feeding on fish and plants, sometimes squawking at each other like old washerwomen. I reached down to snatch up a fat frog, one sharing my space but otherwise acting indifferently toward me. I only meant to offer up my "good Canadian morning," but he quickly hopped away, diving beneath some water lilies before I could grab him. I then slipped on a wet rock and almost fell. Escaping the personal sting of frogly rejection, I walked along the shore for some distance, noticing that the lagoon was framed on three sides by impressively tall Douglas fir, stately western red cedars and the exquisite western hemlocks, all thriving in perfect harmony and making for a picture of nature that only God is capable of painting. It was a very beautiful and picturesque place, and it made me think highly of my Canadian neighbors.

Suddenly, I heard a loud whistle. It was Rick standing near the water, close to where the frog had ditched me. "Hey, lover boy!" he shouted. "Stop communing with nature for a minute and come and get some grub." He then disappeared as fast as the frog.

I was for that, quickly bidding farewell to my Lost Lagoon friends but not before commenting on how very much I liked their digs, adding that I hoped to someday have just as nice a place to settle in and maybe bring a girl from a trailer park with me. We would sit by our own soft, lovely shores, eating peanut butter and jelly sandwiches and kissing. A lot. Yes, someday. It all sounded very reasonable.

After wolfing down an entire box of fresh donuts, between gulps of rich, hot coffee, we cruised downtown Vancouver for an hour watching all the pretty girls go to work. Rick made up a new love speech for each one or group of them, all of which were poetic, eloquently rendered, and skillfully romanced. I let him go about this freely and at length, enjoying and laughing at his Latin love swoons, while I tried my best to avoid eye contact with them. I was embarrassed, unshaven, hair dirty, clothes soiled and wrinkled from sleeping in them, and my teeth needed a good brushing. Rick was a smaller carbon copy, but his appeals to love remained steadfast. He absolutely adored women, no matter his own appearance, at any given moment, and at the moment he looked like me, in need of careful repair. He whistled a number of times at some of them and received a variety of reactions, from, "Oh, please, you must be joking," to the kinder smile, bemused look, and quick laugh that is—God bless a man's good fortune—much more common. It doesn't seem to matter which borders one crosses, some things never change.

"I think these girls are going to like me, Cosmo." He was right about that, especially sweet, tragic Jane. We met her soon after finding a Launderette and washing our big pile of dirty clothes. It had been building up in the back of the Princess since we left home, and Kim's trailer was without a washer, so she couldn't help. Jesse had even used this mountain as a prop for the dragon on his arm, while chatting to us about his prison years and apple picking travels with his dad. I was already beginning to miss his good company and the bright outlook he had about most things, especially his future, despite the multitude of sad reasons to think that the odds, regardless of Jessica's help, were still stacked against him. Still, hadn't he bragged proudly about his future? Because he was, of course, "A much more mature man now, and ready to have a real crack at life."

Then I heard a knock at the crack of my window, startling me from near sleep. I had been headed there while thinking about these things and more, waiting patiently while Rick shopped for bread and cheese. Attached to the knock was the voice of someone associated with the grocery business, and this someone looked like a store manager, or what one might look like, had I not known.

"Excuse me, sir. Will you please step out of the car for a moment?"

I rolled my window down, halfway. "What's this all about, mister? How can I help you?"

He insisted, "If you'll just step outside, sir, we can talk better."

"OK, watch out for the door." He stepped back and let me out cleanly. I'm tall but he stood two inches above me. "What can I do for you? Is there some sort of problem?"

"One might say that," he said. "I'm hoping you can help us identify someone. He's a shopper inside the store. He says you know who he is."

I followed him inside, where housewives were shopping with curlers in their hair, little or no makeup, and small children running about their legs like little savages. A young girl, about seven, collided smack into me, careening to the floor, unhurt, giving me an embarrassed, befuddled smile, missing front teeth included. "Sorry, mister," she said. Her mother was soon assisting her up and dragging her off, but I heard the girl mutter, "Gee, mom, he's a big guy."

The even bigger guy turned out to be Greg, an assistant grocery manager. He had walked briskly and a little in front of me, so I had to hustle to keep up with him. Once past the obstacles of undisciplined and unruly children, I was led to an office in the warehouse, surrounded by boxes of ripe fruit, pallets of canned goods and containers of fresh milk. Only one other employee was there, the produce manager, inspecting big crates of different colored vegetables, with great precision: an eye for what best suits man.

Then I caught my own eyeful of Mr. Ruiz, chatting casually and a little intimately with Jane Silver, the store's inventory control specialist. She was one of those women that my brother describes as "almost pretty and the only kind any guy should marry." She had an especially big, packaged steak in her hands, waving it around in symphonic fashion, as she leaned near to Rick. It was an odd scene, and I didn't know what to think.

When Greg opened the door the two separated to a safer distance. Without coming in himself, he just said, "This is him, Mr. Anderson. You sure I can't do anything else, Jane?"

"Thanks, Greg. It's under control."

"OK," he replied, and marched off in the same military fashion he had used to march us in.

"Pull up a chair, Mr. Anderson, and sit down." It had a disciplinary sound to it. "I hope you are feeling better today?" Her countenance shifted immediately to one of concern for me. I didn't know exactly what she meant by her question, but I found it easy to agree with her. She continued, "Rick, I mean, Mr. Ruiz, here, tells me you can identify him, Mr. Anderson. Is that right?"

"Yes, I can. He's my friend. We are Americans and crossed the border yesterday."

"Can you please show me some identification?"

"I'll have to go back to the car to get it."

So I did. Upon returning, Jane, the almost pretty girl with long, straight and thin blond hair, and a slender physique, reviewed my newly obtained documents with much interest, and with—from what I could surmise—some humor.

"So, neither of you has a picture ID. Is that right?"

"It's a long story, Jane—is it?"

"You can call me that."

"Listen, Jane, if Rick hasn't said so, we are just a couple of guys visiting Canada for a few days. We happened to lose our IDs but got these papers at the border. Would you mind saying what's going on here?"

All this time Rick had been leaning back in his chair, in a very relaxed manner, smiling at me and nodding his head in affirmation to everything I said. From his general demeanor, he looked just like Rick always looked: handsome and composed, except when kicking a suitcase. Someone once described him as a brown Glenn Ford. He wore a cocky but friendly grin, his bright eyes flashing between me and Jane. It would have been impossible to tell that he was in big trouble. He just beamed and let me do the talking. He told me later that he was hoping I'd use my love speech on her and save the universe. Obviously, it wasn't the universe that needed saving.

Amazingly, just like that, the same as the outcome at the border, the cosmic knucklehead was saved, set free and pointed to the door, completely exonerated of all crimes, national and international. It was the darnedest thing.

Once outside, he began to tell me the story. He was caught shoplifting, trying to stuff the aforementioned steak down the front of his jeans. It was going to be his little present to me, a prime-rib addition to our usual diet of bread and cheese. In all honesty, it was just Rick's display of *spontaneous human combustion*, as my mom once coined it for me, although I didn't think she would have approved of his specific kind. It was, in short, a cost saving measure. At least that was his boneheaded excuse for reckless stupidity. A practiced thief surely would have gotten away with it.

By the time Rick finished telling Jane—only 20—his sad American story, she was in love with him. He had presented it something like this: The poor boy had worked so hard to surprise Rosie; smeared his driver's license while risking his life to save a three-legged dog from drowning; cleaned up gooey, disgusting whale blubber to save a desperate town and an esteemed professor's reputation; spent most of his own money fixing a distressed, pregnant woman's car—that was true—and then once again risked his life teaching the frantic girl how to drive. Furthermore, he had dug up a tree stump by himself, while his injured friend sipped iced tea in the shade—me, of course,—and, well, the story was just getting stranger and stranger. Then, after all this and more, he was wrongfully accused at the border of attempted murder, kidnapping, car theft, and draft dodging. Can all these things get a girl to fall in love with him? It sure seemed to have happened.

I was astonished upon hearing all of it, as anyone might be, thinking she must have easily seen through him. "Well, convict, after all those heroics, how did you then account for being a common steak thief?"

"I told her that we needed to save our money to buy medicine for your injuries."

"What injuries?"

"The injuries you got when Kim's car fell on you while we were fixing it. And I had to lift it off!"

"Oh, man, Ruiz! I can't believe you! Tell me you didn't really say all those things."

"Yeah, lover boy, I threw the last part in on the spur of the moment. I needed to get out of there because I wasn't looking to get arrested today. I had to shoot all the bullets I had, bro."

"I'll say. And this story is the reason she let you go? Seriously?"

"Yeah, what else? You should have seen me, Rusty. I was at my best."

"Your lying, thieving best?"

"Come on, man, I was just trying to save us some money, since the piss brain left his in Seattle!"

"This is all somehow my fault?"

"It was just spontaneous. I saw a chance and took it. Besides, she liked me, and you haven't heard the best part yet."

"This gets better? God save me!"

"Yeah, I think he saved us both. Anyway, dinner tonight, courtesy of Jane and yours truly. Steaks, me boy! What do you think about that? And don't give me any sanctimonious bullshit. It turned out all right, and you would have done the same."

"How do you pretend to know that? And what's this about dinner?"

That's right. Not only had she set our hero free, she invited him to dinner tonight. A steak dinner, wouldn't you know it. All I had to do was play dumb and fake an injury, which I wasn't sure I could remember to do. Well, I've got to say—without going into all the particulars, which I think I just did—the whole gag had an unbelievable twist of madness to it. The very steak that should have gotten him thrown into jail would now digest easily on his conscience and belly tonight, and then Jane would make passionate love to him. Ironically, what I said would happen to him earlier actually did happen, although all of it was very odd and quirky and sad—yet still very reasonable.

After kicking around Vancouver for several hours, including a trip back to the park, we headed to Jane's place for dinner and infamy. When she answered the door of the large two-story house, one that she shared with her recently deceased father, she welcomed us warmly, giving Rick a hug and me a cordial handshake.

I sat in a chair and Rick on the couch with Jane. I could smell dinner already cooking. While waiting, she began to tell us a little more about herself, and we listened politely to her story of loneliness, tragedy and deep despair. She was only a young girl when her mom passed away, and now her poor dad was dead too. According to her loving account of him, he had been an alcoholic, but the type who could still function in the world on a day-by-day basis, hiding his disease as well as any alcoholic can. He went to work every morning, put in a full day, and after stumbling back home after the bars had closed for the night, he got up and did it all over again.

"I just don't know how he ever managed it, but he did," she said, woefully. Her spirits picked up a little when she started filling in some of the details about their close relationship and their plans for the future, together and individually. She had a profound love for him, and he was a good man who wanted only what was best for both of them. He had died of a massive heart attack only a month before, and she was terribly lonely, still in some mild shock and glad to have our company. We were the first two people to be inside the house since the day he died. Moreover, she had just broken off a long-term romance with a guy she hoped to marry. She had caught him cheating on her and would not absolve him, as she had done for Rick. With no other relatives around, and few close friends, she found herself suddenly alone in the world. We should all hate it when that happens. I found myself wanting to ask her if she had found any support at work but decided, uneasily, to let it go. Such a question would just throw things back onto what happened today, and if she wasn't willing to say already, then the answer must be one she didn't care to share.

Just the same, I was a bit overwhelmed to hear all this, and the picture was finally becoming clearer to me. Sweet, tragic Jane, as we forevermore called her, was in the black mire of desolation and needed someone to comfort her, hold her close, help her cope with the dire sorrows of her recent life—if only for a few hours. In many ways she reminded me of Kim, and I was surprised to recognize the close parallels. Now here were two American boys on the loose, understanding and sympathetic companions, here and gone, and never to be seen again. She had been immediately attracted to Rick. It was this attraction, the timing of it, and her present, mournful state of mind that set him free, not the nonsense he tried to feed her. Some might call it luck. Hadn't I been lucky to find Kim? What was so different about this?

Anyway, although it was part of her job to catch and prosecute shoplifters, in Rick's case, upon hearing his dramatic account of things, believed or not, she had given a rare, compassionate reprieve. As I said, I really think it had more to do with her than him. Just the same, more power to her if she could provide one, a sorely needed one. It made me like her very much. I still thought she must be very odd, in a good way. Really, from my end, it was impossible to know how much of his story she actually did believe. Rick had sprinkled most of it with some truth and if she believed any of it, I hoped it was those parts. If it's a tip-off, she never once asked me again about my supposed injuries or if I was feeling better. It just didn't matter much to any of us right then.

The rest of the evening was both complicated and straightforward. After dinner, which included two full bottles of delicious wine, French Merlot, I think, we all sat outside by the edge of the pool. Rick sat very close to Jane and tried to splash water on her with his bare feet. She retaliated by jumping in and pulling him in after her. Their playful touching and grabbing lasted for about 10 minutes, and, of course, it meant that his street clothes were now completely wet.

Sweet, tragic Jane invited Rick into the house to change and dry his clothes. I walked to the car to fetch him some replacements, but when I slipped back through the screen door there was no one to see. The only sign of life was the soft hum of a dryer and the distinct, annoying sound of clunking, which a metal button makes on each pass.

OK, then, Mr. Ruiz's quirky luck had turned out better than he ever could have expected and in the most unbelievable of ways. There was nothing else to do except grab my sleeping bag and stretch out on the back lawn. I wanted to sleep outside. It was a beautiful summer night, just after nine, and thousands of shimmering, crystal stars crowded the sky. I decided on a position where I would have to turn my head to see the light in Jane's bedroom window. It went out soon after I zipped up, but the love making lasted well into the morning, I imagined. It wasn't until later that I found out how completely wrong I was. I spent my last waking moments pondering the things one can't make up in life and how they always seem to surpass anyone's fiction. Rick's luck today, or whatever it might be labeled, was such a thing.

The next morning at breakfast, just toast and coffee, they acted like newlyweds, holding hands and kissing freely in front of me. They did so without embarrassment, and I was touched by how quickly they had bonded. It was a reminder of how quickly I had swooped up Kim and how young people display little inhibitions when love is in the air. She had thoroughly occupied my mind since last night, especially when I first saw sweet Jane's light go out. God, how I wanted to be like Rick and not some schmuck who couldn't even get a proper goodbye kiss.

Jane allowed me to shower in her spare bathroom, and not long after I was standing at the back of the Princess loading my gear. I then sat in the passenger seat for a few minutes, feeling melancholy, trying to understand all that just happened and was still happening. My thoughts ran the gauntlet, much as they had the morning I left Cottage Grove. They only produced more questions that were impossible to answer, creating some real gloominess for me. The whole trip, if it hadn't been so already, became very surreal, and I could only imagine what wacky stuff might happen next. Life doesn't always ask us first what we think it should do.

I had thought the same as Rick had thought, two or three days driving, another day at Wesley's, a few more days in Canada, then back home by now. It would have put us there three days ago. I should be in a dark driveway with my girlfriend. Then I should be right where I was presently sitting. She wouldn't be Kim.

I was invited back in for a few minutes to say goodbye to Jane, already my good friend. I carried away a few bags of groceries she was sending along with us. Rick's goodbye to her was short for someone who wasn't likely to see his lover again. Then again, it may have been fitting. Perhaps Jane didn't want to be seen in a public encounter on her doorstep, with a mysterious, dark stranger, one she might have to explain time and again. Whatever it was, I said farewell and thanks first, then watched them from the car, hugging for the last time. Jane blew us kisses as we left, the way Jessica and her girls had done. Then I was sure she didn't care what anyone thought, and I liked her more. When speeding away, I burned a little rubber for her, catching her broad smile in my rearview mirror.

"What an amazing thing to happen, eh, steak thief? It puts the stuff at the border to shame."

"You know what she asked me, Rusty? She wanted to know if I believed in God."

"What did you tell her?"

"I told her I sure did. Then she wanted to know how I knew he was real. Fancy that, Rusty. It's a small world. So I told her as much as I could remember about what you told me at the park. You know, your love speech and how nothing ranks higher."

"Maybe I'm not as big a schmuck as we both think I am."

Schmuck or not, this totally unexpected encounter had been as bizarre for him as it had been for me, and he added it to the long list of things he said he never counted on, "But this is a new number one, Cosmo." I agreed completely with his perspective this time, and not because I had just been trying to put together the pieces of the puzzle myself. It had been a very strange but exciting trip. We were actually beginning to feel like two real international men of mystery.

For the next several minutes we discussed and analyzed the whole trip from every angle, especially those things that happened to us since landing at the border. We could only laugh at all of it, coming to the conclusion that we were just struck with uncanny, dumb luck. Finally, it was refreshing that Rick never spoke about Jane as only a sexual conquest, or even bragged about it in such a way, as he might have done in the past. The soul of sweet, tragic Jane had attached itself to both of us, it seemed.

So that's the way it was at the stunning park near downtown Vancouver, flirting with pretty girls going to work, doing laundry at a Launderette, trying to steal a steak at a grocery store, and finding an almost pretty girl with a crushed, broken heart, and my friend who was so willing to help mend it. I think he did. Yes, they liked Rick Ruiz in Vancouver, and he's living proof that crime sometimes does pay. God surely did watch out for us.

[11]
THE TURNING POINT

Jane lived very near English Bay and only a few miles from Stanley Park. From her place we quickly found Broadway Street, turning into Highway 7, and followed it directly east, the first several miles amid the hustle and bustle of buildings, people, swarms of cars, too many traffic lights and loud noise. They were the common sort of hazards one encounters when trying to escape a big city. From then on, and just before the district municipality of Mission, the road cut free and burned fast. Impatient, again, I put the pedal to the metal and screamed for another 85 miles, fast approaching the divine community of Hope, surrounded on three sides by succulent, forested mountains, and built at the confluence of the Fraser and Coquihalla rivers.

"You are going to get a ticket doing this, Mr. America. 'Oh, can I see your driver's license, please, sir?' It's going to be fun hearing you explain that, Cosmo. You better slow the hell down. You've been pushing it hard for a while." Rick had been quiet for almost an hour, window shopping the countryside at high speed. There was much of delight to see in resplendent British Columbia, right now a pristine valley and lake to my left, and the lazy Fraser River with its soft, quiet banks, and clean mountain water to Rick's right.

"Criticism coming from you is absurd, even if it's right, Mr. Canadian Steak Thief."

"When are you going to stop being so stupid and quit calling me that?"

"Stop calling me Mr. America, and I'll lighten up on you."

We always condemn each other for the same crimes, and it was a crime how hungry I was. Sleeping outside has that result on you, I believe, and have been told. So I told Mr. Thief about it. "Speaking of which, Mr. Thief, I could use a good steak about now. What about you? Let's have another one and sign a truce over it." We were both mildly grumpy from the sting of hunger and love that bit at our souls and bellies. In truth, Rick wouldn't have normally been bothered by my driving, but the circumstances of the past few days made him wary of the police. We had passed a few sheriffs near Mission, some miles back, and the Mounties a number of times in and around Vancouver. I was relaxed, counting on our papers acquired at the border to be sufficient. But, of course, I hadn't been suspected of ruinous crimes.

All in all, if we were going to have steaks this morning, we were going to have to buy them. Our scrimpy breakfast of toast and coffee was rapidly wearing off, and we were too lazy to dig into the groceries Jane gave us. Getting Rick's vote of approval, I took the only exit I saw into Hope, crossing an awesome bridge and the Fraser River, gearing down to second and letting the Princess purr her arrival. Three young boys with fishing poles were heading to the river, and I stopped to let them cross in front of us.

"That's a really boss car, mister," the one nearest me said, the other two nodding their heads in eager approval and waving.

"Thank you," I shouted to them, out my window. They moved along, headed for one of those days that they will talk about when they are old men, trying to remember who caught the most fish and who was lying about it, and, "Didn't the river look so much bigger and faster back then, and do you remember that a hamburger, shake, and fries were less than a loonie (one dollar) at Babbs'?" Then they would remember mysterious older men from that country down south, I was sure, and ask and answer each other, "I wonder what they were doing in Canada back then? Draft dodgers, probably." Still, it was hard to find fault with the Princess, and they had not, so I hoped they would recall her too—and then reflect on us with kinder remembrance.

"Boss?" Rick asked, in some disbelief.

"Yeah, I haven't heard that one in years. I guess news travels slowly to the Great White North."

Coincidentally, the news at "Babbs' Diner, On the River," as the sign read, and where all that stuff was still less than a loonie, was robust and loud, traveling fast between the locals, all of them wanting to give their version of events at the same time.

"It's just a crying shame. I knew something like this was going to happen," an elderly man said, dressed in black jeans and a white western shirt, busily cleaning his sunglasses that had fallen to the floor. He displayed obvious sorrow.

"Yeah, it's real sad, and I hope he's going to be all right. I heard that the doctors said he may lose his leg," added our kind and soft spoken waitress to be, a woman in her 40s, heavyset but pretty, and who seemed to know everyone.

"I saw it coming all along. You can't treat power saws like damned toys," said another man, probably in his late 50s, a day unshaven, and never once did he look up from his plate while making the snide remark. He displayed no remorse or sympathy for the victim of interest, only gorging himself on his food.

The conversation came from all directions, several others chiming in, sad and worried. In the dark about the terrible trouble, I finally asked a young couple seated at the next table.

"He's Bob Davis, a local artist. He almost cut his leg off yesterday. He carves art with chainsaws."

"No kidding. How did he do that?" Rick asked, beating me to it.

The man, slightly older than us, seated with his young, introverted girlfriend, who remained shyly silent throughout, couldn't hide the obvious snicker on his face. At the same time he showed real concern. I imagined he was laughing at calamity, as some do. "He slipped on the grass at the park, giving a speed carving lesson to a large crowd. As I said, he almost cut his leg off."

"Damn fool," the hungry man said, to no one in particular. I wondered what had caused him to have grown so obviously bitter, certainly no one is born that way. Are they?

Then Rick said, "That's too bad. I didn't know such a sport existed."

"It's a sport for damned fools and idiots," the bitter man said, very loudly, in exuberant disgust, but this time it was a closing remark to his rapid-fire editorial outbursts. Good riddance, he was getting up to leave. I had found the first Canadian I didn't like. He struck me as a man without a soul and probably a hater of everything.

"Just give me a man with a soul. That's all I want," my middle sister had sometimes said, in lament but great hope, and I always thought it a poignant cry. Oh, she found one. Good for you, sis.

It was about then that our waitress delivered our food. The place was beginning to clear out, including the couple next to us, the morning coffee break in Hope having run its course. She showed kind interest in us, and asked, "Where are you young men from? I've never seen you around these parts before."

"We're from the United States, Miss," I said. "Just visiting Canada."

"You called me Miss. How sweet you are! What state?"

"California," I said. It was something of a mistake. With the place almost empty and her cleanup chores done, and time on her hands, she proceeded to tell us all about her friends in Monterey County, more than 100 miles south of where we lived. I didn't mind hearing the story, but I was hungry and probably eating my last steak for a while. Wanting to enjoy it, I didn't listen to her as intently as I might have. I merely nodded my head in vague acknowledgement to most of it, chewing ravenously, only picking up bits and pieces. Business owners, they were, and wealthy Americans, it seemed. In another year or two she would visit them for yet another time.

In our case, I doubted if we would ever have the chance to see her another time, and so did she, because when it came time to bid farewell, she actually hugged both of us, and requested that we please be careful on our journey. I figured her for two or three kids, around our age. Only this kind of motherly woman hugs you, despite how little time she's known you. Such moments were always awkward for me, and I know Rick felt the same. But we let her do it, assuring her that everything would be fine, and expressed our hopes that she would have fun in Monterey, when the time came. We told her a bit about our extraordinary luck the previous day, but didn't, for obvious reasons, provide clear details, and there was little time for them. Nonetheless, she was pleased to hear what we did share with her, and wished us more of the same kind of good fortune. We were for that, we agreed, especially Rick. We enjoyed meeting her, very much, indeed.

When I turned onto the bridge that led us in, heading for the Trans-Canada Highway, north, I saw the three young boys directly beneath it, using it for shade, and casting wildly into the river while standing on the big rocks near the bank. I blew my horn at them a few times but never knew if they noticed me. I hoped they did. I wanted to say goodbye to them. They dug my car, making them friends for life. I wished for them to remember us and the Princess, especially.

Highway 7 turns into the infamous Trans-Canada Highway, Highway 1, and the next 120 miles cut through steep mountains of vertical cliffs and sheer drops, the curving river snaking along at every turn, never far from our sight. It was the most enjoyable stretch I could remember driving since leaving Northern California, were the roads burn through the mountains in the same fashion, and one is overcome by the astounding beauty of nature and its absolute wonder and vastness. None of it can be done justice by even the most vivid of poets.

Two miles outside of Hope, we came upon a surprising site: Lake of the Woods, a Walden Pond twin. I imagined Henry David Thoreau working busily in his small garden, close to the lake's edge, and still striving "to live deliberately, to front only the essential facts of life." As I slowed down, I acknowledged my own desire to understand these same essential facts of life. I hoped my delicious pursuit of them, despite how I was going about it, would be judged worthy enough by the great man of Concord, and he would see it as a fitting account of self-resilience and personal adventure. Three cheers and hooray! We couldn't share personal stories, but we were united in the idea of seeking personal freedom, his by a lake and mine on the road, and it was pretty much the same quest.

It puffed me up a little, as one can tell, to know that I was doing what he had done, only a century later, and if in a slightly different way, at least on my own terms, like him. At the very minimum, there were transcendental similarities to our thoughts and private ambitions—I was sure of it. Such musings were perhaps a bit romantic and stretching things, as Rick pointed out to me when I shared them with him, but it all sounded reasonable enough at the time. Who doesn't want to be like Thoreau?

Other than to check out the lake, I don't think Rick took his eyes off the darting river since we left Hope behind, and I wondered what he was thinking. Then he told me. "Pull up over here, Cosmo. I want to see the oldest church in British Columbia."

"How's that, Mr. Ruiz?"

"I said pull in at the next exit, lover boy. A sign back there says the oldest church in British Columbia is nearby. I want to see it."

So that's what I did. I pulled into the small community of Yale. We were only an hour outside of Hope and already stopped again. I couldn't imagine why he wanted to see a church, unless it was to repent. So I asked him. "Feeling a little guilty, are you, handsome?"

"None of your business. It's for historical research. It might be Catholic. I can tell my folks about it."

It wasn't and there was no sign indicating what other denomination might hold services here. Perhaps it only mattered to the locals milling about. We were in a very small town, and they were beginning to take close notice of us as we lingered for a time. It didn't worry us much. Rick needed to get something off his heart. He got out and tried the door. It was unlocked, which surprised me. Good for him. Upon entering, he glanced back at me with a leave-me-alone look.

When he came back some 10 minutes later, he was uncharacteristically silent about the whole affair. Whatever was going on with him was solemn and deserved no pretense of tease from me. He got into the car, and we sat silently for a few minutes, not looking at each other. Then I hopped out suddenly, with no warning to him, ducking inside the church. I wanted to see it myself. It was primitive and small, containing only a dozen wooden pews and a tall black podium standing center stage. The barest of basics for God to work with, but I could tell that services were still held here. There were a few old Bibles sitting in the pews and someone's personal items strung about, an old coat and a woman's shabby hat. There was also sheet music scattered on the floor, as if the devil had broken in and tried to rout the good hymns of the Lord. Then I thought of Thoreau again, and how it was most likely the kind of church he attended. Its ambiance was pared down to front only the essential facts of life and God, all that anyone really needs. It would have suited him well. I said a quick prayer but not one with much passion, admittedly, and was out the door.

I broke our sober silence after several minutes back on the road. I felt the need to say something, like we humans do, sometimes. Except I couldn't think of anything clever or witty, so I tried an old standby that fit my mood. "You want to hear my love speech again, Rick?" I said it with as much pastoral passion as I could mimic.

A short laugh and then, "What is love, Cosmo? What is love, really?"

"Love is God and God is love," you said it yourself. "And it is alive. He's alive, like I told you."

"But he's probably not real happy with me."

"You are a good Catholic to get it off your conscience today."

"And you are a lousy Protestant to console me about it. How do you know what I was doing?"

"An educated guess, macho man. Hey, do you think God cares what denomination we are? I mean, in the end, do you really think he gives a shit?"

"No, unless you are a theologically misguided Protestant and a love struck schmuck to boot, like you," he laughed, reinvigorated by church, grabbing me by the cheek and pulling hard.

"Damn you, convict. That hurts! Here I am trying to be nice to you, and look what I get for it." I recoiled, slapping his hand away, putting my arm up in self-defense. "You're the demon Mexican from hell!"

"Wait until the real devil gets his hands on you, lover boy!" He laughed heartily again, and I knew his pious visit had given him a new birth. I wanted to go for his chest, but he was wearing a T-shirt. I would bide my time. Until then, I didn't feel the need to offer any retaliatory protests to his religious errors or personal and physical attacks, actually glad to take the punishment this time. Just knowing that he got to take care of his business, no matter what church it was, as long as God was there, was good enough for me.

"I never made love to her, Cosmo," he suddenly blurted out.

"What?"

"You heard me clear enough, lover boy."

"Wow. I mean, why not?"

"I couldn't. I mean I could but I didn't. I just held her close all night and we talked."

"About what?"

"About life, bird brain. About life, that's all."

"Oh. OK. Do you want to tell me more?"

"No. I told God, just a few minutes ago."

"I see. Do you think he's happier with you now?"

"I don't know."

"Why not?"

"Because I really wanted to make love to her. The thought never left my head. He knows our thoughts, too."

"Yeah. He must think you are a great man."

"You think?"

"Sure I do. Life is more than sex."

"Yeah. Anyway, I hope Jane will be fine in the future."

"God has a way of working things out for us, Mr. Ruiz."

"Yeah. That's what we talked about all night."

We drove on in sweet silence. Still, I knew that God must have thought he was a great man to shine so much light on him. I thought so.

~~

PART 2

Our next order of business was to gas up and we did so in Cache Creek, a junction community connecting the Trans-Canada with Highway 97. It's also where we changed direction for the final time, heading directly east to Calgary. At the moment, there was no real significance attached to Calgary, except that on the map, which we finally looked at, it seemed like a nice place to go to complete our Canadian odyssey. It was going to be a blazing trip, our Mountie deadline looming, and we planned it to the hour, expecting to arrive back at the border at about the same time we left it three days earlier. All of this was a doable goal, as long as delectable speed burns were occasionally available.

Calgary just happened to be in Alberta, the neighboring province of British Columbia and hundreds of miles inland, as already noted. So, altogether, such a destination gave us some real bragging rights, and our travel stories back home would grow into local legend and fireside folklore. Then life happened, once again, and changed it all.

I came out of the small convenience store, which also served as a gas stop, just in time to see Rick toss some beaten-up travel gear into the back seat, while speaking with a young woman. She was our age or perhaps a few years older, and she was also a traveling American hippie. The first I had seen. She didn't notice me, so I had the chance to watch her for a moment, taking a closer look. She was a dead ringer for the actress and singer Judy Garland but with unshaven, long hair on her legs and a disheveled look that didn't speak of the privileges of Hollywood and recording contracts. This lookalike also wore granny glasses that fit her slim face and nose perfectly, and her complexion was pure and clear. A straight auburn ponytail partly covered her sunburned neck and shoulders. She was tall for a woman and extremely thin, as if starving herself was a normal routine. Hollywood or the dusty road, I thought her attractive and wondered who the heck she might be. I was soon to find out, walking over to introduce myself, her apparent friendship with Rick firmly established.

"Oh, hello," I said. I could smell stale incense on her, mixed with sweat and dirt. Her faded knee length skirt and tie-dyed blouse had grimy stains on them from sleeping where nature and circumstance might accommodate her best. What stood out were her new, sturdy hiking boots, slightly scuffed and probably purchased for the long walks that would be mandatory on this trip. They were men's boots, worn by a hippie girl looking for her new home in a foreign land—a fresh, more welcoming altered state of consciousness.

"Hello there, handsome," she said, always a good beginning, meant or not. "I'm a fellow American going to Kamloops. Your friend here—I mean Rick—says I can ride along. Is that OK with you?" Her voice was anxious.

'Sure, glad to have the better company."

"Right on," she replied, happily. "I'm Jane, glad to meet you." She held out her slender hand to me, rings on four fingers. I thought of my oldest sister, also fond of wearing them.

I glanced at Rick, now pumping gas and driving, trying to pick up on his visual reaction to the coincidence. "I told you it's a small world, Cosmo," he said, "especially in Canada."

I casually mentioned it to her, in fun, and she said Rick had beaten me to it. We shared the normal things people do at first, formal introductions and current quests, right or wrong. She thought our adventure was a grand idea, and a stroke of luck for her to meet up with us pursuing it. She had spent a hard night on the ground, sleeping in front of the store, waiting for morning to hitch a ride. She had been trying for almost four hours. What does a girl have to do?

We were soon back on the road, chatting casually, sharing more things in common. Kamloops was just an hour away and Jane's final stop on her long journey of hitchhiking in the heat of hot days and scorching roads. I was startled to think she had made the trip alone, a girl taking dangerous chances. She said she was headed there to meet up with her boyfriend, an American draft dodger, the two of them hoping to begin a new life hiding safely within the beautiful bowels of Canada. It seemed they had been living and working on a pot farm in Humboldt County, in far Northern California. Then he suddenly got the news that he was needed to serve his country, by military conscription, and bolted within a few days of getting the letter. Jane had voluntarily stayed behind, agreeing to manage their final personal affairs and then catch up to him later. She talked freely and openly about all this, and I was glad to let her speak, not being asked to recount my own questionable tale of hitting the road. She needed somebody who would listen to her story, and we were an interested audience of two. Upon hearing it, I started to feel more like a child, one only worried about the small, insignificant details of life, not such tragic ones as I was hearing about now.

So, here is Jack and Jane, abruptly uprooted from their homeland, and it was going to be no joyride for them, not in the beginning and not for many years. I wondered what they would eventually tell their parents, or like me, say nothing at all, and just write letters and give doubtful assurances from afar. It all might turn into a whale of a story as the years passed by, should they never get to see their families and friends again. Jack was now an American outlaw and coming to his rescue was his sidekick Jane.

What a bummer, I thought, and when I glanced at Rick I could tell he agreed. We both expressed our sorrow for her, from time to time, as she explained things in more and greater detail. She welcomed our concern, assuring us that everything would be all right. In case you are wondering, we didn't disapprove of their working on a pot farm. Neither of us got high, but it wasn't anything out of the ordinary for others our age to do so. Not that we condoned it, or even considered it a good idea, but it was a rather accepted practice with our generation. Nobody thought you were an axe murderer because of it.

Near the end of our brief time with her, or so we thought, she asked if she could read my palm. I told her that I didn't believe in such things, but I would do it anyway just so I could hold her hand. She giggled, grinning broadly at me. She had such a quick smile and was already very comfortable with us. She was also delighted, she said, to have our company and assistance, trusting us immediately. Moreover, she suddenly didn't look like the dirty, road weary girl we had picked up not long ago. Her countenance seemed greatly improved, although, as I said, she was already pretty. Judy Garland was pretty. She was just glad that she had stumbled upon a couple of young Americans, and friendly ones too, with no judgmental axe to grind.

She moved a little closer to me from her relaxed position in the backseat, asking me to give her my left hand, my birth hand, as she noted with importance. She wanted to read about my life, telling me what fate might have in store for me. I was game to play along and did as she asked, jokingly, enchanted by her attempt at enthusiastic friendliness.

"Wow," was her first reaction. "You have a deep and long fate line, much more prominent than most people. Maybe there is some spiritual reason to why Rick calls you Cosmo." She laughed brightly at her own joke, and I joined in.

"You can call me Mr. Cosmo," I said. She laughed again, and I half expected Rick to chime in with the real reason why he called me this name. It was based on some cartoon character he liked, although I never quite got the joke. He had turned reticent again, enjoying the drive and Jane's company. She was a breath of fresh air, and by the time we left her we would love her too.

At the moment, she was very calculating in her examination of me, via my palm, and said that fate would be good to me in the long run, but I would have to overcome a serious tragedy or some challenging event in my life, very soon, perhaps. There were external forces at work on me, she added, and could not be stopped. She noticed that this seemed to bother me, hastily moving on to the other lines in my hand, explaining that I had a very straight heart line and would be content with my love life. Also, my life line was long and curvy, so that I was a person who freely expressed his emotions and feelings, and this she thought a good thing. She finished by saying that my head line, where the river of fate all begins, was a little curved, and this meant that I would be creative throughout my life, perceptive to the feelings of those around me and that my thinking would be clear and focused. That was all flattering and nice to hear. Still, it didn't concern me. I was only interested in what she said first, so I asked her to explain about my fate line in more detail. But when I did, Mr. Ruiz ruined it for me.

"I thought you told her you didn't believe in such things, Cosmo—the spaceman! Let the schmuck worry, Jane. I'll always be there to save his butt." He laughed robustly at me.

"Like three-legged dogs," I bet.

"Exactly. And heavy cars too." More laughter.

"He's right, forget it. It doesn't bother me. I don't believe in such things." Nonetheless, she could read on my face that I was still troubled.

"Rusty, please don't worry about it," she said, trying to put me at ease and taking pity on my name. "It's just a silly game that one of the girls at the farm taught me, and I'm not sure if I even did it right. It doesn't mean anything, really. I don't take it seriously. Whatever will be will be." She then leaned back in the seat and added—further trying to comfort me—that I had strong hands and they would take me far in life, accomplishing much in the long run. She was very glad that she could tell me about that part and extremely sorry if she had upset me.

"That's great," was my initial thought. The first thing I will be forced to accomplish with them is strangling Wesley for dragging his sad butt back home and ruining my fate in the short run. Or worse, I would have to confront Kim, making it doubly bad on her for claiming that she loved me—and then throwing me away because Wesley was the father of her child and deserved another chance. "What can I do?" she might say. What else could I do but think about what she might actually do or feel obliged to do. It sounded sure enough like a serious tragedy and a challenging event, and it could easily happen very soon. I was sorry that I had let the silly game upset me, immensely disappointed in myself for letting it do so. Rick was right. I was a schmuck. Maybe I should have said a better prayer.

Life has an odd way of changing the subject on one, and at the pinnacle of my concern, when I was going to speak up again despite my embarrassment and stated disbelief, Jane spotted Kamloops Lake on our left, calling our attention to it. It was striking, as most things are in British Columbia. It was immeasurably wide and stretched on endlessly, adorned with embankments of thick bunchgrass and pockets of Douglas fir, including ponderosa pine and spruce trees. The blue sheen coloring the water reflected radiantly in the sunlight, and this ocean gloss spoke of its depth, which we later learned to be 500 feet. Jane was thrilled and said the area would be a great place to go hiking and camping, adding that it was a sterling first sign of her new home. Jack's stock was rising, and Jane's mind was now on the exhilaration of finding him soon—not my palm. I feared there wouldn't be time to ask her again.

For now, we would settle on finding Jack's place. Practiced gentlemen, for the most part, we offered to deliver Jane safely into the arms of her lover. She had an indistinct map on her, a hand drawing of the highway and a few streets, plus a river, which turned out to be the Thompson River. It was a surging waterway that eventually fed into Kamloops Lake, and its two main branches originated from a smaller lake and a distant northern glacier. Jack lived within 150 yards of this pulsating torrent, one with a life force of its own and a direction with real purpose. How odd that it would share the company of four wandering Americans, all dispossessed in a peculiar way, with only a hint of their budding direction and purpose to come.

Coincidence also had its own life force and kept right on flowing. Jack rented a dilapidated trailer, a ramshackle one very similar to Kim's, but standing alone, not suffering the indignity of better dressed neighbors. No other dwellings were within throwing distance of it, and sitting just off the river's bank it was easy to find. On this side the bank was sandy and flat and some 40 yards broad. Sightseers passed by occasionally, walking slowly and smiling merrily, enjoying the leisure of an idyllic afternoon. Near the middle of the river numerous water skiers enjoyed perfect weather and skiing conditions, room enough for all, the lovely Thompson appearing to be at least a mile wide.

To say that we surprised Jack is an understatement. He was busy hanging laundry in the hot sun, a long cord tied to one corner of the trailer and attached to a tall, thin metal pole, about 15 yards away. We parked in an open space only 75 feet from where he stood working, but he didn't hear the Princess, her catlike purr overtaken by the noise of river machines and skiers yelling at each other in an unknown tongue. It turned out to be French.

"There he is!" Jane shouted, jumpy and anxious, more than pleased that we had found him so straightaway. We had all gotten out of the car before he finally turned to see us, and for a few seconds there was no recognition of who we might be. Jane stooped low behind me, holding onto the back of my belt to keep her balance, giggling like a schoolgirl.

"What's he doing, Rusty? Can he see me?"

"He's doing what anybody would do, staring at us in confusion," a smile and laughter coming to my face. Without another pause, she popped out and screamed his name, and the two rushed at each other in a burst of happiness. If Jane was a dead ringer for Judy Garland, then this scene was a dead ringer for the one at Jessica's house, when we delivered Jesse in much the same way. Roscoe came to mind once more, and what was it he said about everything in life coming around to itself, again and again, like a circle? The lesson of his spiritual wisdom kept returning to me, never far from my thoughts.

Watching the two lovers hug and dance gaily around the open yard was tender and heartwarming. This must have lasted for five minutes until Jane waltzed Jack over to us, in triple time, both almost falling as they continued to embrace and kiss madly. He was a tall man, as tall as me, very slender, with long brown hair and a week's growth of beard. The features of his tanned face, a good looking face, were sharp and thin, and his cheeks slightly pockmarked from a youthful case of acne, gone now. A tattoo of a mermaid covered half of his exposed chest— he was wearing only shorts—and another, a portrait of his mom and dad, was inked skillfully onto his right thigh. He must have loved them very much.

"Right on. Thank you, fellow Americans," he said, with exuberant gratitude, reaching out to shake our hands briskly, employing the '60s handshake, which was standard for our generation. "Jane says you are two cool cats from California, and you have done her a great service. Both of us, in fact. Very glad to meet both of you. Thanks again. Right on."

We traded introductions and said we were glad to be of assistance, naturally. They then invited us to stay, Jane insisting, and talk for a while and have a cold beer down by the river. They said they wanted to do at least that much to repay us. Such an invitation was too hard to pass up. We still had a long drive ahead of us, and a cold beer and good company sounded like a fine start to it.

The two of them disappeared inside the trailer for about 10 minutes, then emerged just as happy as that first moment together, apologizing for the delay before walking us to the river. We headed to Jack's favorite spot, 20 yards from the river's edge, and downriver from the skiers, still shouting to each other in great fun. I relieved Jane of the four beach chairs she carried, leaving her with only odds and ends. Rick helped Jack carry a large cooler and a bag full of eats, chips and cheese and such. It looked like a party.

So it was and all very reasonable. Jane took over at first, a skilled host, spreading out a towel for each of us, moving any sharp rocks that might poke through. Then she put down another to make sandwiches on, arranging the paper plates and plastic utensils in tidy columns. She was as meticulous about it as Kim had been by the other river. Jane coached me on how to line up the chairs, strategically, so that they faced both the river and each other. I followed her instructions precisely, and I was pleased to see her so happy and so much in love. I wanted Kim to love me the way Jane loved Jack.

After ingesting cold ham sandwiches, cheese and chips, and downing a few beers, while still sitting on our towels, we then moved to the chairs and watched the energetic river sweep by, commenting on the beauty of it and what a fine Canadian summer day it turned out to be. At one point we all gathered flat rocks and engaged in a water skimming contest, Jack easily winning. He had a slingshot for an arm, saying he had plenty of practice during the long, lonely weeks of waiting for Jane. Mainly, we just sat around comfortably and talked. Jack was eager to know all about us. We filled him in as far as we thought polite, taking into account the delicate nature of some things, as we had done at Stanley Park. In reality, I doubted either of them would have been shocked or surprised by anything we shared. Most of it was likely ground they had already traveled.

After hearing about us, and in the same manner as Jane, he told us his own story with some rigor. It was interesting to hear it from his perspective, but we could sense that he didn't want our sympathy. He was 21, and after three years of college, and Jane too, they both decided to take a break from their studies and work full time. Their goal was to save enough money so they could visit Europe for a summer, following their senior years, climbing rugged mountains and languishing in the soft, quiet valleys, as they discovered them. Many young Americans had already done the same, and hiking Europe was much the fad in these days. It sounded much too flamboyant for me, a guy who might not have even made this trip except for the perils of a dark driveway and a big mouth.

Their plans fell apart when the United States Selective Service System caught up to Jack. He thought he could safely take a year off and not be found, the pool of available draftees wide and deep. He had misjudged the government's focused diligence, obviously, and within four months of quitting school he was promptly located. It was then fight or flight. Of course, he was opposed to the war and voiced his many objections to it, all of which he articulated masterfully and at convincing length. He was very bright, part of the generation of young people who would help change and mold the culture in Canada in the years to come. I agreed with some of the things he said, and not so much with others, but remained silent and just listened.

Jane sat in the chair next to him, their arms interlocked, nodding her affirmations, now and again, correcting him about small details at college and the farm. We found out that neither of them were serious potheads. Working on the farm was just a lucrative job and immediately available. By taking it they got to do the one thing in the world they loved most, hiking long distances. To add icing to the cake and cinch the deal, and considerable risk, they got to do that job together. Their daily chore was inspecting and repairing miles of irrigation lines that led from the main water source to the thirsty and thriving plants, spread out over hundreds of acres. They only smoked weed on occasion, Jack remarking that the high usually made them paranoid, causing Jane to laugh and add, "We spent a lot of money on munchies!" She was funny, and I liked her more and more as I got accustomed to the gentle womanly traits she possessed, coming to light one at a time, and blended nicely together with her obvious ruggedness and resolve. She was so young. I wondered where it all came from. She must have been extraordinarily brave to hitchhike so far, alone, and uncertain of what awaited her on the road. Her intellectual talents were also abundant. She would go on to be a skilled doctor—I learned later—in years to come, and Jack would finally get the engineering degree he always wanted. Then both would become accomplished professionals in Canada. Yes, one day, a decade from now, they would return home and tell their families a whale of a story.

Presently, they had not yet communicated with their families about their new lives in a foreign land. Jack made no apologies for the move, telling us that there was plenty of time to inform them, and the more pressing issues of life needed to be settled first. His family would just have to wait to hear from him, knowing he could take care of himself. Jane excused herself for a moment after he said this, walking downstream by herself and weeping. Jack had been unknowingly curt when addressing the subject. It obviously struck a deep nerve in her, the enormity of the prospect of never seeing her family again. His words had been a torch of pain, burning hot enough to cause her to walk away and cry.

"She'll be fine," Jack said. "Until we are married, she'll always have the option of going back. This life might not be permanent for her. Anyway, I can't worry about it too much right now," he added, dejectedly. He picked up a loose stick and started drawing figures in the sand, and my compassion for both of them grew. I began to understand that this was serious business: life in the fast lane and perhaps no turning around for them.

Otherwise, Jack was hopeful and optimistic, sitting back in his chair and straightening his spine. "I'll be working steady at a local pulp mill in a few weeks and be able to support us pretty well. We will see how things go in the States with the war and plan from there. I'm not dying for any phony brass bastards. I can assure you of that."

Yet having Jane walk away deeply saddened him. It showed. I sensed he was afraid he might lose her in this whole mess of war and country, bravery and cowardice, love and family, or however Jane might come to see it and then finally decide what to do. To bear up with what faced him in life—now that he was on the run and forced to reinvent everything at only 21—would be unthinkable without her. He ultimately said so, adding that his situation was pitiful if he lost her. I was overwhelmed with grief. I just wanted to hug him. So, without much hesitation, I leaned over and did. I tried to comfort him, saying that one day the war would end and all would be forgiven, and in due time he'd find himself hiking in Humboldt County again, with his sidekick, Jane. He thanked me and wiped a tear away from his cheek, not expecting this display of compassion from me. Rick reached out and gave him an affirmative handshake, and said, "Right on, brother, it's all going to be fine for you two."

In all the chatter of love and country, we lost track of time and several hours had passed, so I quizzed Rick about our plans to reach Calgary. He had a good buzz going from the beers, now numbering a half dozen apiece. In fact, we all did, so when I asked him my words came out slurred and broken.

"You're drunk, Cosmo," he laughed, "and I'm close to it. I'm not going to Calgary with either of us."

"Good, then it's settled," Jane said, surprising us by her unobserved return. "You can stay for dinner and spend the night. They don't need you in Calgary."

Now that she had found us, and Jack, she wouldn't let us

go. She was as sweet as Tupelo Honey, a woman with a soul. Furthermore, she was right. Calgary had flourished well and long enough without us and running into any Mounties right now, in our condition, would have neither of us laughing. "I agree with you both," I said, winking at Jane, then reaching out to grab Rick by his chest hair, latching on and pulling hard.

"You son of a bitch, Cosmo!" he yelped, reeling back, knocking himself off his chair and falling to the sand. Oh, what a good chuckle we all had.

"I guess I'm not as drunk as you think I am, eh, convict?"

He jumped up and kicked sand on me, running down the beach and then mooning me, the way he had done in Oregon. Jack and Jane howled with laughter, urging him to come back. It was getting to be time to leave.

I was sober enough in a few hours to take the four of us on a tour of Kamloops. Jack was already familiar with many of the local landmarks and would tell us if he had hiked in a certain area, speaking of what new things he discovered. This pleasant town, amid the river and lake, and lovely pockets of forested mountains, looked to me to be about half the population of my hometown, making it 25,000 or so. It had been built on timber and fur, as most of the early outposts were in this region. Before returning to his Taj Mahal, a nickname that I had also given to Kim's trailer—in the sweetest of sarcasm—we drove by the pulp mill where Jack would be working soon. Jane got excited and noted that it was within walking distance of the trailer, and she could meet him daily for lunch, while she looked for work. We all found that reasonable and romantic, telling her so.

That evening we barbecued hamburgers in the fashion we had done at Kim's. I longed to see her again and told Jane, in a private moment, a bit about her. She was shocked and mortified by Wesley's betrayal, but was pleased to know that we had hit it off so well and in such a short time. Then she quickly jotted down her new address and urged me to write her after I returned home, bringing her up to speed on my travels and love life. She scolded me for not telling my mom I was leaving, saying in a twist of irony, "Mr. Cosmo, it's not like you are running from the draft."

She knew her new place in life and her man's, intimately, and it had only taken her a few hours to learn. I was touched by her soft, sisterly tone and her sincere concern for me. After all, she was just a young woman but apparently as tough as nails, if she could hitchhike hundreds of miles by herself and then act so composed and wise, as she did now. She read palms, too? What kind of a woman was she, really? I regretted later not asking her about the more sensitive things she might have had on her mind: the pitfalls of establishing a new life in a new country, and perhaps what she might have thought about Roscoe's view of home and travel. At the time, I thought doing so might be too painful for her. I think the two of them would have liked each other very much.

The rest of the night was spent sitting outside the tiny trailer, in the warm night air and starry sky, talking about our collective lives and dreams for the future. All of them were grand, of course, the four of us ambitious and not to be satisfied with the ordinary accomplishments in life. There wasn't a secondhand Jane among us. Rick had plans to expand his father's restaurant business and recapture Texas in one weekend. Jane spoke of studying medicine and finding the cure for broken hearts, and Jack gave a delightful description of his design for a bridge spanning the Atlantic, exotic hotels and restaurants attached to floating barges. I was going to teach history in college and instruct my students in the finer nuances of Western civilization, giving philosophy seminars in my spare time. We stuck pretty close to this kind of inspiring discourse, saying nothing more about the war or Jack's flight or fight with the U.S. military. We focused on positive things, which was a generational trait, and ones that would someday, through our hard work and true grit, make us happy people. We were all for that, we declared. Such ennobling chatter lasted until late evening, and finally the young lovers said goodnight to us, off to show more tender affections for each other. Then the thought of sweet, tragic Jane crossed my mind, and her handsome Mexican-American savior who was getting very sleepy. I purposely left myself out of it, except to get mad at Kim for a moment, having sent me packing with nothing more than a kiss on the cheek. I was determined to fix that. Overall, I thought of all my new friends and my dear old one, and the lessons Roscoe said I might learn on the road.

The two of us sacked out in our bags, comfortable enough behind the trailer, facing the river. I soon spotted the silhouette of two jackrabbits near the water's edge, motionless, watching the river from heaven pass by, and I wondered where their journeys in the animal kingdom might take them. Then something spooked them, and they shot off like rabbits do, fast and frantic, darting, changing directions on a dime and disappearing into the night. I thought I had an answer to why they fled, or at least part of it. They would run away from things in life if they got too dangerous and there were no other options. It was much the same for the 40,000 American draft dodgers now in Canada, young men running away from their own real or perceived danger. They were truly children of a common mother. Thankfully, this one would not require blood as payment for their freedom. The Peace Arch really meant what it said it did. I imagined that I wasn't in a foreign country at all, other than it was throwing me out in another day.

It didn't always feel good to be an American in these times of great social unrest, not knowing always who to side with. It was an odd feeling and unfair to my country and myself. The Fourth of July would be here in two days, and I had never before thought so passionately about freedom. It had come so naturally throughout my life. Now it wasn't natural. A dirty little war was proving that in spades and much more. I had been sure in my response when Rick asked me how one knows that God is real, but I was sure about nothing when it came to knowing what made freedom real. I said the word out loud, and it was the first time it left a bitter taste in my mouth.

"Rusty, shut up. I'm trying to sleep, and I don't want to hear any freedom speeches from you right now."

"Was I thinking out loud?"

"Yeah, and you always got some transcendental shit on your mind, like that Thoreau crap you tried to give me earlier. Now, shut up, and give that kind of stuff a rest, will ya?"

"Yeah," I said, softly. "I was just thinking about freedom and what our country is doing to thousands of good men like Jack."

"It's a grand problem, lover boy," he answered, in a serious, thoughtful tone, but he still sounded a little impatient with me. "Listen, the war will end, like you told him today, and he'll get to come home soon. All will be well in America. Stop fretting about it like an old woman. You don't even know the guy."

"What is freedom, Rick? What is freedom?"

"That sounds a lot like my line. I think you're the thief."

"Perhaps I am."

The next morning we all plowed into the Princess and cruised in search of coffee and donuts. Jane looked twice as pretty in her clean bellbottom jeans and tight fitting T-shirt, braless and becoming. We let her and Jack do most of the talking, and it was much the same as the night before. Sober or tipsy, they would take their freedom where they found it, and make the best of the situation, using their considerable American know-how.

I loved both of them, and when we finally said goodbye it was as if I was losing part of my own family. I never got to ask Jane to read my palm again, hoping she would claim to be in error. It would have relieved the burden of my heavy heart. It didn't matter, I reasoned, nobody skates through life clean, and I was resolute to make it through whatever befell me. If Jack and Jane could endure their challenges, then I could endure mine. So I became determined to focus on what she predicted would be my contented love life, and as far as I was concerned, that meant spending it with Kim. With such a woman by my side nothing could defeat me. Still, what my fate line hadn't revealed to her, or what she hadn't said, was that I was taking Rick with me. Or perhaps he was taking me with him. Our very lives and fates would be intertwined closely and more intimately than we ever dreamed possible. Very soon, just as Jane had said.

We wished them well, giving Jane a long and warm hug and Jack a firm handshake—no hugging a guy when sober. Then they were gone from our lives, just like that.

That's what happened after meeting hippie Jane and her American outlaw, Jack. I have already told you what fate had in store for them, in the long run, and I wished I could have been the one to read Jane's palm and tell her about it. Perhaps she already knew what her future held.

"Do you know where we are going?"

"You know, Rick, I vote for home. We are not needed in Calgary."

"I'm for that," he said. "Let's go home."

[12]
A RUDE RETURN

We agreed that the drive to the border would be nonstop, gas only. It would put us slightly ahead of our Mountie target time, a concern that had never been far from my mind. We spent part of this time discussing the irony of Jack being allowed to stay in the Great White North and welcomed for it, and on the other hand, the two of us in clear possession of our deportation orders.

"Nothing has happened on this trip that I expected, Cosmo. I told you that, didn't I?"

"I'm with you, moony man. I can't explain it either, and I can't explain it away."

"I don't think I'll even bother," he said, in a heartsick fashion.

"You're not going to mention sweet Jane in Vancouver to anyone and just leave the tragic part out? It must be the luckiest thing to happen on this trip, minus my true love for Kim." After saying this, I was jolted by the thought of Jane's recently deceased father and how the tragedy hadn't left her out. It was appalling that I could be so casual about it. God save me from myself. I wished I had held my tongue. Rick slightly misunderstood me. Still, it provided little relief.

"Yeah, well, that's what I took care of at church," he answered. "And it's not like I killed anybody, so I'm back in good graces and want to keep it that way. I figure the worst is over." The entirety of what happened with Jane was still touching a sensitive part of his young soul, and I didn't need to pry it apart to get a better look. I had said enough. Still, in due time, the worst would be far from over.

"We'll have to stop at Jessica's place to fetch my wallet. It will give us enough money to make it home in style," I said, glad to change the subject.

"Maybe we can stop at the DMV and I can get a new license. Something to remind me of the real Mr. Ruiz. What do you think about that?" The idea excited him.

"I'm not thinking about killing myself trying to find the DMV in Seattle, bro. Can't you do that at home? Besides, I'm pretty sure you'll need to be in California to get a proper license."

"What if the other Mr. Ruiz is still on the loose? At least I can inform them that I'm not him."

"The Mounties cleared that up for you, nicely. I wouldn't worry about him. Besides, when I have my license, I can vouch for you." He had that sorrowful look people get when they think they have just been patronized or undervalued. I relented, a little, "Just the same, if we happen to drive by it, speak up. Maybe we'll get lucky and have time to stop." Those sacrifices, again.

"You know, you're right, Cosmo. I rather do it in Cottage Grove, now that I think about it. It will give me a good reason to hitch a ride from Bonnie. Patch things up if I can, m'boy."

"How do you figure that if I'm there? And I still think you'll need to be in California."

"Are you kidding me? She'll do it just to keep from dragging your love sick butt away from Kim. She knows you're the one who can make it all happen. I know. I overheard her saying it to Kim." He paused at this point, shaking his head questioningly at me. "You know, Cosmo, I hope you're not being a chump over all of this. You've known Kim for a total of two days, and this is some serious shit she's dealing with."

"I'm for that, Rick. And I don't think so, and I know that." I was trying to be lighthearted in the midst of his suddenly serious demeanor. His concern had sucked some fun out of the air for me, but I understood what he was driving at. The sweet boy didn't want to see any hearts get broken. This was his way to express it best. Nonetheless, I didn't want to be pinned down on the whole issue of Kim. So I changed the subject again, pointing out some eye-popping sights we hadn't seen before now. He was soon fast asleep in his seat. Oh, Canada!

The long drive to the border was the only time when there was any extended silence between us. It might be what happens to all travelers on the dash for home: a time of rest and quiet reflection—and sleep. If that was the case for me, and it was, then I reflected on how this road trip had been paved by fate and providence, exactly the way I should have expected it to be. Except now there were decisions to make.

Throughout much of the hushed silence, even when Rick wasn't asleep, I swam in the magic fountain of my fanciful daydreams. My heart and soul were swelling and swooning in great anticipation of seeing Kim. I laughed inwardly, thinking it must be what happens to a schoolboy on his first crush, when he can hardly control himself, waiting to find his heartthrob at the next recess. I've noticed that when people first fall in love it dominates every thought, every waking moment, holding the mind and emotions captive, leaving the victims weak and useless in all the other important things in life. In fact, there aren't any other important things in life, and a man would rather be in love than conquer the world. So it was for me. The race was on and my path was clear, and Kim Warrens waited at the end of it. I was ready for her to take my breath away, as she had done those first few moments at her trailer, when I walked beside her, and all I could smell was vanilla, craving to know how it tasted on her. In all the miles I couldn't think or plan anything long-term, beyond what might first happen to me, us, if this was for real. I was truly smitten, enjoying every notion of first things first.

Nonetheless, from time to time, I was robbed of this delight. Jane's palm reading and its prediction of pending gloom and doom nagged at me, like a blood sucking mosquito that buzzes your ear in bed and no matter how many times you swat at it, you miss, and don't know when the little bastard is coming back. I know I said it wouldn't plague me, but alas, it still did. I imagined the worst of all dreadful outcomes, relating directly to Wesley, of course, and what I would do to him if ever we met up. They were very ugly thoughts, and I had to fight hard to repel them. Each time they came to me I'd admonish them, "This has gone on long enough!" The devil will find all kinds of ways to get at you, the slimy worm that he is. So with respect to all of this back and forth emotional bouncing, and the long hours I had to devote to it, I kept myself busy, the miles tumbling by. Our eventual arrival back home also seemed incidental, of no real consequence when I thought about it. It was Kim Warrens or bust.

Rick had considered things differently. He mentioned, early in the drive, that he was getting very homesick. To stay fair to him, I decided to make our stops as short as possible, should his attitude stay as it was. I figured Bonnie would take care of this problem for me, and a few days at Kim's would be pleasurable. So I ignored his comment. We weren't there yet.

The border was there yet, here I mean, suddenly rushing upon us with small warning. I was startled to realize that of the hundreds of miles we had just driven, and the long hours it took to accomplish it, I could recall very few of them. Even now, it took a heads-up spark of warning from Mr. Ruiz to help me see the light. "There it is. I see the big light on top of the Peace Arch."

"Wow. That was fast." I really meant it.

"I don't know. I slept most of the way."

"Did you? I hardly noticed." I meant that too.

"Where do you plan on stopping?"

That was a good question. The border crossing on the American side was 300 yards beyond the Canadian crossing. Still, it was close enough for the Americans to see us. "We'll find a place on the shoulder, and you can run over and let them know we are back." It was really just a suggestion but came out like an order.

"Over my dead body, Mr. America. You're going with me!"

"Someone has to stay with the car."

"Then you go! I'll stay with the car."

"OK, we'll both go! But don't say something really stupid like you did the last time, Mr. Show Business. You screw this one up, and I'm leaving your butt here to rot." I was just a little jumpy. I wouldn't really leave him.

It was a tight fit on the shoulder of this busy two-lane highway. After parking, I turned on my hazard lights and carefully inched my way out of the door. The two of us bolted across both wide lanes at the first opportunity, not coming until the last of four semi-trailer trucks swooshed by, the blasts of air blowing dust in our faces. They were only now downshifting, their drivers getting ready to chat their way casually through their international crossing. They came and went as they pleased, mostly, and I figured many of them, if not all, were on a first name basis with the guards.

Our case was different, and I must confess that we were both nervous about meeting up once again with the Canadian side. To make it worse, we would be barging in from the opposite direction and taking them by surprise. Luckily, despite our haphazard and modified manifestation—racing as we did from around the corner of the building and appearing from out of nowhere—it caused little harm. Just the same, my apology and explanation to the nearest border guard was awkward. I tried to make known to him the reason for our abrupt appearance, and as I went on and on my babbling seemed to amuse him.

"He doesn't care what your story is, Cosmo. Just get inside!" Mr. Ruiz simply had no respect for border guards.

The next moment we were inside the primary building, the location of our original discombobulation. We were still a little wired up from racing across the highway, having done nothing but sit for long hours, and we didn't stop running until we reached the building, 100 yards away from the Princess. It was a boyish sprint and our blood pumped fast. The profit of it was only disappointment—there wasn't a familiar face here. It bruised my ego not to see the same crew, anxious that they should all know of our safe and speedy return. I suppose I was looking for a grand Mountie reception for being such a well-mannered guest, an American who was smart enough not to overstay his welcome. Let the brass band play and the parade begin, please!

It was not to be. The current embodiment of all Mounties heroic appeared only mystified as he listened intently to me, examining both of us closely and letting me ramble on without interruption. He then walked briskly to his desk, sitting down and reviewing our paperwork, smiling from time to time. In another minute he was standing before us again, grinning. I guessed him to be 40, short and stout, and he turned stoutly straightforward when addressing us. "It appears that everything is in good order, gentlemen. I hope you enjoyed your stay in Canada. Have a nice evening."

That was it. There would be no brass bands or parades. Just then, another fellow, dressed like a highway transportation worker, popped his head in and barked at us, "You two need to move your car. It's a road hazard!"

"Where did you men park?" Our Mountie asked, in a tone of grave concern. We told him. "Geez, then you better be getting along. I'll call the American side and tell them what to expect."

What to expect? I doubted any of it would make mention of a parade, so I finally let it go. Darn it, I suddenly wished I hadn't rushed through Canada, obeying the law, just to come back and be labeled an American, "What to expect." Just a minute before everything had been in good order. Once outside, we debated all the things the great man in red serge didn't have to say to us and how quickly we had been able to alter his good mood. "How were we supposed to know we could have crossed the American side and not stopped at all?" I finally said to Rick.

"Cosmo, did you once think to ask them the first time?"

"No. I just assumed they figured we would stop on our way back."

"What a schmuck. It looks like we didn't have to worry about when we got back at all, did we?"

"I was obeying the law. And any occasion I'm with you, I have to worry."

The next occasion began right away while crossing the highway again. A serious traffic jam was upon us, latecomers to the border, all seemingly anxious to get home for the Fourth of July. There were loved ones, turkey dinners, their own parades and fireworks, and a proud nation to celebrate. All those cool American things. In turn, no one was pleased that we were crossing in front of them, most of them impatient in the close bumper to bumper traffic, and some took the opportunity to tell us about their impatience—in less than patriotic overtures. We darted to get through them, and once safely in the car we joined this holiday procession. I felt like we were going from international men of mystery to prodigal sons on the doorstep of home.

Finally, it was our turn to cross, and the guard seemed to be both amused and annoyed to meet up with us. "Welcome home, gentlemen," he said. "We got word of you a few minutes ago." A wry and knowing smile covered his face. It embarrassed me. I thanked him, cautiously, asking if he wanted to see our Canadian paperwork. His response was purposefully demeaning, and I wasn't prepared for it. "No, I don't. I'm familiar with it. You two aren't the first to get into this jam." He said it stiffly, overly sarcastic. "Just move along and keep the paperwork in your possession until you get squared away here." This part was an order. With that, he waved us through. We were back in the USA, with all its faults, but no better place to call home.

～～

PART 2

The next stop homeward bound, one of keen significance to us, was Jessica's house. We were now close to Seattle, and our arrival would be a great reunion and a needed payday. I looked forward to regaining my American identity, which meant a formal driver's license. Although I still felt bad for Rick, I would be proud to let him ride on my shoulders, one real American bracing up another. It had a patriotic feel to it and made me think better of myself for considering it this way, having so casually rebuked his idea of finding the DMV. And, heck, we would even have enough to spend an extra 10 bucks at Kim's, going to the fireworks at the fair and eating. We would make it home and still have a half tank of gas.

My mind sprang still another bonanza when I thought about my $300 in the bank, and if I sent it to Kim it would help ground her for six months. One can buy a lot of diapers and baby food with that much money. I could then work at home and save everything I earned. It would be perfect. I would meet her in Cottage Grove in six months and enroll in school, perhaps working part time at a gas station or a retail store. I would be just in time for the little bugger's birth. I would become a family man, happy, responsible and wise, and build a new home: a real home away from home, like my friend Roscoe.

There might be the lingering problem of Wesley, of course, unless a way could be found to off him—permanently. Then it occurred to me that if the Zodiac had already done it, I might never know. Yes, the whole subject had its very unpleasant side, as you've witnessed me experience it, but I still needed to weigh it out some and be ready for any possibility. In my worst moment, I decided I'd arrange his murder myself, if needed. Yeah, that's a smart thing to do! All in all, I despised him for leaving Kim and his child, and loved him for it too, and hoped to despise and love him this way forever. The road that one takes to love can be very curvy.

I wasn't sure what curve to take into Seattle. I could only guess. If I hadn't hit the exact exit, at least the one I took had a familiar look about it, despite the opposite direction. Within a few blocks we found a neighborhood gas station, and when conferring with the attendant, I realized we were close. Our luck was still holding for us. On the downside, all that either of us could remember is that Jessica lived on Douglas Avenue, on the east side of the city. We couldn't remember her address or even a cross street. Douglas Avenue ran for miles. There was nothing left to do except start searching the long blocks one house at a time.

We headed east on this protracted street, at a crawl, not wanting to miss a single home. Jessica's car, a newer, white Oldsmobile, had the kind of look to it that blended in well with the general population of cars, and the entire avenue resembled a huge used car lot. It would be easy to miss both house and car in all the similarity. We did actually pass her place at one point, finding it only when we doubled back. We were very glad not to have missed it a second time. Unknown to us, there never was going to be a car to spot.

"Cosmo, I recognize the porch and the yard, but I don't see her car."

"It doesn't matter. If she's not at home maybe Jesse and the kids are."

No one was home, or would be, for a few days. They had all gone to Bremerton for the Fourth of July. That was tomorrow. They wouldn't be back until the day after. We found this out by reading a note taped securely to the inside door of Jessica's front porch. It was meant for a friend, but I had no idea if that person had already read it. It was crafted in such exquisite handwriting that I wouldn't blame anyone for not tearing it down. At least it was out of sight of foot traffic, outside.

"Great, what are we going to do now?"

"I don't know, Rick. I'm thinking."

"We're out of money and almost out of gas, so think of something good, will ya?"

We decided it would be good to check all the bottom windows in the two-story house, nightfall approaching. Our hope was that one was unlocked and no one would see us break in. Obviously, no matter how blameless, such an entry was still a crime. If caught, we would have to rely heavily on our recently refined powers of oratory, especially those belonging to Mr. Ruiz. After all, he had sharpened them to a razor's edge on a steak and sweet Jane. We would proclaim the innocent virtue of our actions, crowned by a healthy dose of what we thought made up innocent, virtuous actions. The ingenuity of youth and all that. We had come to believe we could rely on these qualities. Fair enough, we pressed on.

We didn't have to wait long to test them. We began our search at the back of the house, intending to work our way to the front, but before we were finished with the first few windows, he was there, standing on the side lawn, waiting for us. He was a slight, well-groomed man, probably in his early 60s, with close cropped white hair and a marvelously trimmed handlebar mustache. I will never forget him: He was a thing of beauty and a national treasure. Dressed in new, dark blue jeans, a red blazer, white T-shirt, and red loafers with white socks, he topped his national splendor with a checked red, white and blue duck hat, with a prominent and shiny Old Glory pendant pinned to the bill. You could have strung him up like a flag! He was precious, and I was glad to meet such an American. He was glad to inquire of us, as well.

"Can I be of help to you, young men?" He was friendly enough, but cautious with the question, wearing a very inquisitive smirk, not knowing what he may have stumbled upon. Thankfully, he didn't appear to be afraid of us.

"Oh, hello there," I said. "We are friends of the family and noticed that they are out of town. We were looking to retrieve some money we left here. We thought first of an open window as a convenient way to get in." Boy, I hoped it didn't register with him as bad as it sounded to me. Really, the innocent truth shouldn't sound that bad. I had managed to blurt the words out, nervously. So much for oratory skills. To him, the inquisitive treasure, we might as well have been two inept cat burglars. Then again, reason told me that even inept cat burglars wouldn't say such a thing.

Rick was useless to the cause, adding nothing more than an embarrassed look, just standing there motionless and taciturn, his arms at his side, ready to be handcuffed. Luckily, it wouldn't get that bad.

"Well, that's an interesting story. Why should I believe it?" the American said.

"Because it's the truth," I said, in my best, return American.

"Always a good place to start. I thought I recognized your Camaro. Are you the two boys who were hanging around here a few days ago?"

"Yeah, that's us! I left my wallet here by mistake. We brought Jessica's brother here, helping him pull a tree stump in the back. Then you remember us?"

"Yeah, I think I do. Didn't know about the tree stump, though. Was it a bugger?"

We both laughed. "Yeah, that's one way to put it. We still have some scars left over. At least I do." I raised my arms to show him my barely visible scratches.

"Bugger," stone face spoke. He was completely healed. It didn't matter. The American believed us.

"Well, you probably shouldn't have been trying the windows. If someone has called the cops, they'll be here any minute. I'll wait with you. I might be able to help."

I didn't know if he said that to cover himself, in case we really were lying, or if there was real truth in what he said. The cops? We were in eyeshot of a half dozen other houses, God bless us, but I hadn't seen a lot of people milling about, spying around. Many were out of town for the holiday. Still, I wished we had chosen a better way, my fear of getting noticed now front and center. So we waited, making senseless small talk, until enough time passed to make us think we got away with it.

"It looks like I'm the only one who saw you. That's good."

He shook our hands, finally, and introduced himself. His name was Steve Smith, and I'm not kidding, it was all I could do to keep from laughing. We were graced by the presence of a real American, with a real American name, doing what real Americans do best: protecting life, liberty and the pursuit of happiness. Right now, we were what he was protecting them from.

"Well, I don't have Jessica's address or phone number, wherever that might be in Bremerton, but I think the name of the street is Carson Street. The town isn't that big."

"How far away is Bremerton?" I asked him, having never heard of it.

"It's about 50 minutes away by ferry, probably a little more by car."

"There is a ferry?"

"Each day, I hear tell, goes right across Puget Sound, due west. It even comes back. That's the best part!" He liked this little joke, warming up more to us, enough to risk a little humor. "The ferry is nice and relaxing, to tell you the truth, and the kids like it. If you want to get there by car, you will have to travel south to near Tacoma first, then head back north on Highway 16."

"But you said it was longer by car?"

"Well, you have the drive time but not the hassle of loading and unloading at the ferry. Even though, as I said, it's a lot of fun."

"How big is Bremerton?" I further quizzed him.

"I'd guess 25,000. It's a shipyard town, mainly. They'll be having a huge fireworks celebration, just off the water. Happens every year. It might even top Seattle, but the one here is good." He sensed the way I was leaning, by my questions, and had a word of warning for me. "But let me remind you, young man, I only said I think the name of the street is Carson Street. It seems she mentioned it to me once, awhile ago. I think she had just returned from there. But I wouldn't bet the nation on it."

"Does she have any other friends around who might know?" Rick asked, having worked up the courage of multiple words.

"No, I don't think so," Mr. Smith said. "She pretty much sticks to herself and her kids."

"Do you live close by, Mr. Smith?" I finally thought to ask.

"Yeah." He seemed surprised that I would even inquire. "Right across the street. As I said, I recognized your car and saw you two poking around. I try to keep an eye out for everyone."

"I want to thank you for believing us," I said. "I know our antics might have been harder to explain to the police."

"No harm, guys. Good luck to you, then. Break a leg, and whatever you do don't break it over trouble. Happy Fourth of July." He felt good that he had done his patriotic duty, and he had, and I felt good for him too. With no more fanfare, he turned and promptly walked back across the street, where he had promptly walked over from, ducking into a newly painted white house with silver trim and perfect landscaping. His quick and informal exit did leave me slightly befuddled, yet I was certain that if we decided to hang around it wouldn't be the last we saw of him. I hoped not.

Our own inalienable rights a bit on hold, I looked to Rick for sound advice and inspiration. "What do you want to do? I say we should look for them in Bremerton."

"It might be bad, lover boy. If we get over there and waste a lot of time searching, we might not have enough gas to get back." It was a warning to me that I had already considered, but I was traveling the path of love's sweet allure, sprinkled with denial, a sometimes fatal combination if not caught early and treated. In other words, I would take the chance if it meant seeing Kim sooner.

"Do you have any money left?"

"Cosmo, I have seven cents. That's it."

"I saved 35 cents to use the phone. We can keep it for our last gallon of gas." I was confident. It was the same amount I had when entering Canada.

"To drive where? To a telephone booth we can't afford?"

"That's funny, convict. But listen up. We have a quarter tank, and with another gallon, we'll have a good shot at it."

"A shot at what?"

"A shot at finding Carson Street and finding them, Herr Einstein."

"What are you going to do if you find them? Are you going to drag them back home to get your wallet?"

"Then what do you suggest?"

"I vote we stay here until they get home."

"What? I'll be eating my shoelaces by then, Rick. Let's just give it one shot and make sure to save enough gas to get back."

"And if we don't?"

"Listen, we can go as far as Tacoma and then check the gas. If it looks bad we can turn around then." He still remained doubtful, but the plan wasn't all that unreasonable. I tried to sweeten the pot. "And we'll turn around before we have to spend the 35 cents. A candy bar and soda for you—on me."

"OK, Cosmo. We'll take a shot. Let's just be careful. I don't want to get stuck in the middle of nowhere."

"Great. Let's get going. We only have an hour of daylight left."

We blasted out of there without thinking to inform Mr. Smith, saying goodbye and thanks for his trust. It wouldn't have hurt to show some additional gratitude. I guess we figured we'd see him again, soon enough, if things went wrong. I still felt bad about it. Plus, it would have been good to have his phone number. A last ditch lifeline to a new friend isn't a bad thing.

Just the same, my confidence was high, getting another boost by finding a close onramp to Highway 5. In no time, it seemed, we were just outside Tacoma. "The gauge looks great, just under a quarter tank," I boasted to Rick, eager to press for pressing on. "I think with an extra gallon, we'll be OK."

"We better find Carson Street fast. We might be cutting this close. All this in the name of love, eh, Cosmo?"

"You know you want to get back to Cottage Grove as fast as I do. You wouldn't have mentioned the bit about Bonnie helping you with your license. She's who you are shooting for, isn't she?" I tried to indict him with the same charge, a little put off by his harsh, unexpected retort, even if he was right.

"Yeah, but I'd actually like to make it back, my gringo friend. I know you're pressing this because your skin is itching to see Kim, but your eagerness is going to bring trouble with it."

"So you rather starve on Jessica's porch for two days?"

"It would have been a safe place to sleep. We could have got some grub from the neighbors. I'm sure at least Mr. Smith would help us out."

"We can still get some grub from him. It's only another 25 minutes to Bremerton. We'll be fine." Love can just tie one into knots, if you let it.

Then I made an expensive mistake, spending the last of my meager change. We made Bremerton by the predicted time and stopped at a small market for directions. Sure enough, Carson Street existed, and our luck seemed to be holding together. Making a spontaneous decision—figuring we'd find Jessica and family straightaway—I splurged, buying two candy bars and a soda to share with Rick. We hadn't eaten since leaving Kamloops, having given our extra food to Jack and Jane, assuring them we'd be at Jessica's dinner table tonight. We took a moment to enjoy the treats and then readied ourselves to head out to find the much-sought-after Ms. Jessica. Rick hadn't objected to my lavish spending. We were both hungry.

Bremerton was a lovely, picturesque town, and proud quarters of Puget Sound Naval Shipyard. I couldn't have been more at home, and I detected that Rick felt the same, despite his present apprehensions. His spirits had lifted noticeably, and he had been joking around. One can't have enough sugar. From where I still stood, at the side of the market, I could clearly see the shipyard across Navy Yard Highway, appearing much the same as the one in my hometown. Hammerhead cranes dominated the skyline, as they do at pretty much every naval shipyard, excluding the ships. When I was a young boy a scary story was told of how the cranes turned into gigantic, fierce monsters at night, roaming the city streets, spying on the bedroom windows of young children. They would find them easily and quickly, then snatch them up in their vicious steel jaws and devour them as midnight snacks. Moist, crunchy and delicious. Because of my siblings, fond of sharing the story, I pretty much spent my childhood years scared to death to go to bed. It was the one place too dangerous to be. When it was quiet, I could hear every creak in the house, and it sounded like the walls were crumbling down around me, and then the cold, steel, jagged teeth would have me. Eating me! Unmercifully! I couldn't bear the thought of being eaten alive by such a terrible fiend as a crane monster. I know others would think the same.

"It's just down a few miles, on the left. We will be there before you can blink, macho man." I said this with great personal assurance, still sure that we would find Jessica and the gang, quickly. An employee at the market had drawn a small map for me, and I studied it closely. It appeared simple and straightforward enough. I tossed the tiny map to the car floor, after giving it one more look. I could smell Carson Street but soon found out that Carson Street wasn't a street at all. It was a cul-de-sac, eight houses in total, with well-manicured lawns and very quiet at the moment. Despite being slightly misinformed, success was success, and that was good enough for me. So I darted my eyes from house to house, trying to spot any sign of Jessica or her children. Surely young children still play outside at dusk, don't they? Unless there are none, and that's how many I saw. I didn't see the Oldsmobile, either."

"Man, this place is a graveyard," Rick said.

"Yeah, I don't see a living soul."

"Well, what now, Sherlock?"

"I don't know, Rick. Knock on some doors, I guess. It still might be the right place. Somebody might know them." I was thinking about Mr. Smith and how he also missed the cul-de-sac part. I was looking for anyone to blame, except me.

"What do you want me to do?"

"Just sit here and look suspicious, like a common steak thief. That should be easy for you."

Rick had been driving, but when I got out he deliberately moved to the passenger seat. My crazy uncle once told me that it was a common strategy used by thieves, gangsters, and the general sort of bandits and burglars and no-accounts, when scoping out their target. It made them appear as only innocent passengers waiting for the driver to return. I must have shared these doubtful words of wisdom with Rick and he hadn't forgotten. It probably doesn't work out so well when someone rushes out and tries to shoot you. He must have already thought about that, leaving the keys in the ignition, at the quick, proving how smartly he could think things through. Then he adjusted his seat to its convenient backward position, practically a full recline. It was a great feature the Princess possessed, one we had both taken advantage of many times.

"I'll be right back, convict. Maybe someone around here knows her."

"I'll keep a sharp eye out, Cosmo, like they do in the movies."

"You'll make it in show business yet, Ruiz."

Of the eight houses, only three owners answered the door. It wasn't until I spoke with the last one that I clearly understood our new problem. When I returned, Rick was dozing, keeping a sharp eye out. I rapped my knuckles on the window, shouting, "Time to wake up, senor. This isn't the place, but a lady said she thought we should check at the waterfront. All the local children should be there tonight and tomorrow night. Apparently, there is a carnival in town for the holidays."

He slowly rolled down the window, not looking impressed by this news. "Quit shouting, Rusty. I can hear you. And what do you mean this isn't the place, and we should be at a carnival?"

"She doesn't know Jessica or her children," I told him. "But she said this is the only Carson Street, I mean cul-de-sac, she knows of in town. But the good news, amigo, is that Jessica's kids are certain to be at that carnival, and that means Jessica and Jesse will be there."

"You're quite certain of all this, are you, inspector?"

"Come on, man, think about it. It makes perfect sense. They were coming over here to have a good time, right? That means kids at a carnival. I think our chances are good on this one. Let's take a quick ride over there and check it out." He gave me an incredulous stare and meant to do it. "Why are you looking at me like that?"

"I don't know, Cosmo. You're really starting to worry me. Shakespeare didn't write about love with this much tragedy in mind. You are itching to bring down trouble on us. And you still haven't told me what you are going to do if you find them."

"You've just lost your sense of adventure, Rick." It was the only thing I could think to say. He was right about how I was acting, but I wasn't ready to cave in to reason. "Listen up, Mr.

Ruiz, the carnival is close by, she says, so it won't hurt to drive a few more miles. Let's just get over there." He should have put his foot down, right then, but he didn't because of his friendship with me. Friendships can cost plenty, sometimes.

"OK, but then we are going to have to make a smart decision. This is it, Cosmo, and then we head back to Seattle. No argument!" Sadly, the smart decision would elude us in the end, as they are apt to do when love is heavy in the air.

There was sure enough a carnival, and it was sure enough packed with hurried kids and beleaguered parents. I imagined that Roscoe would have called it a real barn burner, everyone clamoring joyfully at each other's side, excited and eager to make the next attraction. It was a large, electric cavalcade of wonders, packed with this large and anxious crowd in search of them. Only a short distance away, I could see the pyrotechnicians, very near the water's edge, busily working away, preparing for the following night's spectacular gala of fireworks. There must have been 25 of them, all scurrying about, sometimes in groups or sometimes alone, but all with a defined purpose and a resolute look. The show must go on. I had always been impressed by their unstated courage. It was, in many respects, a dangerous job.

Rick dropped me off at the curb, and we agreed that I would run through the carnival one time and then carefully walk it. It sounded like a good tactic, thought of by Rick, and better than standing around hoping they would bump into me, which I actually did for a few minutes. The plan was to meet him back at this exact location in 30 minutes. He would have to circle in the car and because of the heavy traffic, barricaded streets, and a significant police presence, it would likely take him that much time. So we were in agreement, off in different directions, one to fight his last stand and the other to have his nerves stand on end.

It was going to be a rough ride for him, but I wouldn't know that for more than an hour. At first, he was obligated to idle in traffic while the police and a tow truck driver were busy trying to move a stalled semi-trailer truck, one belonging to the carnival, clogging up the center of the main intersection. It had broken down only yards in front of him and just as he was pulling away. It was 30 minutes before his path was clear again. During this time, he shut the engine off but was ordered by the police to turn it back on. His choices were to sit and wait or sit and wait. This seemed unreasonable to him, but he needed to follow instructions, not having a legitimate driver's license and not having possession of the car's owner. It made him nervous and angry to waste precious gas this way, but there was nothing he could do about it except grow fretful and apprehensive. And he did, cursing me behind my back, and he would have done so had I been there in person. In fact, we had both been on edge since our recent stop at the border where we had been lectured and laughed at for being American oddballs. The oddity was growing larger and threatened to consume us unless Jessica and the gang magically materialized. I pressed on in hope.

This time I didn't turn out to be any good at magic or hope. The carnival was a body-to-body people fest, and half of Washington State must have been here. I was fatigued to boot, suddenly drained from the long day and the extended drive. So I just stood at the front entrance for several minutes, dizzy and off balance. The swirling atmosphere of the hectic and raucous festival attacked all my senses, leaving me disoriented and lingering too long in one spot. I scanned the group of people nearest me, three dozen or so, with a great sense of futility, able to spend only a fraction of a second studying each face. There were hundreds of faces here to study.

As I began to move along, I tried looking for six people, at once, a happy group of family members gaily strolling along. Then I finally realized that it wasn't the way kids usually do it. They were probably off by themselves, scattered in different directions. So I switched to looking at only the adults, ones with young boys tagging along. Robert would surely be stuck to Jesse like glue and close by would be mother Jessica. I thought hard about where I would go if I was still a kid like Robert. I ducked into the Insane Asylum and the House of Horrors but was quickly bounced from both of them, not having a ticket. I checked the bumper cars, the Ferris wheel, and the strongman booth, where Jesse might show off his physical prowess to the young lad and where the proud eagle could stretch its wings.

Thus, I found myself searching in this desperate way, bending the rules, so much so that I almost got into a fist fight with one of the carnies at the Screamin' Swing. I kept colliding with numerous patrons as they tried to exit the ride. Each time I strained to look past someone, I ran into another, the world being generally of a much shorter breed. To cap my folly, I spotted a pretty girl or groups of them, every few seconds or feet. The distraction was terrible, and it didn't help one bit. There are always those who unintentionally blind you and make your heart stop beating.

Having searched from one end of the carnival and back again, taking about 25 minutes or so, I headed to the street to look for Rick. He wouldn't necessarily be able to pull over, as when he dropped me off, the crush of traffic even heavier now, the busy policemen waving their arms and blowing loud whistles. There were two main intersections, one leading in and one leading out, and they were now log jammed with cars and trucks and people. I waited for him another 10 minutes, and it was useless. He was no place to be seen. On a lark, I decided to search again, cutting my effort to five minutes this time. I did the same thing twice more. Finally, on my fourth trip to the curb, I spotted him in traffic, three cars from where I stood. It wasn't a happy reunion.

"Cosmo, where have you been? I had to circle around three times. Now we're driving on fumes. Like in out-of-gas fumes! Good going!"

It would have been a great moment to have good news to share with him. I had really done it this time—out of money, out of gas, out of friends. "Well, what took you so long?" I countered, not knowing what else to do or say, except try to defend the undefendable. I still hadn't gotten into the car, barking at him through the open window. "I've been to this damned curb four times. I never saw you before now!"

"Fine! We're still out of gas. What do you think about that?"

"Shit."

"That's it, shit?"

"What do you want me to say?"

"Tell me how we are going to get back to Seattle?"

"We'll find a way. Just don't dog me over it!"

"Oh, you're a dog all right. And I stepped right into the big mess you just made!"

"OK, calm down, will ya? I'm trying to think. I got you to Canada, didn't I? I can get you back to Seattle."

My best idea was to find the nearest gas station. I reasoned that I could leave my driver's license with them in lieu of payment for gas. I would then return from Seattle and clear the debt. Brilliant, I didn't have a driver's license. Obviously, that spoiled the idea. I was right on top of the thinking game. Then I considered just using my registration papers, but realized that wouldn't pan out either, not proving much, except that the Princess had a real owner, and I may or may not be him. My Canadian paperwork was useless. It just proved I was irresponsible, so much so that the entire nation was eager to be rid of me in three days. Three strikes and you're out. Swell, what a mess. I was a spaceman and worse than just an alien on an Oregon beach. Nonetheless, I ran through the useless strategies, all three, and Rick confirmed that they were stupid. I had to say something to him, no matter how wretched.

"Then I'll tell them that I don't have a driver's license either, or I'll let them see the one nobody can read! I'm sure they will fall all over themselves trying to help us. Damn it, Cosmo."

"Are you finished? My ears are beginning to hurt from all of your shouting."

"Just get in the car, and don't tell me another fricking love story!"

We quickly found two gas stations in town but both were bogged down with heavy holiday traffic, long snarling lines of hungry gas guzzlers. We might run out of fumes just waiting to beg. I told Rick to pass them up, suggesting it might be a good idea to shoot for a less crowded station near the freeway, leading back to Tacoma.

Like magic, one appeared. It sat on a small hill, adjacent to a western style motel, itself distinguished by a large parking lot in front and a huge expanse of dirt acreage in back. Beyond this field, also covered in thick foliage, was the freeway leading back to Seattle. Our savior Seattle, the city we never saw, where we could sleep on a secure porch and hustle food from Mr. Smith or a different neighbor. What American would turn us down on the Fourth of July weekend? Certainly not Mr. Smith.

I finally got the chance, after waiting several agonizing minutes, to speak with one of the busy attendants. Like the others, this station was suddenly awash in the hectic movements of traveling patriots, all interested in only two things, the freedom to move along quickly and the freedom to celebrate it. We had neither. I was out of luck, money talks and bullshit walks in America, or any other place, as one knows. I was soon reminded of this by enrolling in Capitalism 101, taught by a chubby, rosy-cheeked young man about my age. At first he expressed some sympathy for our plight but insisted that he was only an employee and couldn't make any executive decisions. He might lose his job if he gave us gas and we didn't return quickly to pay the bill. Then the real zinger came, crushing my already bruised ego. In a fit of final frustration with me, he said, "You know, we get guys like you in here all the time. There's a motel down the road. I bet you can sell something there. Maybe somebody needs some tools or an extra flashlight. I can't let you try it here, though. I might lose my job." With that he walked away to tend to another car, thus securing his job, and ridding himself of me and my "all the time" problem. Terrific. I couldn't say it wasn't what I was expecting. In the end, I thought his idea had some merit, and I offered it to Rick.

"I have a much better idea, Cosmo," he said, his enthusiasm for it lessening his anger. "I'll call my folks, collect, from the motel. They can wire us some money. Nothing to it. We don't need much, and they'll be glad to hear from me—us."

"That's not going to work, Rick. Did you forget that tomorrow is the Fourth of July? This is a small town and there might not even be a Western Union office here. Even if there is one, we'll still have to wait an extra day, no matter how you figure it." I was absolutely opposed to calling home for help, and his idea displeased me. I thought if that happened, and we had to be rescued in such a manner, it would ruin the entire trip for me. I told him so. As a practical concern, he knew I was likely right about the lack of any wire service tomorrow. Rick considered the logic in all this, after listening to me insist upon it, and I think the idea of ruining my trip didn't appeal to him much, either. That friendship thing—again.

Within a few minutes, and the Princess beginning to choke on fumes, we rolled into the motel parking lot. I thought if nothing else good happened, it would be at least a safe place to sleep in the car. Then there was the open field behind it, and it looked like a good place to stretch out in our sleeping bags, if we dared.

Sitting there, lost for answers, we discussed the idea of trying to find Jessica at tomorrow night's fireworks, and how we were still close enough to hitchhike into town. We even deliberated searching the carnival again, together, in the daylight. It might be a good opportunity to pick up a day's work and something to eat. Hell, perhaps we'd earn enough money to get us home in style. We wouldn't need Jessica at all. We would become salaried roustabouts for a brief time, and proudly brag to Roscoe about how we tripped over a way to light a fire in the tent. A real barn burner—break out the buckets, boys! It was a grand thought and would have made a grand story, but life was soon to happen again and change everything.

In the meantime, while we considered all these exciting possibilities, we watched numerous cars drive in and out of the old motel's parking lot, nearly full for the holidays. There were plenty of chances to approach someone, but we stayed in the car for now, firm in our determination to keep our prized tools. I don't know why we adopted such a profitless, dumb attitude. Perhaps it was the generational mindset that schooled us not to lose a single, valued instrument, unless it was pried from our cold, dead fingers. There's something about young men and their tools, and we always have a heavy reluctance to part with them. Beyond the truth of that, it might also have been true that I was embarrassed by the disgraceful idea of approaching a complete stranger and begging to barter. I had never done it. I don't think Rick had, either. We had made our decision and seemed prepared to live with it. Go figure.

By now it was pitch dark, the night encasing us in its brooding blackness. The usually intrepid moon hid behind murky clouds that blew an eerie, biting breeze through my open window, defying the season. Suddenly, I was chilled and put on my heavy jacket for the first time this trip. I felt nauseous too, the life sustaining power of only a candy bar and half a soda now dying inside of me.

It was during these despondent moments of near starvation, sudden cold and some justified self-rebuke, that I noticed a beautiful Lincoln Continental sedan drive past us, very near, eventually disappearing around the corner to the back of the motel. It was painted a lush and lavish midnight blue, the huge body laced with fine chrome and adorned with canted headlights and stylish, scalloped fenders. It also featured jumbo, whitewall tires, pinstriped in gold, and an engine with the sound and rumble of a young, proud lion. This big daddy looked all the part of one, and it was a car truly in a league of its own. Such a bad-to-the-bone Continental reminded me of an awesome beast on the prowl and one that only real men can tame: dark, mysterious men, mostly. Naturally, there were two dark, mysterious men in it, cruising with their stereo turned up very loud, blaring out a tune by country music legend Hank Williams. I was a generation behind those who loved and adored him, late to explore his music, but it was easily recognizable. I didn't think they noticed us.

Usually, I might not have paid a lot of attention to such loud music, but by an awful stroke of bad luck the stereo tape player in the Princess quit working earlier in the day. This forced us to listen to the radio, and the endless, mindless commercials: the yackety-yak that insults your intelligence and sucks your soul dry. Anyway, their flamboyant ride and the blaring music, plus the coincidence, caused us to start joking around about how easy it would be to steal a car's stereo. We even teased each other about who would be best at it, both of us voting for ourselves. We could sell it to someone in town tomorrow morning or at the carnival. I imagined that some carnie would snatch up a car tape player fast, not asking any questions, and be out of Dodge before the sheriff and posse were even saddled. The two intended victims—we first considered these mysterious men—looked like rich fellows, so it would only be a minor inconvenience to them and something that could be replaced without a second thought. Fun stuff, like that.

Whatever fun might have been involved was brushed off as just an entertaining idea, and we settled back in our seats and rested. Later on, we took a walk to stretch our legs, going as far as the open field and dirt parking lot behind the motel. Eventually, well past these, we came to the fence line at the freeway and had to turn around and start back. The ground was wet and muddy from a recent water encounter of some sort, perhaps ferocious rain dropping from a single renegade cloud—a summertime anomaly I've seen happen in California's great Central Valley. Whatever the cause, we decided not to walk through it again, taking a different path back, circling our way around tall brush that commanded a large portion of the landscape.

Then it happened. Rick spotted the fabulous Lincoln parked alone, hidden within the high brush, out of view of the motel and its bright neon lights. Still, it was facing toward it, at a peculiar angle, a direct line of sight to one particular section. See but not be seen.

What happened next was truly a combination of spontaneity, fatigue, hunger, frustration, vain imaginings and a heightened sense of desperation. A dynamite recipe for disaster. We were about to cook up one for ourselves.

"This is our chance, Cosmo."

"If you are thinking what I think you are, then you got to be kidding." I was thinking the same thing and then thought how crazy it was. I told him so. Talking about stealing someone's tape player and actually doing it were far different things. My response had been one of disapproval, but the idea excited me, nonetheless.

"It didn't sound so crazy to you when you were bragging about it earlier. I thought you had a carnie already lined up? But, really, look at that thing. It is just begging for you to rob it!" He shoved me along, playfully, adding a footnote, "I've seen the door locks on Lincolns before, big round things that you can open with an eyelid."

"What about that butter knife you always carry, steak thief?" If you are so hot on the idea, why don't you just use it? Give it a try. Seriously, why don't you? If you can't handle it with such a fine weapon, I'll come and open it with my eyelid." I had to tease him about the butter knife. It suddenly came to mind. He had been carrying it in his pocket since we first made sandwiches on the road and shared them with Roscoe. I hadn't pressed him for the reason why—and maybe there wasn't one. Even so, he had developed the habit of lugging it around. I had let it be up to now. After all, it's hard to cut off your legs or privates with a butter knife, accidentally or otherwise.

"It doesn't matter who does it. If I'm not mistaken, we are both in the same jam." He actually sounded serious about it.

"Then there's motive and opportunity for you. Go ahead, macho man, prove that you deserve the name. You must be good at stealing something." I hadn't intended these comments to be a challenge to him, but they struck a sensitive nerve, flaming a fire that had been simmering since we first joked about stealing one. I hadn't thought much about it before, but his pride must have taken a bit of a hit over the steak business, having been caught so easily and by a woman. Anyway, whatever it was, he was out to prove that he was a better man, capable of setting things right.

"I bet you I can have that tape player in two minutes or less, Cosmo. This ain't a busy grocery store, if you haven't noticed, and there ain't no leaky steaks to give me away."

Bingo! The joke was on, and I foolishly decided to fuel the fire. "Really? Steak stains? That's how you got caught? I thought it was the huge bulge in your pants that nobody could believe!"

"You're sure pushing the subject for the loved crazed moron who got us into this jam, Cosmo."

"Go ahead then, John Wayne. I'll wait here in the grass. Show me a little American know-how."

We sat down on a dry portion of the ground and waited for another 15 minutes, watching the car closely for any movement, with unintended lapses of joking around. I couldn't imagine why it was parked out here and finally asked Rick's opinion. "What do you think they're doing way out here?"

"Probably hiding their car from stereo thieves. What else?"

"No, I got it!" I said. "They don't want their wives to see it. The motel is probably a place to meet up with their secretaries for a game of poker."

"Poker? Right. That's good, Cosmo. Strip poker, maybe. But, you know, I've heard about married guys meeting up with women at motels and trying to hide it."

"You've heard of that, eh? Wow, what a novel idea."

"I'd probably just come in a taxi if it was me," he said, coyly.

"What if your wife came looking for you in the same taxi?" I asked.

"What do you think, you dope? I'd invite her in for poker and make sure she won enough for the fare home. Aaaaah! Take that!" He picked up some loose soil and grass and threw them at me, then tried to pinch my cheek. I barely avoided him and returned fire, hitting him square in the chest with a dirt clod.

"Damn it, Cosmo, this is my last clean shirt!"

"You can buy a new one with the money we get from the tape player or stereo."

We were jousting and jesting around like this, brazenly, to pass the time, but I was beginning to feel a lot like a criminal for just sitting here and observing. Nothing, no movement inside the car. If anyone was in it, they sure fooled us. It appeared that all was quiet.

Rick finally got up, tossing me the butter knife. "Here, hold this while I check it out first. Try not to stab yourself in the eyelid."

It relieved me to know that if he really intended on using it, he would have to return. I gave him a last word of caution, "How do you know someone isn't in the car, convict?"

"I don't. But nothing has moved in 15 minutes, has it?"

"So what. They could be sleeping or just relaxing low in the seats."

"No, I doubt it. If it's those same two guys we saw pull in, they're most likely in the motel bar whooping it up and listening to Hank Williams. It's the holiday, Cosmo. People are drinking and having a good time. I'm just going to look. Relax, take a nerve pill, will ya? I'll be right back."

In a moment, I could have used one.

[13]
WHAT IS FREEDOM?

At first sight, Carter's Wrecking Yard came with all the familiar belongings one would think common to the trade. There were trashed cars and trucks and vans, and the occasional recreational vehicle, all stacked in hellish piles of broken and twisted metal. Leading up to all this dereliction was a graveled entrance saturated in squalid grime, the putrid leakage of a mishmash of engine lubricants. Such waste spoke of the last breaths of life to cry out from the once proud, venerated steeds that adorned our fathers' driveways.

The common mixture of sickly, stray cats ran about frantically, hissing loudly and clawing at each other, battling for the best place in line, recognizing our approaching headlights as their ticket into this barbwire hell. I saw an old dog chained to the fence, never moving a muscle at our arrival, content to let the cats bask in all the glory. He was pitiful to look at, mangy and lethargic, disinterested in us, only alive enough to lift his head to see who was coming. At least he wasn't vicious, and it was the first good sign. If there were others, I hoped they were like him.

Still, the worst part was the rank air, the poison that penetrated through the car windows, nauseous, reeking of scorn for the naivety of love and vanilla expectations, mocking me in the fragrance of its brutal finality. With each breath the finality got a little closer. It wasn't supposed to work out this way. Yet, here we were, and my mind and emotions fast approaching a frantic state.

Moe stepped out of the car and into the dim light, strolling deliberately to the gate, kicking and cursing at the wretched cats now rubbing against his legs, competing for the affections of a madman. One took the point of his heavy boot squarely in the face, screeching and reeling back in intense pain, momentarily stunned, before disappearing swiftly into the invisible night. The others stayed the course, continuing to mill about but at a safer distance. As Moe reached for the lock, about waist high on him, Charlie suddenly sprayed him in the bright glow of the car's high-beam lights, causing him to turn in anger, growling and waving his arms in a threat of severe retaliation for such nonsense. It pissed him off, in short.

Then the psychopath turned off the lights, altogether, laughing crazily, then turned them back on again, taunting Moe and mumbling something unintelligible about him. It had the tone of acute hatred. Moe gave him another sharp glance, a murderous glance, and it spoke to the fact that Charlie's antics were close to caving in on him. I thought Moe might have hated him more than I did. He then fumbled about with some keys he carried, finally locating the right one, and was soon pulling the gate open wide. The cats made a mad dash for the office, some 25 yards away, where they started feeding on scraps of food, bits and pieces of dried, stale sandwiches, likely left there by Mr. Carter and his crew. They capped them off by lapping up any sour beer that had been left outside to rot. Mr. Carter must have been an alcoholic. Dozens of beer bottles and cans were strewn around and about the large heaps of junked metal, in the most haphazard of ways. I could see the cats examining them thirstily and fighting over those that still contained any remaining drops of an easier life.

We drove slowly through this endless patchwork of rancid wasteland, never once seeing any kind of flair for organization. I thought Mr. Cater was a sloppy junkman, no doubt. I further thought it peculiar to spend even a moment thinking about it. It wasn't the time to worry about Mr. Carter's self-improvement issues, but who can account for the petty tricks that the mind plays on one.

The sloppy junkman owned a large tin shack in the back. In another moment we were there. It was lit up by a dim light dangling loosely over the front door. Charlie got out this time, leaving the car idling and briskly approached the unlocked entrance. It was obvious that he was glad to be here. He poked his head inside for a few seconds, then returned to the car. "This is the place all right, Moe. I can see it's been used before. Thanks, kid. We couldn't have done it without you." Then the maniac laughed, and it sounded like the hiss of a rattlesnake. I truly despised him.

"Let's just get inside, Charlie," Moe barked. "You can talk to the kid then."

I much preferred talking to Moe, and I hoped what he said didn't mean he would leave us to the vile mercies of the deranged Charlie. I was once again convinced that all he wanted was someone to kill tonight. He planned it to be the colonel, but we screwed that up for him and perhaps a nice bonus on top of his normal pay. That was encouraging to think about. His loathing for us was just beginning to spike.

From this moment on, the two goons seemed to work together with some precision, as if they were suddenly transported into their own natural realm of things: what they did best and most often. Charlie reached in and turned off the ignition, and then the two of them opened each back door, simultaneously. Moe shoved me aggressively from one end, and Charlie dragged Rick from the other. I had managed to loosen the ropes once more. So when Moe pushed me I slammed hard into Rick's side, colliding with his broken ribs. He cried out in anguish, cursing me. I pleaded with Moe to show restraint.

"I'm just getting warmed up, pissant. Stop your bitching and get inside." He slammed the door behind me, while Charlie untangled us from the ground. We both had fallen. Rick recoiled once more in morbid pain as Charlie jerked him to his feet. I jumped up as quickly as I could to take the pressure off the ropes, hoping to lessen his agony. When doing so, I slipped and fell back down, taking him with me. It was Moe who lifted us up this time, using only one big paw and the other to check the ropes. He immediately pulled them tight again and another scream came from Rick. The big bastard was suddenly showing no mercy, and I judged it the end for us. My heart sank when thinking of his unpredictable and precarious mood swings and what might happen to anyone who got caught on the wrong end of them. I feared that whatever previous compassion he had for us had run dry.

I hadn't offered any verbal resistance the entire ride back, only giving the two thugs directional help, which felt much like a rustler volunteering to string the rope that hangs him. We sure could have used the assistance of Sergeant Renfrew and a few of his Mountie friends about now. Alas, they were in a different country tonight, perhaps sitting comfortably around a campfire and retelling heroic stories about when they were the most brave and in the most peril. Of course, they would finish by saying how they saved the day in the end. Canada would sleep safely tonight.

Oh, but a Mountie to be. I should have stayed, divorcing my native land, pursuing and capturing the red serge of courage. It has always been the emblazoned, scarlet jacket of invincibility, and I would know what to do now. I would know how to escape to safety at once, disbanding and disarming the two repulsive heathens, doing away with them on just a whim. It would be the perfect, exotic ending, thus earning my rightful place in the bookshelf with Sergeant Renfrew. Sergeant Anderson and Sergeant Renfrew team up to destroy evil, again! I would even get top billing.

Wishful thinking, at best, and pointless. I would save my courage to believe in what Moe said earlier, "Hell, kid, you won't even hear it, like a pinprick before falling off to sleep."

Death might be my terrible reality, nearer now, and so unexpected. Despite Moe's assurances, I still feared a long, torturous and painful one. My head was flooded by the tormenting questions that came naturally to me. Will they kill us one at a time or together? Maybe they might torment one of us first, to let the other see what level of inhuman suffering was in store for him. And who the hell is the colonel, anyway? Maybe, like Charlie, who was just tired of the bullshit, they would do it quickly and be done with it. A shotgun blast to the face would do nicely, leaving nothing much left behind to identify or bother about. The thought sickened me beyond any horror I could imagine. My mind raced over all these things before I hit the ground.

Once inside, Charlie had given me a final shove and Rick a hard kick, sending us both tumbling to the splintered floor. Rick fell on top of me this time, his right knee lodging into the small of my back, and a lightning bolt of searing pain shot up my spine. The terrible sensation pulsated through my neck and face, rendering me completely numb, paralyzing me for a moment. I had never experienced the complete loss of bodily control, and in another moment I was throwing up in a spastic seizure. I didn't have much on my stomach, so it ended up as dry heaves, a number of them, leaving me sucking for breath and struggling for air. A real bummer.

Seeing my debilitated condition, Charlie waited until I could recover. I did so in a blaze of curses, to no one in particular, and I think more to myself. Charlie laughed at me, quickly hustling us to our feet, untying the rope and then pushing us back to the hard floor. Constantly being shoved and falling to the ground was unnerving, and his savage ass knew it. His conscience was sealed as with a hot iron. This was just the cake before the frosting. He had been overly quick to pronounce judgment on us tonight. Now that he had us imprisoned, I was certain he would enjoy the execution.

Moe suddenly showed up with two chairs, found in a dark corner of the room, slamming them down next to us. He lifted us to our feet, one at a time, dropping us on them. The hard landing produced another screech from Rick. We were finally untied and upright, but the noose was still tight around our necks.

Then Moe quickly walked away, leaving us alone again with Charlie. The big man began to examine the shack and its contents, dangerous tools left scattered about the floor and hung on the walls. He stopped at some old shelves covered in foul dirt and grease, overflowing with sharp metal files and blunt ratchets, including several corroded, dead batteries, still oozing decayed acid. There was an assortment of other lethal things that could easily maim a human body. His weapon of choice was a scarred crowbar, one of its claws chipped. He raised it far above his head, slamming it viciously on top of a tattered battery charger, exploding it, bits of glass and metal flying through the air. It scared me. He appeared out of control, not the benevolent Moe I had come to know and desire. No, it didn't look like he would need his knife tonight. He grinned and said, "I'm sure glad to get that off my chest!" Then he purposely looked over at me, giving me a wide smile and a wink, and I was instantaneously back to thinking he was really on our side. It was maddening.

In the meantime, Charlie pulled two rusted chains off a near wall, draping them around our shoulders while laughing hideously. They were about eight feet in length, very heavy, and made of steel a half inch thick. "Hey, kid, do you ever feel like you have the weight of the world on you?" He continued laughing. The seething sound of it was pure evil.

"Screw you!" I said, looking him hard in the face, searching his eyes for any glimmer of sanity. There was none. So I decided to challenge him again, with a loud shout out this time, hoping it would startle him enough to delay the inevitable and perhaps finally convince him of our innocence. "Mister, none of this is going to change anything! You can throw a thousand chains around our necks or shoot us in the face, and it still doesn't change the fact that you are wrong, and we don't know the damned colonel!" I continued with more and louder. "Can't you see that we are telling the truth? We don't have a reason to lie to you! We are just a couple of guys who were trying to get gas money to go home. Damn it! What the hell is wrong with you?" It was of no use. I had made a similar plea so many times that even I couldn't hear the words any longer, shouted or not. If I couldn't hear them at this volume, what was left for the psycho to hear? Then it got even worse. Charlie dropped the bombshell.

"Screw me, huh? Then let me screw with you a little more, loudmouth. I don't care if you don't know the shit-sucking colonel. I'm going to kill you anyway! How's that for getting screwed? We can find the little weasel without your help, punk."

"Then why won't you let us go? Why do you have to kill us?"

"Because you can identify us, kid! But that's not our fault, is it? So tough shit for you! This is your reward for being stupid."

"But we are not going to tell anyone about you. Can't you figure that out?" The words were muted, coming from Rick, finally able to breathe well enough to utter them softly. It was good to have him back, in any condition. Unsurprisingly, his condition looked extremely bad. Besides his broken ribs, he had a swollen, purple eye, the other completely closed. A dark, frightful bruise painted one of his cheekbones, and two deep cuts varnished his forehead, a larger one and a smaller one. Both slashes bled some, the rivers of blood joining streams, matting near his right temple. These were his undeserved trophies, ones he had not wanted, but I helped him to win. I could see them clearly for the first time. What had I done?

Rick's words just made Charlie laugh more. "Who do you two punks think you're screwing around with here? Like you put it, kid, nothing is going to change the facts. I'll still do what I have to do. You know a little too much about me and my friend. Like I said, tough shit! The talking is over!" He was ice cold, grabbing the chains and viciously yanking down on them, then shoving the rusty steel hard into our faces.

Wow. He was right. All of this was my fault. I was stupid. It was my reward and the brass band and parade I had wished to have. Poor Rick was marching in line with me, side by side, to our ugly demise. I couldn't fathom that in my careless rush to find true love, and be the hero of my own story, that I only found impending death, instead, staring me in the face. The staring face was that of a schizophrenic killer, one with no remorse or single shred of feeling inside of him. It was a cruel ending I had brought down upon our heads for simply running out of gas, while running for love. Rick was also right.

Shakespeare had never written about love with this much tragedy in mind. It far eclipsed the boundaries of any blunders I could have imagined making.

It was in this defeated state of mind that I made my final plea to Charlie, needing to know if I understood exactly what intentions he had in mind. Of course, the point couldn't have been made clearer, but like love, hope can't be killed. "Do I really understand you right, mister? My God, we don't know anything about you. It doesn't make any sense at all—none of it."

He confirmed that I understood him. "Yeah, and it doesn't make sense that you two just accidentally ran into us. I'm not buying it, Buttercup. You can count on that. We'll catch up to your friend right after we finish with you. And just so you know, colonel or no colonel, we are not in the business of leaving stray evidence behind. Something has to be done. Right, Moe?"

"Yeah, something has to be done, Charlie." It excited Charlie to have Moe on his side.

"The Butter Knife Stereo Thieves!" Charlie bellowed, in glee, as he had first done earlier in the night. "Or is it, *The Buttercup Stereo Thieves*, kid?" He taunted me, moving his face close to mine, pleased at reviving his old cleverness. Did I tell you that he also had bad breath? I didn't answer him, except to turn my head after giving him a caustic look. "Whatever," he said to me, giving me a hard shove. "We got a menace off the streets of America, just in time for the Fourth of July. Hank Williams should write a song about us."

"He's dead," I said, sarcastically.

"Then you'll get to meet him first, kid, and he can write a song about you," he shot back, chuckling, Moe laughing with him. Still, something about the big man's countenance had suddenly changed. It seemed different this time. Even his laugh sounded forced. Something was up.

Moe unexpectedly dropped down on one knee and leaned close to us, like a stern schoolmaster about to drive home a lesson, very hard but fair in the end. "You two California shitbirds, draft dodgers, stereo thieves, whatever the hell you might be, should know by now that you got your butts into a tight sling tonight," he said. He paused as if to ready himself for the dramatic closing—and it was. "If we let you pissants go now, and you tell the cops about us, it will be big trouble for us here and back home. People tend to get brave when the cops are around. So it's best not to give them a choice." He stood up, tall, as a lawyer does when he knows he's in full command of the courtroom, turning to look at Charlie and then back at us. "Now, we need time to stay in town until this thing is done, and you two are a problem. But in due respect to Sammy the Sucker and Charlie, here, there just may be a way out for you two."

It's still the greatest single thing anyone has ever said to me, but I had little time to enjoy it. It was all Charlie needed to hear, too. He didn't want to hear about a way out. "No way out, Moe! We can't take a chance on these two going to the police. Are you crazy? They know too much. We got to eliminate them!" The words came out of him defiantly—not to be negotiated.

Moe retaliated, anyway, "They wouldn't know nothin' about nothin' if you hadn't shot your big mouth off about the colonel, Charlie. Now you're telling me you're going to kill them for your mistake, and you don't care what I say about it?"

"You just agreed that it's best not to give them a choice, Moe. Don't go getting soft on me. It's time to get the shotgun. We have orders not to take any chances!"

"What do you know about our orders?" Moe fired back, incredulously, disdainful of what had been the most serious challenge to his authority. "I give the orders here. You'll do what

254

I say, Charlie, and nothing else. And I'll change my mind whenever I want to!"

Amen.

I had bad feelings before about these two fighting, but Moe was on our side again. At that moment I wished he'd smash Charlie like he had the battery charger. It would be nice to see his brains explode like flying glass. Just the same, Moe had proven to be excessively puzzling, and his mood swings were like juggling sticks of dynamite, not knowing which fuse is lit.

As one knows well by now, Charlie was truly insane, and I suspected that he could turn on Moe and strike first—at any second. What these two were doing together was impossible to comprehend. It was obvious that both of them were keenly interested in wanting to settle the matter of who was in charge. Charlie's contempt for Moe, and his so-called softness, exceeded purely professional considerations and rather went to the heart of his debilitating psychosis. Moe knew it.

What I didn't know, but would find out later, is that Moe had been living with Charlie's hair-trigger lunacy for more than a month, while they chased the colonel across the country, starting in New Jersey. He didn't reveal how a military officer got involved with the Mafia, and perhaps it was better for me not to know. Nevertheless, the colonel had somehow managed to steal a ton of money from them. He had also been sly and elusive and virtually impossible to catch.

Not regular partners in crime, Charlie had threatened to act on his own, time after time, during these weeks of teaming up together and regularly questioned Moe's authority. There were even stints when he tried to humiliate Moe, as he had done with the car lights, and over time he had exposed himself to be a blood thirsty animal: a rabid dog not to be trusted and perhaps, one day, to be put out of his misery. But for now, this same misery wanted us dead and for less reason than Moe had considered the same for him. Although murder was part of Moe's business, it hadn't completely taken over his nature. He murdered but Charlie did it randomly. Anyway, at this moment, the tension between them was at a fever pitch. Then the end came right out of the blue—and savagely.

Charlie's reaction to Moe's perceived betrayal was to punch me hard in the face, without warning, blood spewing from my nose and mouth. I reeled back in my chair from the blow, almost falling over. To my shock, and that of Charlie, Rick suddenly jumped up and threw a retaliatory punch at him. He missed, but the vigorous swing put his chain in rapid motion, and it didn't miss, striking Charlie directly on the left elbow. It had that awful sound that metal makes on flesh and bone. The sound I learned to avoid at the racetrack. It wasn't a fatal blow but it certainly hurt him.

"You little piece of sorry shit! I'm going to kill you for that!" The enraged lunatic launched a swift, wild backhand with his damaged arm, but Rick ducked—he was always a good fighter, as you may have noticed in the beginning—and Charlie's intended blow hit Moe squarely in the nose, drawing blood and making him wince. It had been a solid, violent whirl, and the violence was returned.

"That's enough!" Moe boomed. Even faster than these words came out, he drew his large switchblade knife and stabbed Charlie directly in the heart, the long blade disappearing deep inside his chest. Charlie emitted a terrifying shriek, and he took a last, fruitless gasp for air, dropping dead on the spot. The look on his face had been one of indescribable horror and astonishing surprise. The move had been so fatally fast and ferocious that I hardly had a chance to blink—and it was over. Rick had crumbled to the floor while trying to save me, and I now reached down to assist him, never taking my eyes off Moe.

"Shit!" Moe said.

Shit, that's it? Without attending to us, he dragged Charlie's dead body into one corner of the shack and covered him up, as best he could, using a gunnysack he found on the floor. Then he came back and said, "Well, pissants, this changes things and we need to get out of here." He said it without emotion, adding nothing more. He was cool under fire.

"Does that mean you're not going to kill us, too?" I immediately regretted asking it. I was beyond relieved that Charlie was dead but hurt and confused enough to remain wary of Moe's mood swings. I shouldn't have been, the mood had swung our way. Needless to say, the big man had finally come through for us, twice in a span of two minutes, and I shouldn't have doubted him. I thought I detected some personal disappointment in his response to me, but he opted to have fun with it.

"Kid, I just did me some killing, and before the night is over, I might have to do me some more." He paused for a moment to watch my reaction, knowing that I wasn't sure who he meant. Then he laughed his booming Bunyan bellow, and I knew we were finally safe, at long last. It wasn't the kind of freedom I struggled to understand at Jack's trailer, but it would do nicely for now. "Happy Fourth of July, pissants!" he shouted, with great enthusiasm, pumping his fist high into the air. It reminded me of what he had done for James. It was now early morning on the Fourth.

At that very second the fireworks exploded for me, and suddenly my own personal brass band and parade showed up, in the spirit I had first wanted and imagined. I was thankful and relieved to have Rick marching in it with me. It truly was a moment to celebrate great personal freedom, and I would live to do it again—for my country.

It had been a very close call. I couldn't help but stare at Moe in sheer wonderment. He was a killer and a brute and unpredictable but nonetheless still an American hero in my eyes—and on the right day. And don't they just come in all shapes and sizes? "Yes, happy Fourth of July, Mr. Moe."

Rick had exhausted all of his remaining energy throwing the wild punch but with my help was back in his chair, fading in and out of consciousness. I wasn't sure if he had seen what just took place. Regardless, had he not tried to defend me, things might not have worked out so well. It looked as if God was still watching out for us. I always liked to think about it that way. I put my arm around his shoulder and asked, "Man, how you doing? Are you all right? Can you talk?" He pressed his weight against mine and mumbled something I couldn't understand, except my name. He later told me what it was, "Don't forget to thank him, Cosmo." You know, I don't think I ever did.

"I'll help you get him to the car," Moe said. "He'll live." With that, we carried Rick to the Lincoln and placed him in the back seat. Moe motioned for me to get into the front seat with him. Up to this point I had said nothing more. We left on the narrow roadway we came in, and Moe stopped at the office. "Hey, kid, there's a pen and some paper in the glove box. How about fetching them for me?" That's what I did, and it was a reasonable request. He got out of the car, scribbled something on a single sheet of paper, folded it once and slid it under the door.

"You sure got quiet on me, kid," he said, when he got back in. "I hope you're not in mourning or something like that? I didn't think you liked him."

"I didn't. He deserved what he got! I would have done it myself, if I had the chance."

"Oh, alive again, are you? That's better. I believe you would have, kid. I surely do believe that."

"So," I asked, emboldened by his confidence in me, "what happens now, do we have to notify his parents?" It was the last thing I expected to say but there it was.

"Notify his parents? Hey, that's pretty good, kid. I'll have to tell the guys back home about that one." He slapped me on the shoulder, playfully, and added a line to Charlie's obituary, "Naw, the crazy prick didn't have any parents. Some mad scientist invented his ass in some laboratory, somewhere. I should kill him too just for doing it." He laughed at his own joke and then instantaneously grew serious, as only Moe could. Showing almost a fatherly concern for me, he said, "But I'm glad you brought up the question, kid. Because what happens now depends on you." He rested his arm on my shoulder and then patted it. I swear to you, as untimely as it may sound, my next thought was how glad I was that he didn't pat me on the head again. We stopped once more at the gate, and he turned off the car and lights. The cats had disappeared, and the dog had crawled under a wrecked truck. It's said that animals can sense death.

In the next few, dark moments, we just sat there, and I listened to what was expected of me. I was to carry out his instructions—without question. Rick was to be informed of every word. It was a final lesson on the road and a lifelong one. It went very close to this: We were to keep our mouths shut about absolutely everything, never to reveal a single detail to a single person as long as we lived. If we did or if we went to the police, Moe would come back, find us and kill us, and if he couldn't come back himself, he'd send someone back. This rule would be in force forever, and whether we saw Jesus or the devil when we died, they were not to know, either. I was reminded that the two of us got our butts into and out of a real tight sling tonight, as he was fond of putting it, and pissants so lucky shouldn't press their good fortune. As before, it wasn't the Sermon on the Mount, but I embraced it.

Convinced that I understood these terms fully, word for word, he then asked me a question that almost made me laugh. Had it not been so sad, I would have.

"So tell me the truth, kid. You two aren't really draft dodgers, are you?"

"No, we wouldn't do that," I said. "We love America."

"I don't blame those boys for trying to get out of this war. It's a real mess."

"We don't blame them either, Mr. Moe. They love America, too."

"Well, happy Fourth of July again, kid, one American to another."

"Same to you, Mr. Moe, one American to another."

EPILOGUE

Moe, on the way to the motel, told me the full version of his travels with Charlie. Upon arriving, he handed me gas money and then helped me with Rick. Within a few minutes more, he circled to the back, a place I would never step foot in again, and disappeared from our lives. Of course, I don't know what became of him or the poor colonel. I fear that it ended badly, but most days I don't even think about them or what happened that night. I've been able to put it out of my mind, the only reasonable thing to do.

Rick has never dwelt much on it, either, as far as I can tell. Over the years we've talked about it but not with any regularity. When we still do, we are able to have fun with it, somehow, as morbid as that may sound. I think it's just our best way to deal with it. If time can't completely erase memories, it can sometimes do a good job of fading them. It's a blessing to remember what happened only in the light of God's good fortune and the boldness of youthful passions gone astray. When one of us is bothered by it, the other is quick to point out that we decided, long ago, not to let a dead madman have any lasting control over our lives. We then joke around and say to each other, "But you two pissants sure got your butts into a tight sling that night!" To this moment, we still laugh to think that we can remember a killer with great fondness. Life is very odd.

To fill you in some, we headed straight to Kim's, neither returning to Seattle nor extending our futile search for Jessica and family. Wherever they were, I hoped they had a good time. It was a few weeks later before I received my wallet in the mail, the money still in it, and I have never spent those bills. I just can't. There was plenty of sympathy for us, as well. Kim fawned over me, and Bonnie helped to care for Rick at the Cottage Grove hospital. All we ever told them was that we had been in a scuffle, and it was a close call. They were more concerned about our injuries than what might be the actual truth. Luckily, this paid off well for us in the end, and by the next time I saw Kim it was a thing of the past. There were plans to make.

So that's what we did, and 10 years later we are celebrating the fruits of those plans. We have three children now and the first, sweet Jessica, I adopted when she was four, after six months of marriage to Kim. When she was seven we told her about her real father, thinking sooner was better than later. After we did, she embraced me and said, "But you're my real father, Daddy." How heavenly sweet it was for me to hear.

It made me think of her great Seattle namesake, also adopted, who had spoken so highly of her new father. It was because of him, she stressed, that she grew up in the midst of opportunity. She said something else to us that night on her porch, after the hard day's work was done, a line I've never forgotten. It came at the end of her comments about him. "He was the first real man I ever knew, and I've only known a few." I never asked her to elaborate on what she thought a real man was, or who the others in her life might be, but I've often wondered about it. I could only hope that one day my Jessica might say something like that about me. I planned on giving her every opportunity to do so. Her name was a daily reminder of that goal.

We have never seen Wesley, and that's been a really good thing for us. Still, as I grow older, I regret more and more having wished that the Zodiac had gotten him. It's not what a real man would hope to happen. By the way, I fall more in love with Kim every day, day after day. Despite our close call, the joke was still on me. When we reached her trailer, my mouth was too busted up to kiss her. By the time we left, seven days later, I was almost healed, and our last kiss was the kiss of the century. The passion of it was like nothing she had offered me before.

"OK, then, Mr. Cosmo, there is something for you to remember. You see, my fine prince, if you don't come back, then I'll have had the last laugh!" What can I say about such a smart woman? It had the exact same impact on me that getting a little peck on the cheek had: a mad yearning to return for more. I was a sitting duck, a smitten schmuck, as Rick liked to call me. Yes, Kim was a smart woman.

It's only one reason I married her. The list is very long, and it would take me pages to tell you about them. I can sum them up by saying that God really shined his light on me, dropping down the answer early in my life and with such quality. I'm glad I've always stuck up for him. We live in California now, in my hometown, a grand shipyard town, and I work as a reporter at the local paper, writing features. I changed my professional aspirations to journalism soon after returning from the Great White North. Somehow, what happened caused me to have a desire to tell the stories of other people's lives and adventures, the way I have told you mine. It's a very satisfying pursuit because we all have them, and they are all worthy of being told, no matter how fantastic they may sound. I've learned not to doubt the fantastic. It happens all the time and to all types of people.

Every Fourth of July is very special to me. It's usually when I think of Moe and how he wished me a happy one, twice, and how surprised I was to hear it. "The Killer and the Kids," in America. It didn't have the same ring as, "Sergeant Anderson and Sergeant Renfrew Save the Universe!" but it was an authentic American story and not the Mountie fiction my mind had invented. Thankfully, I have not yet been enshrined in a bookcase, next to a killer, so that young Americans like me can read about me, and men like me, hoping one day they might do the same. Sometimes it's best not to have all our dreams come true.

I'm glad to tell you that I didn't lose contact with Roscoe and Rosie. Every year we drive to Eugene to spend Thanksgiving with Kim's parents, and on two occasions we made a detour and stopped in to see them for a day. Roscoe loved to retell the story of our first meeting and how fate had placed us at the same rest stop. He bragged about how we all got along so well, like a tight knit circus act. Then he would get more excited and tell Kim about the details of how hard we worked to surprise Rosie, making sure to highlight the wonderful party we had afterward. Kim never got tired of hearing it, laughing and squeezing my hand every time Roscoe got animated.

Then Rosie would play something for us, and the magic of that first meeting would come back to me. Mrs. Van Hamilton's music. I thought of Rick and wolves and redwood trees, and then I thought of chocolate milk and horses for the children—they have three now. More than anything else, I thought of "The Second Greatest Man in the World." It was an unequaled pleasure to know him and to be in complete agreement with him: The real meaning of life is better searched for at home. I have never forgotten what he first said, "Everything I am lives there, and there lives everything I am."

On a sad note, they lost Frankie to leukemia five years ago.

Of course, he was my partner in the quest for all things chocolate milk. On that first visit—I might have said—I had taken him for an untamed ride in the Princess, ripping through her gears to show off, creating huge clouds of dust on the country roads and blasting Jimi Hendrix at full volume. A smile never left his face the entire time we remained there, and we had become something of heroes to him. Now I wished we could have taken him along, leaving out the bad parts. We have promised to come back and see them again.

On a brighter note, I've written Jane and Jack a number of letters over the years, promising to visit them in Toronto. They eventually settled there, Jane becoming a fine doctor and Jack an accomplished engineer. They have two kids of their own, a girl and a boy, and they finally returned to the states to visit their respective families. That happened a year after President Carter granted full amnesty to all American draft dodgers. In one of Jane's return letters, she mentioned how they have also been able to put the memory of those tough days behind them. What a relief it was for me to read it. I've always wanted to tell Jane about how her palm reading prediction turned out for me. Darn it, I'm then obligated to think of how I can't—my promise to Moe and all. After all, he did save my life, one American to another. Nevertheless, we'll see them in Toronto one day, children of a common mother.

Jimmy James Jesse Jackson? Pshaw. The eagle had landed and nothing would stop him. He learned the auto body repair trade, became a magician at it, and two years ago opened his own shop. Little Robert now works there part time and his oldest sister, Shannon, is the bookkeeper. I'm happy to report that Jessica has become fairly wealthy, her talent at real estate the talk of Seattle, and by this means, and her love for her brother, she was able to help him start his own business. The eagle was on solid ground, and I'm glad I had believed him when he said, "I'm a much more mature man now and ready to have a real crack at life." I still do. Welcome to America, Jimmy James Jesse Jackson.

Of course, I want to end with my best friend and the worst thief in the world. Mr. Ruiz has become a wizard at the restaurant business, working closely with his dad and brother. They now own four, two in town and two in a neighboring town. He got married to a pretty woman from Virginia, only a year ago, a customer he happened to meet in one of his restaurants. Now with the responsibilities of work and family, we see each other only every other week. Nonetheless, I want to keep him close. He has always promised to be around to save my butt, and so far he has a perfect record.

Oh, just another final thing or two. When I got home and walked inside the front door, my mom and dad were sitting at the dining table playing cards. I said hello first and waited for whatever the Pink Wall had to say. She just turned, looked me up and down for a brief moment, and said, "Welcome home, son. There's some cold chicken in the refrigerator." She went back to playing cards.

That's it, cold chicken? Yep, and neither of them have ever mentioned it again. They have little idea how much I've appreciated that over the years. In fact, I've never been more impressed with my mom than at that moment. Women, especially mothers, can be truly remarkable.

Hey, the Princess went to my young nephew, not long ago. Aaron, 18, had been drooling over her for years and had approached me several times about buying her. I retired her to my garage, driving only the family van, with intentions of one day rebuilding her engine. Aaron had enthusiastically offered his help, and then one night he showed up, sneaking out to my garage and starting work by himself. The poor kid was enchanted by a beautiful princess, and it was hard for me to watch. Kim was delighted by it and kept talking about our first meeting, teasing me about how much she was impressed by me for owning her. "You wouldn't have gotten past first base with me, Mr. Cosmo, if you didn't have her. Sell her to the poor boy, you big lug. Maybe she'll bring the same luck to him, as she did us."

One princess praising another—and, of course, this made me cave in. So I agreed, only on the stipulation that he would always treat her like a princess and that she always remained in the family. I turned over the keys to him one week later, on Christmas Day. I had made her a gift to him, not wanting or needing to take money. He was overwhelmed by my kindness and kept thanking me, repeating, over and over, "Oh, God! God! Thank you, Uncle Rusty. They don't make cars like this in America any longer."

"Amen, and you can't get a hamburger, fries, and shake for less than a dollar at Babbs' Diner any longer," I finally thought to add. I was excited that he was so happy, and my comment came in fond remembrance of a little boy and his pals, waving, going fishing, and digging a princess.

"Isn't that a place you stopped at in Canada, Uncle Rusty? I remember you telling me a little bit about that trip. It sounded far out to me."

A whale of a story, and Roscoe was definitely right. Life is like a circle that should always lead back home.

Made in the USA
San Bernardino, CA
04 November 2015